Readers love *Familiar Angel*
by AMY LANE

"*Familiar Angel* is fantastic… a transcendent love story…. Harry and
Suriel are heroes to die for,
and their love is a lesson….
I can only have faith and
desperately hope she will
keep turning out more tales
like this!"
　　—Cindy Dees, *NYT* and
USA Today Bestselling
　　　　　　　　author

Some lovers are as familiar as the family pet.

FAMILIAR ANGEL

Amy Lane

"Fantastic...a transcendent
love story that will sweep you
off your feet."
CINDY DEES,
NYT and *USA Today*
Bestselling Author

"Both striking and sensual,
the thought-provoking
novel pays equal attention
to love, sacrifice, the divine,
and family."
　　—*Publishers Weekly*

"Amy Lane remains one of
the queens of storytelling."
　　　　—Joyfully Jay

"A masterpiece."

　　　　　　　　—Paranormal Romance Guild

More praise for
Amy Lane

Crocus

"It's everything I expect and want from an Amy Lane novel, plus the chance to revisit a favorite couple and their family. Very much recommended."

—Jessie G Books

"*Crocus* is a story of family and love and acceptance. It's about overcoming obstacles and keeping what's important at the forefront. It's about love. So, so much love."

—Diverse Reader

A Fool and His Manny

"I loved every sentence from beginning to end. I got sucked into the story right away, and it held my attention until it was over."

—Joyfully Jay

"Reading this novel is like being enveloped in large, welcoming mommy arms or walking in the door home and getting the welcome you always dreamed about from the family you always wanted."

—Scattered Thoughts and Rogue Words

Stand by Your Manny

"…it is an amazing ride. This is a wonderful addition to a heartwarming series."

—Paranormal Romance Guild

"If you're looking for a nice, sweet romance that has some real obstacles to overcome before a happily ever after, you will definitely enjoy *Stand by Your Manny*."

—Top 2 Bottom Reviews

By AMY LANE

Published by DREAMSPINNER PRESS
www.dreamspinnerpress.com

Published by DREAMSPINNER PRESS
www.dreamspinnerpress.com

Amy Lane

FAMILIAR DEMON

Published by

DREAMSPINNER PRESS

5032 Capital Circle SW, Suite 2, PMB# 279, Tallahassee, FL 32305-7886 USA
www.dreamspinnerpress.com

Familiar Demon
© 2019 Amy Lane.

Cover Art
© 2019 Reese Dante.
http://www.reesedante.com
Cover content is for illustrative purposes only and any person depicted on the cover is a model.

Trade Paperback ISBN: 978-1-64405-187-0
Digital ISBN: 978-1-64405-186-3
Library of Congress Control Number: 2018960688
Trade Paperback published February 2019
v. 1.0

Printed in the United States of America

This paper meets the requirements of
ANSI/NISO Z39.48-1992 (Permanence of Paper).

To the dedicated few who love my weirdness enough to follow me here. And to the Green's Hill folk, who were gracious enough to come visit. And to Mate. For always. And to Mary, who only puts up with these books so she can get to String Boys.

Author's Note

So, the denizens of Green's Hill were not all created JUST for this book. They, in fact, have stories of their own. If you're interested in Lady Cory et al, please visit DSP Publications at https://tinyurl.com/yao3r8pq and check out her first book—*Vulnerable*.

A GOOD BROTHER'S SPIT

THE MARKET was supposed to be neutral ground.

Edward Youngblood gathered his thin silk scarf tighter around his hair and face, making sure his features were obscured. His bright green eyes and sunburned skin were obvious over the covering, but he couldn't help that.

This was supposed to be a place of anonymity. A sort of "Magic Users Are Us" where those with knowledge of the arcane gathered on a hidden plane of existence to talk shop and trade artifacts.

But that didn't mean the name Edward Youngblood wasn't being whispered fiercely these days, and Edward could feel the sands of time running through his fingers even as he took a step inside the gathering tent and out of the fierce suns of this desert plane.

He really needed this chameleon's tongue.

It wasn't an actual tongue of an actual chameleon—that would be easy enough to gather and downright cruel. What he needed was rarer and bit more just, to his way of thinking. The spell called for Chameleon's Tongue, After Use, which meant the tongue of a spy, a shapeshifter who had betrayed his people, right after the act of betrayal.

He looked up at Cuamo, the barkeep of the Market, and nodded. He had intel—the best—that such a shapeshifter would be in this bar this night.

Cuamo nodded and looked away, catching the eyes of four hooded figures in the corner of the tent, and Edward stiffened.

He knew those brown eyes, snapping mad over a hand-woven scarf, and he knew the crossed blue eyes of the man next to him, and oh, God and Goddess help him, he knew the ginormous shoulders and hazel eyes of the man across from them.

And there was no denying the angel in the corner, with or without his wings.

Edward tore the scarf from his face, all need for pretense gone.

"Goddammit!" He stalked to the corner and threw himself gracelessly into the pile of cushions they'd set next to their table for him. "What in the unholy fuck are you idiots doing here?"

1

Harry Youngblood, his brother, ripped off his burnoose and let the full weight of his scowl fall on Edward, and Edward felt his fury start to subside.

"Edward fucking Youngblood—did you really think we'd let you do this alone?"

Edward swallowed, then crossed his arms on their low table the better to bury his head. "It was supposed to be my quest," he said, as close to apology as he ever came. "I'm supposed to find the items alone—"

"And you did," Beltane Youngblood, the hazel-eyed giant, said earnestly. His burnoose fell off without thought—but then, Beltane barely had to breathe and there were ripples in the world. "You found all—"

"Some," Edward corrected.

"Most of the ingredients here all by yourself, and you put them in the back of my parents' minivan, which got inconveniently…."

"Blown up," Francis supplied at Bel's side, looking dreamily up at the grown young man he and his brother familiars had known since his first breath. "They got blown up, remember?"

Beltane smiled besottedly down at Francis, and Edward tried and failed to avoid rolling his eyes. The Youngblood brothers were not technically brothers, nor related by blood. The thing that had started up between Beltane and Francis in the past year both defied description and was never discussed among Francis, Edward, and Harry—but that didn't mean Edward and Harry didn't spend their time worrying about how it might end up.

The whole lot of them were in each other's pockets far too deeply for a failed love affair to separate two of them—and as steady and loyal as Beltane had been since birth, Francis had always been as skittish as, well, a Siamese cat. Messing with the Youngblood chemistry was not wise.

But Bel didn't seem to worry about that. Ever. "Yes, but it was mother who did the blowing up. I mean, she was getting us all away from psychos with guns at the time, but I don't think she wants reminding." Bel sounded very earnest, as he should. His mother was, well, the reason they were all walking around—not just on planet earth but on this particular magical plane where none of them had any business being.

"I'm just saying, there were explosions," Francis told him mildly. Then he smiled, an expression blissfully cold and deeply disturbing on his narrow, roman-nosed face. "I liked the explosions."

"I helped with those, remember?" Bel said with pride. "Mother had just finished teaching me flourishes, right? A little blue, a little green—"

"I was there, Beltane," Edward snapped, trying not to let their byplay distract him. "I remember."

"But we weren't there, were we, Harry?" Harry's beloved, Suriel, turned big earth-brown eyes to Harry's face. Harry—the oldest of them, the protector—had a jaw of granite and a brow that had been pulled down into a scowl more often than not. In over 140 years of friendship and brotherhood, Harry had proven himself the most aggressive and driven of the lot of them.

Edward wasn't sure he was ever getting used to the faintly befuddled look on Harry's face whenever Suriel turned that limpid gaze his way.

"No, Suriel," Harry told him, a flush washing his Irish-fair skin. "You and I were, uh, hashing things out."

Suriel smiled at the rest of them. "We were making love as often as possible," he told them, smug with it. Something in Edward's face must have changed because Suriel's smile faded. "I'm so sorry, Edward. I know you're getting a bit impatient."

"I was really looking forward to that Chameleon's Tongue," Edward admitted quietly.

"Good thing for you we have it," Harry told him, voice as dry as the dust that surrounded them. Then he stuck out his tongue.

"What in the hell!" Edward flailed. "Put that away!"

"I'm a shapeshifter who betrayed you by telling other shapeshifters what you were doing," Harry said. "And I looked carefully at the spell you showed me—"

"You cracked my computer?"

"The password was only sixteen characters and barely encrypted. You were *asking* for an intervention. Anyway, it didn't say the tongue. It said…." Harry made a little "c'mon" gesture with two fingers.

And Edward sighed, because he was right. "It said the spit of the lying tongue, a traitor of the Chameleon people, after he has lied and before the spit has dried," he recited.

"Yes. So, you were here to collect some poor bastard's tongue in a jar, and here I am, just dripping with unrighteous shapeshifter spit. Did you bring a fucking jar?"

"He didn't have to," Suriel said calmly. "You made me bring one for him." And with that he produced a baby food jar, the kind their mother Emma used to mix her paints. He handed it to Harry, and Harry closed his mouth and made a face like he was scraping his tongue on his teeth. After a moment or so he held out his tongue, drooled in the jar, and then sealed it.

He handed the jar to Edward with what could only be described as righteous superiority.

"Thank you," Edward said ungraciously. "That was awesome. Does it justify the entire lot of you lying to me and then pulling off this dramatic… magical intervention?"

"Absofuckinglutely," Harry snarled, suddenly up in Edward's face.

Edward, who had spent much of his life as an orange tomcat, backed up and hissed.

Harry, who had spent *even more* of his life as a long-haired *black* tomcat, curled his lips back from his teeth and growled.

For a moment there was a standoff between them, and then Edward remembered that reason was his watchword, his mantra, and his creed, relaxed his… uhm, upper lip, and straightened. Unconsciously, he brought the back of his hand up by his nose to make sure his whiskers were settled, and took a deep breath.

Then he hated himself, because not only had he let Harry be the dominant cat, as always, but he'd forgotten himself for a moment and tried to smooth whiskers that weren't even there.

For his part, Harry backed up out of fighting space and rubbed the back of his own neck with his hand.

"Edward," he said, with a voice so tender it made Edward ache. "Did you think we wouldn't understand?"

"How could you?" Edward asked, his voice rough in his own ears. "When I didn't understand it myself. It's not… reasonable."

Harry turned a look on him that was so damned compassionate, Edward wanted to hide. Had his brother always been this kind? "Love never is," he said, glancing at his beloved.

Suriel tilted his head forward slightly. "The mystery is part of the joy," he said, angelic serenity at the fore.

"Part of the bloody-arsed… assed… fuck. Fun. Dammit." Back and forth, from an Irish brat in a gold-rush town to a doctor and practitioner of the arcane who was over a century old, Edward was so undone, his voice couldn't even decide who he was. To his horror, he felt his eyes burn, and he gave his emotions a brutal stomp.

Nobody was more shocked than he was when they rebounded, zooming back up to smack him firmly in the solar plexus, leaving him distraught and gasping from pain.

"It wasn't supposed to be love," he said after a moment, his face heating in mortification and despair. "You don't understand—it was so… it made sense and… then it didn't… and now he's in pain and…."

And Harry, the passionate one, the brother he could always count on, didn't let him down now. He crushed Edward to him in an almost violent embrace.

"We'll save him, brother. We'll save him. Don't give up." For a moment the only sound between them was Edward's suppressed sobs, deep breaths, really, as he fought not to be overwhelmed by emotion. Harry tightened his grip and he gave it up, let loose tears on his brother's shoulder, and Harry's whole body shuddered in relief.

And Edward fell apart, sobbing in earnest as he remembered once again that even if his lover wasn't there, he was never alone.

IMP OF THE ARCANE

140 Years Ago

THE DEMON sagged against his restraints, his beastly head lolling, the very human blood torn from his back running down his ribs. The lash rose and fell again, the very sound making Mullins's skin cringe back from his own beastly head as he hid in the shadows.

Menoch did so love his work.

"So, Leonard," Menoch practically purred, "why are we here again?"

Mullins must have made a sound, because Leonard looked up from his slump and shook himself. When Mullins had first arrived in hell, he would have found the shivering of the man's body in conjunction with the beastly head and feet to be an abomination. After he'd had the skin and flesh peeled from his bones and replaced with his own beastly features, he would have felt it to be even more so.

But not now. Not when this man-beast was suffering the torture of a thousand hells to cover for Mullins's misdeed.

Mullins had to come forward—he had to! Even if he suffered the same fate three times over! He made a move toward the red light of the torturer's torch and saw Leonard shake his head slightly. "No," he mouthed.

"*Answer me, filth!*" Menoch screeched.

"I forgot your orders, oh torturer of hell, demon of shame."

Mullins closed his eyes. Even half-dead, Leonard was lying for him, and if Mullins kept gazing at the spectacle of pain, someone would notice the torchlight reflecting from his slitted eyes.

The lash rose and fell again.

"Why?" Menoch demanded.

"I forgot!"

"Lies!" Menoch screamed.

"Truth," Leonard wept, sobs shaking him as he hung from the heated chains bolted to the ceiling. "I forgot. I'm a demon of learning, milord.

Puny and forgetful. *I* am to blame. *I* forgot to relay the order. *I* deserve the lashes of shame."

Well, Menoch *was* the demon of shame—and his lash was diamond tipped. But Leonard maintained the fiction, right up until his spinal column was flayed open. He gave a howl and a wail and lost consciousness, and Menoch's beating stopped.

"He fought that for a long time," he said to the smallish, wrinkled slug thing at his heels.

"Yes, milord."

"It's always better when they fight, Renotly," Menoch said with satisfaction. "He suffers for today, as long as he can, and by tomorrow he's healed, and he suffers some more." Menoch's form was that of a giant, grotesque housefly, flesh-colored, with pulsing bulges of pox coursing along his broken exoskeletal skin. "By hell, I lust at the thought of it!"

"You want to satisfy yourself, milord?" Renotly whined. "I would relieve you!"

Mullins kept his eyes closed, knowing that if he opened them, *he* might be chosen for the honor of relieving Menoch's urges. Nobody in hell wanted that job.

Nobody but Renotly.

Ugh.

The two greater demons of the twelfth sphincter of hell disappeared to do unholy things, and Mullins came forth, lockpick in hand, to help Leonard down from the chains.

Leonard groaned, and Mullins pulled him up, half carrying his bloodied body into the deepest secret recesses of the twelfth sphincter—an almost clean sector of stone, tidy as a monk's cell. He laid Leonard on the bed and conjured cool water, using the magic that Leonard himself had taught.

Leonard was the demon of learning, the scourge of the cold academic who refused to see the real-life consequences of learning, even when terrible forces had been unleashed on earth.

As demons went, he was not exactly terrifying. And when Mullins had come to hell, on his knees, having made a dreadful bargain to spare the life of his younger sister, Leonard had purposefully asked for him as an assistant.

Hell was… hell. There were no grace notes, could never be mercy.

But Leonard had never allowed Mullins, even once, to forget that they were both human beings under the guise of crazed beasts.

A thing Mullins was beginning to regret.

Using more magic—oh, academia could be a glorious place—Mullins took away Leonard's pain, closing his wounds with only the barest of scars. Menoch was notoriously sloppy about details. Leonard would be expected to heal anyway—he wouldn't look to see that the area had been soothed.

"Give me up," Mullins begged, holding water for Leonard to drink. "Give me up—please. I can't stand to watch you—"

"No," Leonard said, voice rasping.

"But… but…." Mullins's voice dropped to a hoarse whisper. "Emma… she's making plans to pull you out—you can't do it when you're half-dead from beating."

"Emma understands," Leonard said softly. "You need to understand as well, my dear boy."

"I don't." Mullins laid Leonard gently down again. "Why? Why would I understand when… oh hells. Leonard, the things we're asked to do down here—why does it even matter!"

"Because they lie," Leonard said softly. "They tell us we have no souls, and so most of the… the *creatures* down here act as though that's fact. It's not. It's all lies. We have souls—you haven't killed a child yet, Mullins. Nor an adult who was not asking for holy retribution. Your soul, should you escape, is still as pure as the day you came. They want you to think it isn't—that you can give in to fear and cowardice, to cruelty. I did that—for a hundred years I did that, and then…."

"Emma," Mullins whispered. Leonard had been summoned by a witch, simply for conversation. Mullins had been there—and even though he knew the lie that Leonard had succumbed to cowardice and fear because Leonard had never been cruel to *Mullins*, Mullins also knew the truth: that Leonard may have lost his soul completely one day, had it beaten and battered, murdered and raped from his person, if he had never engaged in spirited discourse with a golden-haired sorceress who treated him with kindness…

And then fell in love.

"She has forgiven me for the beast I became," Leonard whispered. "The least I can do is spare you the lash so you need never become that beast."

"But it's hurting you!" Mullins's face, covered in coarse hair, was not meant for any of the human contortions of weeping. They *hurt*, for hell's sake! His eyes burned like a human's would in alcohol, and his nose and cheeks ached.

And still, Leonard's hand on his cheek made all that go away. "My son, have faith. We shall pull you out—"

"Do not," Mullins begged. "One more day of Menoch, and then she'll be ready. We've scouted the church, she's cooking the hex bags…." His voice dropped even further. "She's enlisted the *enemy*—"

"Suriel is kind," Leonard said, his voice dry and mocking.

"He's agreed to come," Mullins said stiffly. It was hard enough to remember he had a soul, much less remember that the angel wasn't his enemy—not really.

"Anybody Emma has faith in will be good to his word," Leonard said faintly. "And that means you, my boy. We won't leave you in this dreadful place—please, son. Have hope."

Leonard fell into a fitful sleep then, and Mullins curled up in a ball next to the hard-slatted bed that he usually slept in. Gah! Leonard had never lost his kindness, no matter what he professed to have been. But Mullins…. Mullins was hanging on by the barest of threads. He'd been told to go lure a young brothel brat into a river, the better to claim his soul now, while it was unformed and still bitter as a child's could be made, and before it matured and learned forgiveness and self-care.

He couldn't do it—not with this child.

In his heart, he knew, not with *any*.

Leonard had seen him, ready to defy Menoch, ready to be beaten from existence, and had stepped forward.

Leonard had learned the art of taking such beatings.

Apparently it was to draw strength from the warmth of his true soul.

EDWARD COULDN'T stop staring.

He and Harry and Francis crouched in the underbrush near the Sacramento River, still shaking from their escape from the Golden Child, the brothel that had been their life and their hell ever since their mothers—in one way or another—had wandered into the pitcher plant of safety that the place offered. Their mothers had passed away, leaving the boys to fend for themselves, and getting the hell out of the brothel seemed to be their best bet.

The *plan* had been to escape from Bertha and Big Cass, and then to hop on a railcar heading for the Midwest. Harry wasn't great with plans, but he'd earned tickets for his sisters to go back before his mother died of pox and a broken heart, and he said there was farmland Midwest, and Bertha and Big Cass couldn't even dream of the boys in their care escaping that far.

That had been the plan, anyway. But Harry had set fire to the trash pile as a diversion and escaped in the smoke, and Edward and Francis had gotten caught in the herd of women screaming as they exited the building.

Big Cass had spotted them in the street, running for the outskirts of the city, and had given chase.

He'd caught Francis from behind and given him a terrible blow to the head. Edward wasn't sure what happened after that. One minute his heart had been racing in his chest and the next Big Cass was stumbling back, blood rushing from his nose. He'd howled and launched himself at Edward, but Edward took advantage of the moment of shock. He grabbed Francis and hauled him away from the scene, ducking around a corner and waiting until Cass's bulky figure shambled by. He'd been able to make it to the meeting place, but Francis had grown increasingly less cognizant of his surroundings as they ran. By the time they'd run into Harry, Francis was barely conscious and Edward was exhausted from dragging him.

When Harry heard them thrashing through the bushes, Edward assumed Big Cass had caught them, and his heart shriveled inside his chest. Harry pulled them to safety, and Edward was honestly relieved to see the beast-man and the witch entering the clearing.

They may have eaten children's souls for breakfast, but at this point anything was better than being a gaping maw at the Golden Child, waiting to be sold to the next filthy miner desperate to dip his wick.

And now, watching as a beautiful woman and a ferocious beast set up hex bags in a pentagram around another beast-man in the center, he was working furiously to realign his world.

His mind—ever logical—saw the pentagram and thought *Witchcraft!* But that logical mind was not immune to the other things going on. The beautiful woman was kind to the beast, and both of them were intent on saving the thing in the center of the pentagram.

And then the beast shed his own blood to make the magic complete.

Edward had shed enough of his own blood in the brothel—had given himself to Big Cass multiple times to keep the brutal bouncer away from Francis, the youngest of the three of them and the most fragile.

He understood self-sacrifice, and in particular, he understood that peculiar wrenching feeling that happened when the self-sacrifice went against the grain of who you were. It was not *logical* to hurt yourself or allow pain in order to protect others, but sometimes it was *necessary*.

In future years, Edward would have the selfishness vs. selflessness debate many times, in salons, with his brothers, with friends and teachers, professors and angels—and in particular, the terrible beast-man he watched disappearing into the shadows on this fateful night.

But in spite of the many years of learning that would come, he would never, ever manage to verbalize the crystal clear understanding of the concept that he experienced watching that hideous, terrifying, vulnerable being limp away to what sounded like a terrible fate.

The only word that would ever come close was love.

His attention on the demon—for that was what he turned out to be— was pulled away when the woman, Emma, summoned the angel Suriel.

The angel.

An *angel* joined hands with this woman, this obvious sorceress, and together, they stood over the figure lying on the ground before them and…

Made magic.

Edward's brain forgot reason in that moment and embraced wonder.

A glorious glow surrounded the figures in the clearing, then spread, a nimbus surrounding the area, encompassing Edward, Harry, and Francis, permeating their bodies, before it simply ceased to be.

When it was gone, instead of Harry, a sturdily built, plain boy of fourteen, there sat a growling, spitting fluffy black cat, fur upright in fury. Next to him, eyes crossed, a mostly cream-colored Siamese cat stared bemusedly at his paw.

They both opened their mouths in surprise and meowed.

Edward sat down on haunches covered in orange fur and stared at Harry in utter helplessness.

They were cats?

Harry went rushing out into the clearing in a cloud of righteous indignation and black fur. Edward would eventually follow—and listen as Emma explained what she had done.

"I can give you a home," she said softly. "I can give you food and clothes. I can teach you to read and give you a purpose. I just ask that you hold my power, be my familiars, use my magic to change your shape and do no harm. I…." Her voice broke. "I just didn't want to leave him, you see. If I hadn't stored my power in the three of you, I would have aged and died right here, and he would have awakened in this world to live a long life alone. I'm sorry. I know it was wrong—so wrong—to not ask you. But please… won't you please forgive me enough to let us care for each other?"

Edward recalled the kindness she'd shown the demon beast, and as he watched, the now-human Leonard sat up, looking plain and gentle. When they all heard the racket of Big Cass thrashing through the woods, it was only logical that Edward allow Leonard to scoop him up and hurry him away from danger.

Harry could run from danger on his own, but Edward appreciated transportation and some caring for.

It was only logical.

NOBODY WAS as surprised as Mullins was, the first time Emma summoned him after Leonard's redemption.

He'd been facing off with Menoch, lying—because that's what demons did.

"I have no idea where he is," Mullins said, as though he hadn't missed his friend every moment of every tortuous day. "He was summoned—"

"By that *woman*?" Menoch spat the word. Of course the demon of shame was a misogynist. Mocking women gave him more power than he knew what to do with.

"Yes—you told him to answer her, remember?"

"Yes." Menoch had beady little human eyes in his fly's face. It made Mullins want to vomit, even though he spent much of his time in hell as this twisted fusion of man, pig, horse, and goat. "I remember. And then she learned his name and he had no choice." A horrible buzz-snort then. "Bloody accords."

There were treaties—old ones—between heaven and hell. Mullins and Leonard had studied them long and hard before they'd risked sending

Leonard up to the surface without a summoning and allowing Emma to transform him back into a man.

Mullins had spent enough time memorizing those treaties, word for word, that he'd begun to doubt their necessity.

Essentially, the treaties drew out the rules of hell:

No demon shall break his word, but lying is perfectly acceptable.

Demons must come when called by name.

Hell may compel demonic actions.

Demons cannot be wiped from existence by not complying—but they may be punished.

A demon's surrender is the only thing that can end his suffering *and* his soul.

And:

Redemption for the atrocities of hell can only happen with sincere sacrifice.

The. End.

That was it.

Mullins had drawn up enough contracts as one of the 666 scribes of hell to know that everything else was window dressing.

It was like the spell for a demon keeping a small chunk of its soul. There were long, involved passages about needing small mammal's entrails, complete with several types of microbial activity, to ward off complete damnation in the heart of a demon's soul.

It had taken two years of intense reading for Mullins and Leonard to realize that the entire passage was about caring for something smaller than one's self. It didn't need to be a cat or a rat with a petri dish in its stomach—it needed to be a *live animal* who had just been cared for.

Once Mullins had deciphered that passage, he and Leonard had looked up the spell for redeeming a demon—which had taken years. But years they took, and they had faith.

Mullins hadn't been paid for this task. He'd worked long hours after his regular duties.

But he'd done it for the same reason Leonard had risked his life and soul to escape.

Emma—beautiful, kind Emma who had so guilelessly offered Mullins a way out—had loved Leonard enough to redeem him from all the evils he'd performed in hell.

Leonard thought being with Emma was worth the risk.

Mullins thought knowing that Leonard was safe was worth the risk.

Just like the Articles of Hellish Redemption, the solution had been so much simpler than the spell that delineated it.

Mullins had snuck Leonard out, past the catacombs of the scribes. Through sulfur, arsenic, and lakes of blood, they had managed to wend their way to the surface without the magic that would have summoned the other demons and given away their plan. Only the imps of schadenfreude at the entrance to the surface had seen them, and while they'd both been wounded, Emma had been there at the portal to help Mullins and Leonard make their escape.

After Leonard drew his first breath as a free man, Mullins had returned, sneaking around the frenzied imps and teleporting back to his place.

Nobody noticed the magic then. They were too upset about the redemption. While nobody knew which demon had been stripped from their ranks, all of hell knew that *somebody* had. It was why Mullins hadn't been able to go with them.

The redemption could only be performed on *one* of them. If Mullins had stayed, the very fact that he was still a demon would have led the others right to Emma and Leonard, no matter how well they were hidden.

As it was, Mullins was there at Menoch's beck and call while all of hell tried to figure out which of them had actually managed to escape.

"Well, the accords gave her the power," Mullins said patiently, breathing through the pain. "But now somebody is summoning me by name, and by the accords, I must go."

Ah, the blessed accords.

Because Mullins recognized the voice of the summoner—and it was low and sweet and kind. Always, always kind.

Emma.

He allowed the world of hell to fade and embraced the reality of the woman who had stolen Leonard from him—and given them both hope.

The room she summoned him to was plain, a log cabin with running water—an anomaly for this place and time, Mullins knew—and two bedrooms. In the distance, he could hear the giant shush of the ocean.

Emma stood next to Leonard in front of the summoning circle, holding a delicate seal-tipped cat in her arms. Leonard was holding a marmalade tom, and a fluffy black tomcat curled up in the back of the room, letting out a low-level tomcat growl.

Emma smiled as soon as he had completely materialized. "Mullins!" she cried, as though seeing an old and dear friend. "We're so glad you could come!"

Mullins nodded and kept tears of relief at bay. Tears hurt, and they looked grotesque, and they did nobody any good.

"I'm happy to be here," he said gruffly. "You have… guests?"

Leonard stepped forward and looked behind him. "Harry, would you like to change form and shake hands like a man?"

There was a mild ring of challenge, and the black cat gave a deep breath and…

Suddenly stood, a midsized compact young man, still in the throes of adolescence. His hair was a black fury around his head, and his black eyes snapped with irritation.

That nonstop feline growl had not yet ceased, and Leonard cocked his head and raised an eyebrow.

Mullins had a moment to register that Leonard, as a human, was a plainly handsome man, with a little bit of gray in his medium brown hair and laugh lines around his hazel eyes, before the boy-who-was-no-longer-a-cat stepped forward, hand extended.

"Harry," he said, voice still growly. "Emma and Leonard say we can trust you. Pleased to meet you."

Mullins took his grip around his goat hoof and was faintly warmed by the way the boy squeezed hard, like Mullins was a human, and shook.

"Pleased to meet you, young master," Mullins said quietly. He let go of Harry's hand and raised his eyebrows at Emma. "Familiars?"

He could feel it now, the way her once formidable power was spread out not just with Leonard, but among the other three creatures in the room. It was an incredible sacrifice—it would cut her lifespan to a fifth of the time she would normally live as a learned and studied witch—but she and Leonard seemed so content, he couldn't even bring himself to ask.

"Edward," Harry said gruffly into Mullins's realizations, "Francis— c'mon ye lazy bastards and fuckin' change."

The marmalade cat leaped solidly to the floor and grew into another midsized boy, not much younger than Harry. This one had red hair, freckles, and stunning green eyes, and for a moment Mullins was…

Beguiled.

His body stilled, his restless heart and worried mind took their ease.

All his fears about facing Menoch again, becoming snared in the lies of hell, grew still.

This boy was looking at him curiously, head cocked, as though the two of them shared a secret.

"Hullo," the boy said cheerfully. He stepped forward and extended his hand. "I'm Edward."

Mullins shook his hand dutifully, but a part of him was lost, back hundreds of years, when he and the smithy's boy had tussled in the grass one morning and shared heated skin, hot touches, a tender, wonder-filled kiss.

Had the boy possessed green eyes like this? Maybe not... but something about *this* boy was mesmerizing, like that one had been.

Mullins shook himself, exactly like a beast, and released Edward's hand. "Master Edward," he said, bowing slightly.

With a delicate little whirl, the white cat in Emma's arms became a younger, slighter boy, with white-blond hair and crossed blue eyes. "Francis," he said, stepping into Edward's space without any self-consciousness. He grasped Mullins's hand and Mullins gasped—but kept his composure.

Later he would tell Leonard that their youngest familiar had a drop or two of truly fey blood in his system. Angels, Mullins could touch at will, but the fey—they were beyond anybody's management.

But the boy—and unlike Edward and Harry, who were on the cusp of manhood, Francis was truly a boy—only gave Mullins the ghost of a smile and practically floated back into his cat form, and into Emma's arms.

"You have a family," Mullins said to Leonard, trying to keep the surprise from his own voice. Demons didn't find redemption and reclaim their humanity—and if they did, they never became foster fathers to a trio of fey and human children.

"Emma's doing," Leonard said, tilting his head warmly toward the woman who had saved him in every sense of the word. "She stored her power in them the night she brought me back. It was...." He grimaced.

"It was the only way," she said simply. "They boys were in the bushes, watching our every move. I needed vessels and I... well, I won't say I did it shamelessly. But as it turned out, they needed us as much as we needed them." She smiled fondly and stroked Francis soothingly behind the ears. "It's worked out very well for all of us, I hope."

Harry shot her a wary look. "You've been good to us," he said, his voice sounding rusty, like he didn't use it enough. "Better than anyone. We thank you."

She smiled gently at him, her eyes troubled. "It's been our pleasure, young Harry. Now please make yourselves comfortable, and by all means get poor Mullins a cushion."

Harry took one from the sofa against the wall, and Edward brought over a chest for him to lean against. Both of them had obviously been schooled in how to handle a demon summoning, because they began mumbling the spell of protection three steps from the pentagram on the floor, and they continued mumbling it as they set Mullins up to sit cross-legged, as was most comfortable for him, on the floor.

They continued the recitation until they were safe on the other side of the chalked outline, and Mullins nodded approvingly.

"Very good," he said. "And your Latin is flawless." He winked at Leonard. "Did you teach them that?"

Leonard inclined his head. "I did. But they've been good students—in all matters."

"Emma taught us to mend our own clothes," Edward said shortly, as though affronted. "And how to cook."

Mullins was delighted. "Well, everybody should know how to care for themselves. Emma does take good care of you, I'm sure, but someday you must care for yourselves, yes?"

Harry and Edward exchanged the glances of puzzled conspirators. "Someday, yes," Harry said carefully, and for a moment, Mullins doubted. The boys were planning to run away already, weren't they?

"Emma said we could stay as long as it suited us," Edward said diplomatically. "We were surprised, you see, to suddenly be cats."

Mullins looked at Emma with some speculation, and she herself gave back a very catlike smile.

"I see," he said politely. Inside, he was thinking that Emma had perhaps done the wisest thing of any human he'd ever known. She'd given the boys their freedom—but had also given them an incentive to stay. Clever, clever Emma.

Wistfully, Mullins thought that if he had been born to parents as wise as Emma and Leonard, he might not be sitting here, a twisted beast, pathetically grateful that Emma and Leonard's careful schooling had never put Mullins in the position of having to choose between his own well-being and tearing the boys apart, as protocol would have dictated had they forgotten their protection incantation while getting him a place to sit.

He hoped with the tattered remnants of his soul that he never had to choose between what protocol dictated and harming Leonard and Emma's children.

He had a sinking feeling he might rather be torn apart himself than participate in harming these boys that the two of them so obviously cherished.

It turned out that the boys were the reason he was there.

Leonard sat down in a hand-carved rocking chair that Mullins gathered he had made himself, and Emma made herself comfortable on the couch. Together they gently urged Mullins to help the boys learn Latin, to build upon the very solid knowledge they had already imparted and to explain nuances that would hinder spellwork and get in the way of their more arcane studies.

"I don't get it," Harry said grumpily, writing with awkward precision on his small chalkboard. "Everybody keeps telling me that it's the intention that counts. If it's the intention that counts, why can't we just think 'Turn into a toad' and have that happen?"

"Language makes your thoughts clearer, Harry," Edward said, concentrating on his own tablet. Francis sat next to him, still in cat form, and moved his paw purposefully on a scattering of dust Emma had brought in when she couldn't coax him to change. "If you just think 'Turn into a toad' at someone, the thought's gonna go wide. You might look at their hat and turn *it* into a toad; you might turn their boots into a toad. But if you say very specifically 'Save the sheep in the wold but turn their owner into a toad,' and you use a different language to focus it, to make it special, the spell is more likely to take effect."

"Exactly," Mullins said, surprised and pleased. Harry was smart and aggressive—but he was also passionate and emotional. Edward was the more logical of the two of them, the calmer one, the thinker.

Mullins was enjoying all the boys' company, but something about Edward soothed Mullins, gave him feelings of peace in the universe. For a demon living in constant fear of Menoch's lash, it was an amazing luxury, this feeling of peace.

Suddenly Francis let out a distracted meow, and all eyes turned toward the little cat who was licking the dust off his paw. In front of him was a slightly hard to read but perfect conjugation of the Latin verb "to eat."

Emma raised her eyebrows. "Feeling a bit peckish, are we, my sweet?"

Francis twitched a tail and yawned, showing teeth.

Edward reached out and smoothed his brother's fur. "Fine," he said shortly. "Let me finish my own work and Harry and I will fetch the cake from the cold box. Is that what you wanted?"

Francis cleaned his paw again, feigning indifference.

"There is also," Harry said mildly, "some fish left over from dinner."

Francis sat back on his haunches and blinked expectantly. Harry held out his tablet for Mullins's inspection. "I botched the last one," he said apologetically. "I'll fix it when I'm back if that's all right with you?"

"It is indeed," Mullins said, nodding. Edward kept working assiduously as Harry moved to the small kitchen area and began pulling out the cake and the dishes, Francis at his heels. Mullins risked a glance behind him and saw Harry feeding Francis small pieces of grilled trout as he worked, and Francis taking them with delicate nibbles.

He'd seen brothers in blood who weren't as kind.

"I *didn't* botch the last one," Edward said with satisfaction. "That should be acceptable."

Mullins forgot the grotesquerie of his expression and smiled.

To his eternal surprise, Edward smiled back. "It's okay?" Edward asked, always seeking perfection.

"Indeed," Mullins told him. "It's very well done."

"Excellent! Time for cake. Would you like some, Mullins?"

Abruptly Mullins became the outsider again, an agent of hell, a creature who depended on tricks and subterfuge and entrapment. "I'm sorry, Master Edward, no. And Emma and Leonard should have taken care to make sure you never offer a demon food in your home, ever."

Edward bit his lip. "They said that," he mumbled, clearly discomfited. "It's not their fault—"

"You were being polite, Edward," Emma said softly. "Just remember you are lucky this is Mullins. Any other demon would have taken you up on it and we would have all been ripped apart in our beds."

If a demon ever ate the food offered to him in free will, he was bound to the offerer. Another demon could have used that bond to return to the home unbidden and do… well, whatever the family was in a state to let him do.

Edward nodded, looking shamed in a way that was far beyond what reprimand Emma had offered, and Mullins watched him go, troubled.

"They're very young," he said to Leonard, and Leonard gave him a bleak look.

"They are—far too young to have gone through what they have." Leonard made a little sign then, with his forefinger and thumb, and looked up and around. Mullins didn't have to look around—his old mentor hadn't lost his touch, and the secrecy spell was very firm indeed.

Mullins cocked his head, wondering why Leonard would block his next words from the family.

"What?"

"They were escaping from a brothel—all three of the boys had been abused or traded. Edward and Harry were running to try to save Francis from the worst of it."

Mullins felt a vague red haze fill his brain. Anger, the devil's favorite sin.

"Which brothel?" he asked, his voice as measured as it had always been.

"The Golden Child," Leonard told him, eyes level. "Their worst abuser, Big Cass, was killed the night we were there—"

"By whom?" Mullins needed to make sure the job had been done right.

"Suriel," Leonard said, not trying to sugarcoat it.

"How long…." Time stretched so oddly in hell. It had felt like a year, maybe two down there, but Mullins had assumed it had been but a day. But this place—this was a well-established home. There were gas lights in sconces on the walls, and the boys had an established routine. Somebody had already taught them Latin verb conjugations, for sweet hell's sake!

"We've been here five or so months," Leonard said. "But don't expect the boys to grow by leaps and bounds. Emma wove that spell good and tight—she and I aren't exactly immortal anymore, but they're not exactly mortal, either. We figured five for every hundred. More if they use their human forms a lot, less if…." Mullins saw he was looking at Francis with worry in his eyes. "They tried so hard to get him out, you see. And he got caught one day while the boys were both… busy. He didn't want to tell them… kept it close. The damage it did to his soul—well, he's going to be a cat for much of his life until it's gone, you understand?"

Mullins nodded, his red haze intensifying. And still he couldn't help ask, "Edward too?" The boy seemed so even, so calm.

"He was pretty—he was treated better than Harry, but yes."

It wasn't a haze anymore. Mullins had to fight it from taking over his entire body. He knew this feeling, this liquid, viscous sludge pouring through his veins.

This was the gift of hell, the gift of a killer's blood.

"Mullins," Leonard hissed. "Your eyes!"

Mullins cleared his throat. "I need to take my leave," he murmured. "Do you have any other names for me besides Big Cass?"

Leonard knew why he asked. "Bertha was the proprietress. And Edward has told me about a few customers who were particularly brutal." Leonard gave him the names without remorse—which reassured Mullins, actually. Rage was not just a demonic trait. He could feel this weight in his breast and still be human.

"Is that all?" Best to be thorough here.

"Yes. Don't harm any of the girls." Leonard nodded decisively. "They worked hard to protect the boys for as long as possible. Think of it like hell—the demons in power have choices and they choose to abuse their power. The demons without power are victims—"

"Until they become abusers." Some of the red faded from Mullins's head. This was Leonard's best lesson, and Mullins would be better off if he never forgot it.

"Indeed." Leonard met his eyes then and made the gesture to take away their little bubble of secrecy. The chatter from the kitchen intruded on Mullins's dark thoughts, and for a moment his emotions were etched in crystal.

Emma was the mother and Leonard was the father—that much had never been clearer.

The boys were their children—of course.

But he had a use too—a service besides teaching them Latin—which he would do many, many, many more times in the future.

As far as he was concerned, this other thing was the reason he'd become a demon at all.

He managed to be polite and kind as they wrapped up the grammar lesson. When it was over, one at a time, they stood and bowed.

"Thank you for the lesson, Mullins," Edward said, so incredibly polite he must have studied.

"'Preciate it," Harry muttered, face flushed. "Wish ye could eat. Would feel better if we could repay ya."

Mullins knew his beast's eyes grew wider. "This was a gift, young master," he said gently.

Harry's mouth worked. "Not good at accepting those." He looked mournfully around the snug little cabin. "I'll try to get better. But you're a good man to come help. Thank you."

"Of course," Mullins said gravely, wondering what was to come from Francis.

Francis sat at the hearth in cat form, washing his paws until Edward nudged him with his sock-clad toe. "C'mon, Francis, don't be an ass."

The cat let out a growl, then abruptly turned into the enchantingly fey and beautiful young man with the white hair, and bowed.

"Thank you," he said, meeting Mullins's eyes with must have been a supreme effort.

Mullins inclined his head. "My pleasure."

And Francis was a cat again.

Mullins felt something in his chest that displaced the rage, if only for a moment. "This family was a balm to my bleeding soul," he said, because demons could speak the truth. "Please summon me as often as you wish."

"We release you," the boys all said as one, and Mullins felt the pull of hell again.

He allowed himself to fade, but he didn't go directly back to his catacomb in hell.

First he passed a spell of deception over himself. Unlike being summoned, when the compulsion was to present himself in his real form, visiting an unwary human allowed him a certain leeway.

In this case, he allowed himself to look like a typical human of the era. Dirty, unshaven, black stubble growing from his jaw, he wore rank and threadbare breeches, battered boots, and a cotton shirt that had seen many washes, none of them recent.

Then he arrived at his destination.

Sacramento was a gold rush city, with ankle-breaking cobblestones in the streets and a dock for ships traveling up the delta to bring supplies. The high boardwalks tried to keep the shops and apartments from getting wet in the floods that invariably tormented the region every ten years or so, but the horse-drawn carts that rolled down the road and the river delta itself left the streets and boardwalks covered with silt and mud and shit.

It had potential to be a town someday, but today?

Today Mullins lumped the whole place in with the wolves and deer at the Golden Child.

He found the brothel on the edge of the town proper, along the railroad tracks, and his heart hurt. The boys had been hiding under bushes, escaping. How hard must it have been to see a train every day, going someplace other, someplace *else*, and to be stuck here in a torment of other's making.

Human form or not, he allowed the red of rage to fill up his eyes.

He crashed through the doors of the Golden Child Saloon and Brothel like the forces of the Apocalypse on the greased wheels of hell.

Nobody looked up. Nobody cared.

A prematurely old woman, face caked in paint, sauntered up to him. "Can I help you?"

"I'm looking for Bertha," he said, voice husky.

"She's in session with Bruno," the woman said, eyes crusted thick with kohl shifting uneasily.

Mullins knew this name.

It was a place to start.

"Show me," he rumbled, and the woman blinked, her mind exhausted by just the command.

"Of course," she said.

Mullins smiled the death's head grin of the beast.

Let the revenge begin.

When he walked away from the brothel that night, he was one of many fleeing. The girls were, as Leonard had asked, unharmed, mostly dressed, running for their lives to the train station in the night.

Mullins had made sure they had as much money as they needed.

There were a lot trousers that would not be put back on after this night.

He hadn't gotten all the names that Leonard had given him—but he would.

Right now it was best to just fade into the night and let others wash off the blood.

Nobody would hurt those boys again. Not under Mullins's watch. Emma was the mother, Leonard was the father, the boys were the children, and Suriel was the protector.

But this family was special, and they needed Mullins in the capacity for which he could best serve.

Mullins was the *avenger*, and nobody would hurt his boys again.

Planning a Demon's Demise

Present

EDWARD MANAGED to calm down, hating that his brothers had seen him this distraught.

He was the reasonable one. One hundred fifty-five years to cement his identity, from birth to the day he was made a familiar, through to the present, and he had always been the reasonable one.

"You are such a nelly," Harry said disgustedly, helping him sit down.

Edward glared at him. "Thanks a lot—"

"No, not because you cried, you ass, because you're all up inside your own head. Oh my God, did you think only you, Edward Youngblood, could go about and find the secret ingredients to make a demon human again?" Harry rolled his eyes and pitched his voice high and hysterical. "This is my quest because I am the scholar and my brothers are too goddamned brain dead to even get out the front door without me—and I'm doomed, doomed, *doomed* because I am doing this all by myself and—"

"You used to haunt the beach for months, you fuckwad," Edward said irritably. "Remember that? Oh, where's Harry? He's walking along the cliffs, gazing moodily into the sea, and thinking that his angel will never be able to come down and be with him." Edward shook his head at Suriel, who was grinning in delight. "He was insufferable."

"He tried to do that with me in his bed," Suriel told them all happily. "A rogue wave almost washed him out to sea in cat form. It was amazing."

Francis burst into peals of laughter, and Beltane's thunderous chuckle practically rattled their desert plane.

"Thanks, beloved," Harry said dryly. "I'm sure they all wanted to know that."

"Oh, but we did!" Francis howled, and Harry smacked him on the back of the head.

"Knock it off." He turned to Edward then, all trace of teasing gone from his brown eyes. "So, what we need to know is how much of your list you've knocked off and what else it is you need."

Edward sighed.

"That's the problem," he said, giving Harry the carefully hand-copied spell he'd managed to make from a singed piece of parchment Leonard had smuggled out of hell. "Here's my list of ingredients—most of which were one of a kind and got blown up in the damned minivan."

He handed Harry another hand-scrawled page. "And this is the list of instructions. Everything here is one of a kind and irreplaceable. The instructions are impossible—particularly in this day and age—"

"A virgin's tears aren't likely to be found," Harry grunted. "That's true. And neither is a… what is this?"

"A horn of a Pyrenean ibex. Huh—aren't those—"

"Extinct," Edward said glumly. "I stole the one I had from a museum."

"Three strands of hair from an elven king." Harry looked at Suriel. "Do we know one of those?"

"I'm sure I don't know what you're talking about," Suriel said blandly, and Harry and Edward met eyes. Mullins had told Edward once that Francis was at least a quarter if not a half fey—but that angels didn't recognize feylings. Edward and Harry had spent some of their formative years gently baiting Suriel to admit what Leonard and Emma guardedly admitted was possible—that the fey existed and were far more common than most people thought. They'd never stopped this game, but watching Suriel draw a complete blank was still mildly entertaining.

"I think you do," Harry said, grim mouth and dark eyebrows doing a figure eight thing in conjunction. "And someday I'll get you to admit it." He turned to Edward, tabling that discussion for the moment. "And you. You're right—some of this shite you can't find anywhere—it really is gone. But… but remember, Mullins *trained* us."

"He taught us to be precise or we might get ourselves or our subject killed!" Edward protested. "How can I be precise if half this stuff doesn't exist anymore!"

"Except precision is not necessarily using *just* the same verb! You remember that? Remember our first munitions spell, Edward? Or did it get shaken out of that egg-shaped head of yours!"

"I remember," Francis said, smiling wickedly. "We almost blew ourselves up. Beltane, you should have been there. If Leonard hadn't stopped us, the house would have been in the stratosphere."

Bel's hazel eyes grew big and round. "It would have? Who cast that spell? How'd it go so high? Why'd it get out of control? How'd Dad stop it? What did Mum say?"

Edward glared at Harry sourly. "Now look what you've done."

Harry shook his head. "No," he said, thinking hard. "It's an important memory. Beltane, you're sure you've never heard this?"

Bel shook his head, masses of yellow hair tumbling over his eyes. "No—I'd have remembered if you all nearly took out my home, wouldn't I?" He chewed his lip then, an uncharacteristic display of vulnerability in a young man who had been confident and boundless pretty much from birth. "So much you all know that I wasn't there for." He smiled uncertainly at Francis, who gazed back with a ton of adoration and not a modicum of self-awareness. "Things you haven't shared that I can only guess."

Edward and Harry met stricken eyes then, over their heads. Was it possible? Did Beltane not know about their pasts? That time before Emma, before being magical beings, was both long ago and so immediate, it carried with it the same weight of fear and pain and regret that it had that night they'd accidentally stepped into Emma's summoning circle.

How was it possible that Bel, the child they'd loved since his birth over twenty years ago, didn't know who they all had been?

But they had other things to think about—Harry seemed to be making a point.

"So," Edward said reluctantly, because he was the storyteller of the three of them and always had been, "this goes back to when we started the family business."

EDWARD REMEMBERED very specifically that, while Suriel had been on board, they'd managed to shock Mullins in the worst way. "You wish to what?"

"We wish to blow up a goddamned brothel," Harry snapped, glaring at Edward. "Someone here needed to go get his wick wet—"

Edward grimaced. It felt distasteful to talk about things so coarsely—particularly in front of Mullins, who, in spite of the horrors of hell, of which Leonard had let loose only a little, had always presented himself as a gentleman.

Mullins tilted his beastly head. "A girl?" he asked, sounding puzzled.

Edward flushed. During Mullins's last visit, Harry and Francis had been giving Edward grief about seducing a local shopkeeper's son. The boy apparently had been horrified by his inclinations, and Emma had ended up magicking him to Paris with a complete knowledge of the language and a job in a shop, just so nobody in their tiny Northern California town north of Mendocino would even know.

Having been raised as a familiar for the past twenty-five years, Edward was beginning to think that actual human beings were terrible, disastrous products of misguided religion and sexual repression who made hells of their own bodies and refused to see the glory they'd been given in the first place.

"I like both," Edward said with dignity. "It's not a crime."

"Sadly not true," Leonard said, shaking his head. "Sodomy laws are still fairly common, but we understand your point, Edward. Biologically an inclination for both sexes is probably more common than an inclination for just the one, but nobody's done the research. And we are straying from our topic."

"Sodomy is way too fun to outlaw," Edward muttered to Harry, and as Harry looked at him in surprise, he realized that everybody was waiting for him to elaborate on what the topic actually was. "Uh, oh. Anyway, the topic."

And suddenly he remembered Marilyn, the forward saloon girl in Fort Bragg who had invited him into her bed just two days before.

Edward had been there to doctor a patient—he and Leonard had a reputation as physicians by now, and people had ridden from as far away as Portland for their services. The patient resting comfortably, the danger over, Edward had gone willingly. Unlike Harry, who took sex as seriously as he took everything else, Edward threw himself rather gleefully into any assignation that fortune gifted him with. However, at the end of this one, as the sun rose, Edward recognized bruises all over the young lady's flank and backside. As he'd run his hands along her mottled skin in horror, she'd gazed at him shyly, biting her lip.

"Don't you understand?" she asked roughly. "That's why I wanted you. Because you'd be kind and make it nice. Mistress Cora lets the men do whatever they want to us. I just… I'd give my time for free, just to have it not be awful."

And for the first time, Edward had drawn the line between the rough-and-tumble saloon in Fort Bragg, where he'd been visiting, and his own terrible childhood in the Golden Child. And indeed, some of the girls were there by choice, and he was all for that.

But some of the girls were not, and Marilyn was one of them.

And he'd been filled with a righteous fury.

He didn't even remember how he spirited the girl away at that point. He'd brought a horse—he supposed he'd thrown her on it and bundled as many possessions as he could find. He remembered the two-hour ride overland and Marilyn clinging to the saddle pommel, trying not to cry out with pain as Edward recited as many healing spells as he could remember to help her make it to Emma and Leonard's steadily growing cliff-side home.

As he'd spilled out his story to Emma and Leonard and Harry and Francis, he'd seen the look pass between their parents, that look that said, "We'll do this, but they have to be sure."

"Boys," Emma had said, breaking into Edward's furious diatribe, "this is important. If we rescue these girls, that might not be the end of it. The ones who still wish to work will need a place of their own. The ones who wish to escape need to be taken to their homes. One of the great paradoxes of a place like this if it's being run badly is that so many people depend on it, whether it's evil or not. Are you prepared? Once we help the girls escape and take down the brothel owners, you need to be on board for whatever tasks come after."

Surprisingly, Francis was the one who spoke. "You rescued us. We can rescue them. We don't need to make them familiars—just make them free."

"And give them resources," Harry said practically. He'd looked at Emma then, a shrewd gleam in his eye that Edward appreciated. Harry was their planner, but he was also their hothead, which made things precarious sometimes. "You have an idea?"

Emma nodded. "I have… contacts," she said vaguely, tapping her forefinger to her full lower lip. "Okay. Here's what we'll do…. Harry?"

"Yes?"

"You, Edward, Mullins, you formulate a plan that involves…." She grimaced. "Not a lot of carnage."

"I beg your pardon!" Edward burst out indignantly. "Did you not see her bruises? Did you not *treat* her bruises?"

"Enough deaths will draw attention, son," Leonard said, the calm, as ever, in the eye of the storm. "We're getting rid of the brothel and getting the girls to safety. Mullins and Suriel mete out life and death and justice. We just help the living."

"Unless they try to unhelp us first," Harry clarified.

Leonard stared at him levelly, but Harry didn't back down. "Define that," Leonard said at last.

"I'm not letting another fuckin' prick use me—"

Leonard recoiled. "Never," he said fiercely. "Self-defense, yes. Nobody hurts my boys. But no offense. No cold-blooded murder. No piles of bodies. Keep yourselves safe and minimize the number of deaths. Glory hallelujah, boys—have we not tried to teach you moderation?"

"I'll moderate him!" Edward and Harry said in tandem, glaring at each other.

Harry had stared him down then, and Edward had broken, as always. Eventually Edward would learn to love being Harry's second, but in the beginning he had felt…

Failed. Like he'd been given this second chance with Leonard and Emma and wasn't adequate to the task.

It was a feeling he'd never been able to shake.

But they'd been too busy then for him to even give the feeling voice.

"I've got an idea," Harry said then, because no surprise there. "But we'll need Mullins to teach Edward a spell."

"Not you?" Edward asked, miffed.

"I'm not as good with them on the fly. You're better with magic and always have been," Harry said without quailing from the knowledge at all.

It was the truth, but Edward had learned then what made his brother the leader as much as he wished he was up for the task. As it was, he and Harry drew up the summoning circle and Edward said the words.

As Harry said, he was the most adept at magic, but there was more to it than that.

Edward just liked Mullins; that was all.

"What kind of spell?" Mullins asked after they'd explained it to him, and Edward took a moment to breathe and appreciate Mullins's presence. Like Leonard, Mullins had a calmness to him that soothed all the boys.

*Un*like Leonard, Mullins also held a sort of attraction for Edward that he couldn't quite put his finger on. Underneath the formal coattails he always wore, Edward suspected his human body was quite fit—but it wasn't that, or not entirely.

It was that his beast's face, which should have been terrifying on the human shoulders, seemed more even, more handsome and noble every time Edward saw him. There was a balance inside Mullins that seemed to indicate both great stillness and great power all at the same time.

Either way, he wasn't sorry to be working in harmony with Mullins.

"We need an explosive spell," Harry said decisively. "We need something that will send, say, a horse trough or a hitching post into the stratosphere. We're looking for a distraction here, not complete destruction. And it needs to happen during the day, when there's fewer customers, because them's our enforcers, you think?"

Leonard nodded. "I agree. So you're thinking a diversion. Edward blows something up, and the customers and girls will run outside to see and—"

"We'll need to prep the girls first," Harry said decisively. "Edward, can you get Marilyn to give you a list of names of the girls who will definitely want to run?"

Edward nodded, but not decisively. "She's not entirely sure," he admitted. "She says some of the girls are scared enough to turn on rescuers."

Harry grunted. "Perhaps...." He brightened. "Suriel—I could ask him for a spell of my own. A truth spell, a veracity spell—something that will let me know which ones are with us and which against—"

"I can scry for that," Emma said casually, and Harry's face fell.

"Excellent," Harry said, masking his disappointment well for a boy who'd always worn his emotions in full view. Edward would learn to hate that stoic mask in the years to come, but he did appreciate how it let Harry think. "We'll get word to those girls, and the thing will go kaboom, and we can hurry the willing away from the brothel down the alleyway. If we have horses waiting, we can have them ride cross country—nobody will spot them if we're not on the road."

Emma and Leonard both pondered the plan, making suggestions here and there that even Edward had to admit he hadn't thought of. Mullins tilted his head, and Edward came to the edge of his summoning circle, grabbed his tablet, and sat down.

"You are certain you want to do this?" Mullins asked immediately.

"Well, yes." Edward took a breath, because Mullins looked so concerned, and given the way even Francis was throwing himself into a plan that already involved stuff getting blown up and horses they didn't have, it was probably a good thing that one of them was showing some restraint. "She was beaten, Mullins. We got her away to a job as a cleaning girl with one of Emma's friends. Maybe she'll meet a husband there, and maybe not—but even if she doesn't, she's in a place where her free will counts, you understand?"

Mullins snorted. "I have to follow the orders of anybody who summons me, Edward. And when I'm not here or being summoned, I'm at the beck and call of a repugnant moron. Of course I understand. What I'm saying is that you put your family at risk here—"

Edward looked up and saw Harry drawing on the tablet and Francis—still in human form, which was a surprise because he rarely stayed so long—all talking purposefully and had his own revelation.

"We need to do this," he said quietly. "Can't you see? We *were* Marilyn. We *were* beaten and forced to do things we'd rather not. That Emma found us? Gave us this freedom, these powers, these gifts? What's the likelihood that would happen? We owe the world, don't you see? This is a gift we can give for all that we've gotten. My brothers think so too."

"But those people are dead now!" Mullins let out a sound like a growl that made Edward jerk back.

"How do you know?" Edward shrugged. "It's not been that long, for certain. Twenty years? Twenty-five? And even if all *those* people are dead, *these* people are still forcing girls to do what they'd rather not. It needs to be stopped. We're… well, gifted. We're gifted in ways that will make it stop. It's important we do what we can."

Mullins just shook his head. "Fine," he grumbled. "Do you have your stylus fixed in your head?"

Edward's stylus was an actual feather quill, scratching black oak-gall ink onto a ready piece of parchment. Harry's was—in his own words—a brand of fire, etching fiery words on a black wall, and Francis's was a stick in the sand, but instead of the water washing away the words, it revealed them written in obsidian.

But Edward's was simple and old-fashioned, and he closed his eyes and envisioned his stylus and medium, and allowed Mullins's instruction to wash over him.

"Do you know what you're going to detonate?" Mullins asked. "Approximate weight, size, density?"

"Horse trough along the street," Edward told him, eyes still closed. "I figure if it catches fire, the water'll put it out." In his head he didn't see the horse trough, though, but the claw-footed bathtub that Emma had Leonard install in their first years in the house. It still stood, cast-iron and adamant—with whimsical butterflies painted on the side.

"Very wise." Mullins's voice was low, kind—almost a handsome voice. "I want you to think about our mathematical studies. What kind of force would it take to propel an object that size into the air? How high do you wish it to go? Make those calculations with your stylus, thinking purely in terms of force and velocity."

Edward's stylus moved slowly, because he was thinking about the difference between cast iron and wood—which was the only thing that saved their house and the tub, which Emma adored.

"Edward!" Leonard snapped, and Edward shook his head, eyes open but out of focus, the concentration broken.

"What?" Dammit—all his calculations, lost in his head—

"Stop trying to blow up the bathtub! It's shaking in its fixtures! Mullins—did you tell him to think hypothetically before he started calculating the damned spell?"

"Fuck." The succinct oath popped Edward's vision into complete focus. Mullins *never* swore.

"Mullins?" he said uncertainly. "Did I... did I do anything wrong?"

"No, young Master Edward," Mullins muttered. "I was remiss. I was worried about you, about the boys—"

"I'm not that young, you know," Edward said, which of all things at this moment, when he could hear his brothers in the washroom yelling as they manually tightened the fixtures that would keep the water from pouring in. He should go and help them—he should—but he'd apparently been dumping power into the aborted spell and could barely stand.

"You're—"

"I've lived thirty-five years on the planet," he said with dignity, although he knew he still looked to be a boy in his teens.

"And I've lived nearly three hundred," Mullins said shortly. "I know how to practice a spell, and I was so worried getting you to calculate mass and velocity I forgot... for something like this, write a practice word—

hypothetical, or tomorrow and tomorrow, or *something* that will make the spell not an immediate happening but a thought exercise. Usually it's not necessary—usually your mind knows the difference—but a spell using munitions is so specific, you're occupied with higher math, and doing things like estimating the bulk of an object takes your thoughts from the hypothetical to the real. It's my fault, Edward. I knew this, and I forgot to tell you and…." He sighed. "You boys will be careful, won't you?"

Edward tried to summon a smile for him, although the knowledge that he'd almost blown up the house would ride him like a near miss for many years. "Of course, Mullins—why would you ask?"

"Because your family is important," he snapped. "Do you think I just sit on everybody's floor and talk about normal everyday things? Do you think everybody brings me cushions and asks about my well-being? I live in *hell*, Edward, and this family gives me just a little bit of earth that I need to not become a sniveling, slavering bestial evil that would devour you, flesh, blood, and soul if you forgot and offered me food."

Edward stared at him, a shiver running up and down his spine. "You must promise me," he said seriously. "You must promise all of us that won't happen."

Mullins returned his regard, the darkness of his beastly eyes limpid and unfathomable. "I can't," he said, voice hard. "Which is why you three boys must take care of this family with all you have. Now they seem to be wrestling the bathtub back into its usual state. Get out your stylus again and write hypothetical or what have you on the top of the spell. Now concentrate on the horse trough in front of your barn, where visitors tie their beasts, and we'll work on blowing *that* up."

Edward grimaced. "That's really a much better idea," he said, feeling dense. "It's a good thing we have you here."

"I doubt it. Why Suriel couldn't talk you out of this is beyond me."

Edward let out a half laugh. "I thought he would," he admitted. "But Harry had caught hold of the idea by then, and all Suriel could do was stare at Harry with this mooncalf expression like Harry had invented being a hero or something. It was sort of revolting, really."

Mullins laughed too. "Well, thank hell you're sensible. You'd never let that sort of *emotion*"—he spat the word—"get in the way of your reason."

"No, sir," Edward reassured him. "Not emotion. Just"—he grimaced—"just my mother's claw-footed tub."

BELTANE LISTENED to the story with wide eyes and enchantment. "That's marvelous," he breathed when Edward finished.

"All except the part where I mooncalved all over Harry," Suriel said, pouting. "I was impressed, was all. It was such a noble direction for you three boys to take your powers, and I *was* the angel bound to service—"

"Don't apologize," Harry said, his usually brusque voice something akin to gentle. "That look gave me the courage to go on our first adventure."

"How did the rescue turn out, anyway?" Beltane asked, as avid as a child.

"It was brilliant," Francis said, eyes dreamy. "Edward made such a ruckus blowing the horse trough in the air that *everybody* turned out, and while the whole town was watching the sky to see if it would come back down, we snuck the girls away who wanted to go. We borrowed some horses and they took off, and just when everybody was thinking about going back into their shops and such...." He giggled. "Edward—oh my God, it was amazing! He brought the trough back, spinning like a top and...." He giggled some more. "And...."

"And drove it through the roof of the brothel," Harry supplied as Francis dissolved into a complete puddle of laughter. "The brothel owners were so busy trying to figure out what had made it do that and what it had destroyed, they didn't notice the girls were gone until they'd cleared the debris. Nobody even put together our presence in the town and the girls' disappearance. Overall, one of Edward's best spells."

"Thank you," Edward said humbly, because his brother's praise was rare and valuable.

Harry turned to Edward with earnestness. "It was our first run. I treasure it. But you see what I'm talking about here, right?"

Edward thought for a moment. "But I almost blew up the house!" he protested.

"But that doesn't mean you can't use that idea for something else entirely!" Harry stood and paced at their table. "Don't you see? You were trying to blow up a horse trough and you chose something with similar weight and mass that served the same purpose."

"So what am I supposed to do?" Edward said, feeling tearful and out of his depth—again. "*Substitute* ingredients? But that's madness—remember what we were taught? Precision—"

"But we were also taught that our will shapes the precision," Harry supplied in a huff. "Look, Edward, the quest for shit that's been gone from our world for centuries can resume at any time, but give it some thought, will you? Work with Suriel on it, and Beltane too. Look at the ingredients, and don't just take them at face value—decide what they're *for*. Once you decide what they're *for*, you can think of an ingredient that will serve the same purpose."

"What do you mean, what they're for?" Francis asked. "And why was I left out of that list of people to help?"

"It's like the witches in *Macbeth*," Beltane said, in an instructing voice Edward and Harry had only heard him use with Francis. "See, everything on the list was something evil, something that spoke of a deliberate choice of someone to be a bad person who did destructive things. It wasn't the eye of the newt that mattered—it was the stealing the sight from something that needed it. It wasn't the dog's tongue that they needed, it was the silence of anything that would warn of the evil to come. So we look at Edward's list and decide what the ingredients *do* that will help spring Mullins, and then we decide what we have that will do the same thing."

Francis wrinkled his nose and batted at it with his palm, fingers curled inward. "But that doesn't explain why—"

"You think too literally," Harry said gently. "Your talents would be better used searching for the things we need to—in fact, that's what most of us are doing. We could use a case too—something that would keep everything separate and in good condition."

"I'm very good at carpentry," Francis said, preening.

"I know you are," Bel told him, so soberly Francis brightened.

Edward and Harry met eyes. Their little brother had developed in so many unexpected ways—but his relationship with Bel was the one most fraught with peril.

"So," Harry said, offering Edward a hand up from the cushion around the low table. "We're going back to earth, because I'm betting Emma's about half out of her mind by now, and then *we* are going to take that list of yours and do some research for substitutions."

"And then?" Edward asked.

"We're going to go find it. The whole shebang. All at once. All together."

"You?" Edward said, feeling bereft. That list had been his life's goal for the past year.

"Yes. We."

"What will I be doing?"

Harry had always claimed to be the plain one of them, but Edward had always thought his eyes—peasant brown—were actually his finest feature. Right now they were bright with intelligence and soft with compassion. "Brother, have you even told him what you're doing?"

Edward swallowed and looked away. "I… I didn't want to give him false hope," he said softly.

"Well we just had a very public conversation in a place where the spies of hell come as cockroaches so they can sample the wine. I suggest you go to the cabin and summon him so you two can have a little conversation, you think?"

"What purpose would that—"

Harry's fist gathering his shirtfront was not really a surprise. "Because this is a bloody dangerous thing we're all doing here, and none of us regret a second of it, but if you blow yourself up trying to pull him out of hell, then he damned sure has the right to know why."

Edward met Harry's eyes then, his heart so sore he could barely breathe. "What if he tells me not to?" he whispered.

Harry snorted and let go of him so abruptly he stumbled back. "Leonard told Emma to do the same damned thing, did you know that?"

Edward stared at him. How had he not known this? "No."

"You know what she did?"

Edward's mouth twisted, and for the first time in two long years, he felt hope. "Ignored him."

"Damned straight." He grinned fiercely, their most bloodthirsty warrior, always, before looking behind him. "We ready, everybody? I've got the spell fixed in my head. Edward, you got your own?"

Edward nodded. "Yes." Harry could boomerang them all out—it was a simple teleportation spell, although it required a whopping burst of power. Edward wasn't good at it yet. He needed to have something more involved at the ready, and he'd come prepared.

"I suggest you summon him immediately, Edward. You don't want to know what he'll be like if he hears it from *that sniveling little fly gut demon that just flew out of here!*"

"Harry—"

"*C'mon, boys, let's track that fucker down!*" Harry paused just long enough to shout, "Edward, *not you!*" before all of Edward's brothers disappeared out the flap of the tent, searching for a demon who hadn't shown more than a twitchy exoskeleton before Harry had spotted him.

Gah! Apparently, Harry was right. Edward needed to call Mullins and they needed to coordinate a plan.

STEP FROM SORROW TO SORROW

VANTH WAS a weaselly little thing for a fly, and as he danced around Mullins's head in delight, Mullins was forced to wonder if, should he lose his temper and squash the little troublemaker against the jagged walls of his cell, anybody would wonder what happened to him.

"Youuuuuu shoulllddd have seeeeeeeeen thheemmmmm…," Vanth buzzed. After a while, Mullins learned to let his mind wander during words or he would have lost his sanity. "All gatherrrrred togetherrrrr… plotting to saaaaaaave youuuuu…."

Mullins froze. "Nobody saves demons," he said, keeping his voice cultured. Inside his head, his *own* stylus—an elm switch scratching designs in rich brown earth—began to work subtle magic. Hopefully so subtle that Vanth—who was infamous for being brain deaf to magic—wouldn't sense what he was up to.

Because if his intel was right, and the Youngbloods were doing something as bloody stupid as forming a rescue team, Vanth spreading his information to anybody else in hell could spell out a death sentence.

"Why would they save me?" he asked, disbelief clear in his voice. "What purpose would that serve?"

In his head the spell—shaped like a giant flyswatter, extending from his hoof—continued in its solid way.

Vanth laughed unpleasantly. "Twoooooooo luuuuuuvvvvv—augh!"

Wielding his magic and swinging like an all-pro tennis champion, Mullins did exactly what he'd written and splatted Vanth against the wall of his cell, where the bug-demon's insides spread across the jagged stone in a white smear.

Mullins knew a cleanup spell by rote, and he'd just waved his hand to peel the whole mess from the wall and send it into a toxic waste dump in the human world when he felt the call.

"Really, Edward?" he snarled, the murder of Vanth working him up into a right frothy head of steam before he even disappeared from hell. "Really? You think—"

He appeared then, not in the Youngblood living room, a place he knew well in spite of the many changes and modernizations made over the past 140 years, but in their cabin.

A place that held its own intimacies.

"—summoning me right now is a good idea? Great hell's fiery breath, Edward Youngblood, who are you trying to kill here, me or you?"

He looked around the cozy space, scowling. Edward. Edward alone had summoned him, which didn't bode well—had never boded well, not even the first time he'd done it.

The bulk of the cabin was a kitchen and a living room, all in one space, with a bed in the corner of the living room and a door opening into a rather luxurious bathroom.

He'd been in this space unencumbered by the summoning circle. He'd been free here, to sit at the table with Edward like a human being and to imagine being with Edward, both domestically and carnally, in ways he didn't want to think about now.

"I'm not trying to kill either one of us," Edward said shortly. "I'm trying to find a way for us to be together. You knew this. I told you about my plan."

Mullins closed his eyes and wished for actual human hands so he could drag them through what used to be thick, curly brown hair. "You told me about your *dream*," he said desperately. "I told *you* not to do it, because it was too dangerous."

Edward was standing, arms crossed, facing away from Mullins but regarding him from a skeptical profile.

"You do know what me and the others spend our time doing, right? Did I not spend enough time begging you to stop Harry from being a suicidal fucking maniac?"

Mullins sighed and shifted from hoof to hoof. Those had been dark times for all the brothers. Suriel's suffering to come back down to earth had been no small thing, but Mullins had to give it to the angel for surviving that test with his skin—if not his wings—intact.

"I'm here to help you survive that," he said gruffly. "Not to make things worse."

Edward kept his face averted, but Mullins recognized the unsteady indrawn breath. It was the sound he made when there wasn't reason enough in the world to shore up his broken heart.

Mullins was reluctantly taken back to the first time Edward had summoned him, and him alone, to this sweet little cabin where lovers whispered promises they never wanted to break.

"EDWARD?"

Edward sat, cross-legged, head bowed, his still-young face etched in grief.

"Oh. He's passed. I'm so sorry."

Unlike Harry, who after nearly sixty years on earth seemed determined to have only the briefest of moments with the mortals he shared the planet with, or Francis, who wandered the world as a wraith, as innocent of sex and love as a child, Edward had thrown himself into a relationship.

For the past thirty years, he and a once-young doctor had lived a few miles from Emma's and Leonard's home, lovers, spouses—true partners. Mullins had met Paul on more than one occasion and had liked the man. Steady, without temper, and pleasantly bemused by the immortals he was surrounded by, he would walk the cliffs and the seaside and the forests of Mendocino with three cats at his ankles or Edward by his side.

Or at least that's what Emma had told Mullins thirty years prior, when Edward had decided to let Paul into their circle, to love him the length of his mortal lifetime, and then to let him go.

Mullins could not have imagined doing that with a whole heart—but then, he hadn't become a demon because he was brave.

"This morning," Edward rasped. "He… his heart gave out. We weren't expecting it. I mean, I'd heard murmurs, but nothing like this and…." He swallowed hard and met Mullins's sympathetic gaze. "It hurts," he said plaintively, surprised as a child. "God… I won't see him again until… until many mortal lifetimes. And… and right now there's just this hole. And all I could think about was you. You'd know how to fill this hole in my chest. And I don't know why—Harry would turn to Suriel, and all I can think about is you."

Mullins let out a harsh breath. "My boy—"

"I'm seventy-five," Edward snapped. "I know I look… hell, twenty or whatever. But I'm seventy-five. I've… I've lived a whole life. I should know this feeling but I don't… I don't understand…."

"Harry would turn to Suriel because Harry's in *love* with Suriel!" Mullins burst out, unable to confront Edward's terrible vulnerability. He'd long ago taught the boys how to guard themselves against a demon, even if they broke the rules of hospitality or the summoning circle, but he didn't feel any of those safeguards in place. Edward had summoned him here, alone, because he sought solace from a friend, and he was either hoping Mullins would kill him and put him out of his misery, or he'd genuinely forgotten that Mullins had orders from a lower power.

Mullins was in a ferocious mood to disappoint both Edward and his bosses, because he wasn't going to kill anybody today.

Edward glared up at him from a face rumpled and blotched with tears. "You lie!" he snarled indignantly. "That would be madness—"

"Like bringing me here without safeguards?" Oh, suicide by demon had never infuriated Mullins more.

And then he felt the faint buzz of Edward hastily erecting the shields Mullins had taken such pains to teach him.

"I'm sorry," Edward whispered. "I… I didn't do that intentionally." He swallowed loudly. "That would be a terrible thing to force a friend to do, Mullins. I'd never treat you like that."

Mullins's eyes burned with tears a beast could never shed. "Thank you." He wiped his face on his shoulder, because he couldn't help the very human feeling that his eyes were leaking and his face was wet.

"What do you mean, Harry's in love with Suriel?"

Mullins sighed and sat down across from Edward, crossing his legs the same way. The summoning circle was unnecessary at this point, and this gave them some intimacy, some gentleness, that the moment seemed to badly need.

"You can't see it?" he asked. "The way Harry seems to light up inside whenever you speak of him? The way he seems to mourn if you go too far between summoning?"

"He always argues against calling him," Edward mumbled, looking at his hands. They were wide-palmed and long-fingered—strong, capable, and surprisingly agile. Between Mullins's and Leonard's tutelage, and lots of practice in this out of the way area, Edward had the hands of a first-rate surgeon.

Mullins let out a snort. "Do you think this thing you do, where you and your brothers displace heaven and hell on your whim—do you think that doesn't come without a price from those of us yanked out of our element?"

Edward glanced up at him hurriedly. "This hurts you?" he asked anxiously. "How does it—"

Mullins shook his head. "Harry knows Suriel's price," he said through a scratchy throat, knowing this because he'd seen Harry's face when Suriel was discussed. "And he refuses to call him. I won't tell you my price, Edward Youngblood, because I don't ever want you not to call me."

Edward nodded and looked down at his hands again. "Paul never told me the price he must have paid. To live with us and grow old and never see me age… I don't understand this world, Mullins, where people give so much and get so little."

Mullins wiped his eyes on his shoulder again, surprised because his shoulder was wet. "Do you think he didn't get something for his currency?" he asked, smiling slightly. "He got you, Edward. He got family. He got kindness. A lover who looked at him as though he was a young man, even when he'd seen nearly seventy winters. Do you think that's nothing?"

A sobbing breath. And then another. Suddenly, Edward seized Mullins's hoof—

And laced their fingers together.

Mullins let out a startled beast's sound, and Edward stared desperately into his eyes.

"They're blue," he said. "Like a lake on a summer day. I can see them… and the outline of your jaw. You were quite a handsome man, Mullins."

Mullins shook his head, unwilling to talk about the semi-transformation Edward was witnessing, because it surely couldn't last. Instead, he tightened his grip on Edward's hand and raised their hands to his beastly mouth, then placed a gentle benediction on the knuckles.

"I'm so sorry for your loss, Edward," he said quietly. "Tell me what you need—"

Edward scrambled across the wooden floor of the cabin, pressed Mullins to the floor, and sobbed on his chest with the full force of his grief.

"Oh."

Mullins wrapped his arms around his boy's shoulders and held on tightly, stroking Edward's hair and feeling the rough satin of the bright orange strands under his fingertips.

"Just hold me," Edward begged between sobs. "Please."

"As long as you need," Mullins promised hoarsely. He would tell Menoch later that he'd been compelled—and it was the truth, but not the way Menoch would hear it.

There truly was not a force on heaven or earth that would have moved Mullins from that moment, holding Edward and offering the crippled solace he could.

"Do you remember Paul?" Edward asked, breaking into Mullins's thoughts with uncanny accuracy.

"And Dorothy," Mullins conceded. Edward's other long-term love had died at twenty-five, a scant year after they'd gotten together. "We grieved for them both."

Edward finally met his eyes. "You held me, both times," he said. "You convinced me that there was a tomorrow without them. You sat on this floor and held my hand, when it should have been impossible, and I saw your face, your true face, when it shouldn't even be a memory, and you walked me through my grief. Do you remember?"

Mullins was shaking with those memories, with the sweet weight of Edward's head on his shoulder, with the heat of their bodies pressed together, with the feeling of Edward's hair under his fingertips. "Of course I do."

"That grief I felt, it was real."

"I know it."

"It was human grief—I have a familiar cave in my breast carved out for that very emotion."

Well, he must have. He was fearless that way, allowing himself lovers, allowing himself to care.

"You're so very brave," Mullins whispered.

"If you were to go, never to return, the pain… it wouldn't fit in that cave," Edward told him, voice past shaking and on to breaking. "It would blow my chest outward, destroy my body, eclipse the sun. I need you in my life. I want you in my bed—but that's secondary. I *need you in my life*. Tell me—tell me truly—that you want to go back to your jagged cave in hell and perpetrate atrocities on the unwary."

Mullins closed his eyes. "I loathe it," he burst out, unable to lie about this—not to Edward.

"Tell me you don't love me."

He made a sound then—a whimper, the tenor of a beast from the throat of a man. "No," he whispered.

Edward stepped into his space and grabbed his hands, his battered human artist's hands, which only Edward could see, only Edward could touch, and laced their fingers together.

"It's time," he said boldly. "It's time to be brave. My heart needs you *now*, beloved. There's no room in here for another human lover to take your place while you gather your courage."

Mullins closed his eyes, and to his wonder, Edward cupped his cheek—the soft skin of it, not the beastly jaw. He rubbed his thumb over Mullins's lips, his soft human lips, and Mullins forgot himself and licked the pad of it.

Edward leaned into his chest then, and wrapped his arms around Mullins's waist, resting his head on his shoulder.

"If you fail," Mullins felt compelled to warn him, "your soul is at risk too."

"I'm not going to hell," Edward said with a confidence Mullins envied. "Hell is without you. If we fuck this up, I'll be wherever you end up. Please tell me you'll try, beloved. Please tell me you'll try."

Oh God. Even as Mullins thought about the deity he wrapped his arms around Edward's shoulders and, counter to all the mandates of hell, began to pray.

"For you," he promised. "Only for you."

FIVE YEARS ago, in Las Vegas, Harry let himself get caught so Edward and Francis could get rescued captives to safety—and Edward couldn't find him. Oh, they knew why *now*. Suriel had interposed himself, voluntarily, for Harry's safety, and other magics were at work too—old and fierce ones, hostile to all the boys, but Harry in particular. But at the time, all Edward and Francis knew was that they couldn't find their brother, couldn't sense him anywhere on the planet, and their misery and panic could be felt through seven dimensions, straight to the twelfth sphincter of hell.

Summon me, Edward. Come on, boy, summon me. I can't help you unless you call!

Mullins remembered thinking the words, fiercely hoping, praying in his way to the one force of nature he could remember believing in. Edward hadn't let him down yet. When he felt the call he practically popped a hole in the roof of hell—and the fabric of space/time itself—appearing before Edward and Francis as they huddled on the floor of their rescue van, twined about each other like furry ivy.

"Boys!" he barked. "Human forms! How am I to convince the lords of hell you had any sway over me when you weigh nine pounds apiece!"

"Francis weighs five," Edward snapped, his orange hair standing up over his head. "And what in the hell are you doing here?"

Mullins stared at him blankly. "I…. You summoned me?" Because obviously that wasn't the case. There was no chalk on the ground, no circle, no safeguards. As Mullins gaped at Francis, huddled in a circle of fur still, he felt the faint buzz of belated safeguards, erected for courtesy and not for true protection.

"I *should* have summoned you," Edward said, eyebrows knitted to a foul temper, "but no. I just curled up in a ball and mewled like a kitten. Thank you for showing up."

Which was exactly what he'd done, wasn't it? He'd *shown up*. Out of thin air. Without any call but the terror beating in Edward's feral heart.

"For you," he said, the realization shaking him more than those rare moments when they meshed fingers, when Edward's capable hands cupped his jaw, felt the contours of a face not visible to man for over 300 years. "Only for you."

Now, in the present, 140 years after Edward's rebirth as a feral cat, a noble physician, and a fearless warrior, Mullins swallowed his terror, much as he'd made the boys swallow theirs before they ventured out in the desert to find Harry.

"Only for you," he repeated. "What is it you need me to do?"

Edward smiled at him, a plan alight in his eyes. "You know the spell you gave me, when I asked you about this years ago."

Mullins felt his face burn. "I never should have done that. You said you wanted to know how Emma had brought Leonard back."

Edward tilted his head. "I asked you about fifteen years after Dorothy passed on. Did you really think I wasn't planning this then?"

"I think you've been unfathomable to me for nearly a hundred and forty years now, Edward," Mullins said with dignity. "I don't know how you can even look upon my face."

"Because you're a truly beautiful man," Edward shot back, a faint smile playing with his lips. "And I enjoy seeing your emotions glow in your eyes."

Eyes that Mullins closed. "Not so loud," he begged hoarsely. "If anyone in hell hears you, I'll be bound to my chamber, never allowed to be summoned again."

"Is that what happened to Leonard?" Edward asked sharply, turning to rummage through a pack on his bed. "Because he was in pretty bad shape when Emma got him, and I remember that you had to haul him around."

"Indeed." Mullins shifted on his back legs. "By the time Emma was ready to summon him from hell, Menoch could see his fading bestiality. I committed a transgression, and Menoch used the excuse to bind him to two rocks and flogged him while Emma tried to pull him into her world. I appeared in his stead and told her I'd get him out, and you boys saw the rest."

Edward nodded, brain obviously busy. "That gives me an idea," he said, chewing his bottom lip. "But only if things get really bad first, yes?"

"No! You are not to boomerang to hell to bail me out!"

Edward pinned him with a hard glance. "My brothers are in on this," he said. "Suriel is helping them because he can't stand to be separated from Harry. You need to understand that this is not going away. How long have we been doing rescues, do you remember?"

"One hundred and eighteen years," Mullins said dully. And three months, two weeks, four days, and six hours. He'd lived every moment in fear for the lives of his boys—Edward in particular.

"Do you remember why the first one worked?"

Mullins racked his brains. "Because Harry stole the neighbor's horses on the way to town. You hadn't been planning on it, but he remembered you needed to get the girls out some way."

"And how did the horses get back?" Edward prompted.

Mullins found himself smiling. "Francis memorized a spell to put back lost items while you were getting notes to the girls. Because…." He scowled. "Because you asked me to teach it to him."

"Exactly. Harry has his way for planning for contingencies, and I have mine. Between the two of us, we manage to cover almost everything. So believe me when I say I've got some Plan Bs, Plan Cs, and Plan Ds up my sleeve, and Harry has ones without letters—Plan Purple or something. That's Harry's specialty."

"Plan Purple Harry," Mullins said, smiling in spite of the seriousness of the situation. "Understood. I'll trust you."

Edward turned to him, eyes bright and shiny. "Really? You swear?"

That took Mullins back a moment. "That what? I trust you?"

"Yes."

His boy—his *man*—who had grown so much in his time here on earth.

"With all I am," Mullins said softly. Even if Edward let him down, if this wild plan failed somehow, Mullins could do no less. The thought of his bare and jagged cell in the twelfth sphincter made him queasy. He would rather be unmade than think he would really return there for all of eternity, particularly when Edward promised him heaven.

Kindness.

Love.

Edward smiled, his ruddy cheeks popping into apples, his green eyes alight with wickedness and cheer. "Excellent. Hours ago I was pretty despondent, you know—but if you trust me, I think we can make this work."

EDWARD FOUND the paper he'd scrawled Mullins's spell on from memory, and then pulled out a legal tablet from one of the drawers in the little cabin.

"Come here," he called, settling himself down on one of the kitchen chairs. "I know the floor is usually our place, but it's far more comfortable here, yeah?"

"Yeah." Mullins smiled shyly, remembering how he'd gone from the floor to the furniture in the Youngblood home, and the boys had been so respectful of every step. "But no tea."

Edward regarded him soberly. "I remember every safeguard," he promised. "We're too close now to take that risk."

They settled themselves down at the little wooden table, and unbidden, Mullins had a vision: Harry and Suriel eating dinner here, lit candles on the table, Harry's wry, self-deprecating smile making Suriel's eyes light up with kindness.

"This is where they honeymooned," Mullins said thoughtfully. He closed his eyes and let himself watch them, just to see their affection.

"Why, Mullins, you voyeur," Edward chided, and Mullins felt his face heat.

"I wasn't watching those parts," he said chastely. But he couldn't help it. He grinned, with no idea what the expression looked like on his beastly face. "But they are both very beautiful."

Edward rolled his eyes. "Harry assures me he's very plain, but I'll take that the way you meant it."

"And how did I mean it?" Mullins asked, confused.

"That someone you loved was beautifully *in* love, of course."

Mullins scowled and allowed Edward to pick up the pen and the legal paper. In hell, he would have made a show of holding a pencil between the cleft in his hoof, but it was tedious and tiresome, and much easier to write with the stylus in his mind. But here, in order to do trial and error work, a tablet was a much better idea.

"You assume demons can love," he said, not sure if he wanted to debate this. It was a rule in hell—an absolute. Demons had forsaken their souls—had given up all finer emotions associated with said soul. Love was one of those. For years, Mullins had been holding on to a half-remembered morality, a sort of list of things humans absolutely could not do and still retain their souls. He'd made them public knowledge to his superiors as things he absolutely would not do. Finally it became more time-efficient for Menoch, Renotly, and the rest to just not ask him to do those things than to punish him until someone else was assigned to the job.

But he'd been schooled and schooled well as to what he was and what he was not.

Whatever it was he felt for Edward, whatever affection moved him to protect the Youngblood family, it was not, strictly speaking, love.

Edward snorted. "You most certainly can."

Oh no. "But… Edward. It's part of the covenant we sign. We sign away our soul—our ability to—"

Another inelegant snort. "And I call bullshit."

"Excuse me?" He really was affronted. The last 400 years of his life had been predicated upon the fact that his morality was a construct and he was clinging to it with the skin of his hooves.

"What do you think love *is*, Mullins?"

Mullins stopped and stared at him, even as Edward opened a "knapsack porthole" in space and started pulling out various tomes to set on the table.

"It's the glorious ascendant emotion that occurs when two people would clear any hurdle, endure any sacrifice, destroy any interloper, in order to touch each other. It's the perfect blend of the angelic aspects of kindness and serenity and the demonic aspects of fierceness and carnality, tempered with the mortal earthiness of mundane, day to day interaction! It's—"

"It's what happens when two people want to be together. Always." Edward shook his head. "And that was a lovely bit of poetry you were spouting there, but have you given a thought to what it means?"

Mullins let out a shaky breath. "I hadn't dared to think—"

"Two marriages," Edward said, as though he were barely holding on to his patience. "I've lost a husband and a wife, and I can tell you what sex is when it's glorious and what sex is when it's a simple need to connect with this person you care for. I can tell you that it does, indeed, make you your more angelic self—that part is true, but not in any perfect or serene way. It just makes you want to be... better. And I was a mess after Dorothy—you remember that?"

Mullins looked away. "You certainly drank a lot."

"I did. And I spent a great deal of time naked with consenting strangers, do you remember that too?"

If Mullins's ears hadn't been pointed like a boar's and covered in coarse fur, they would have been pink. "It was not my job to—"

"My brothers summoned you to drag me out of an orgy," Edward said dryly. "They did it on purpose, by the way. They knew I'd be so embarrassed by having you see me like that, I'd perhaps temper my behavior—and it worked."

Oh, Mullins remembered. He'd lurked far too long in the corner of that room, watching Edward—*his* Edward—holding on to a chain suspended from the ceiling, biceps bulging, fair skin flushed, as a masked Adonis of a man fucked him from behind and lovely, laughing blonde temptress took his cock into her mouth.

For a moment he'd been paralyzed, overcome with lust, wanting more than anything to join in the abandon that surrounded him, just to, for a moment, have his body touched, in spite of the demonic deformities that would make such a joining a horror for his partner.

Then he'd seen the expression on Edward's face—and the world had stopped.

There'd been pleasure, yes—desperate pleasure—and Edward's naked body had been all that was humanly beautiful. Muscles straining, cock erect and prime, his asshole yielding in lovely submission, Edward was what human abandonment to lust was supposed to look like.

Was it Mullins, only, who had seen the grief as well?

Mullins waited until the climax—everybody's climax, including the young lady's—had been attended to, before scooping Edward into his arms from his panting, sweaty collapse on the sordid floor. At first Edward had protested, feebly, but as Mullins pulled him to a bathroom and threw him into the shower there, he had come to his senses.

And wept.

And then he'd found his clothes and dressed, and soberly accompanied Mullins outside to where his brothers waited, ready to move to the next job.

Nobody had said a word about that night, or where Edward had spent a week of his life, or those moments of Mullins holding him close, rocking him like a child and murmuring nonsense into his hair.

Until now.

"I remember," Mullins rasped, acutely uncomfortable. His trousers were cut in the style of 150 years prior, and they were too tight for his cock as it swelled against his thigh, and his tail as it twitched in the seat.

"That thing you did for me," Edward said quietly. "You may tell yourself you were compelled. You may tell your bosses that my brothers laid a spell on you to do the work that they could not. But we all know the truth. You never checked for safeguards that night. You never let a compulsion touch you. You didn't rend the flesh of any of the people in that room to rescue me from myself. You could have done what Harry and Francis asked and borne me from a charnel house, naked and howling and covered with blood. But you didn't."

"No." Mullins's heart beat hard in his breast.

"That's what love is, Mullins. Whether you can say it in your head or not. Whether you can admit it to yourself or not. I think telling you that you have no soul is perhaps the greatest lie ever told in hell. And most of you buy it. Most demons are angry or desperate as humans, and they become angry and desperate as demons, only with magic powers and unlimited physical capabilities. But not you. Not Leonard. Someday you'll tell me what brought you to hell, but right now, it's enough that I know your soul has always been your own."

"This thing you're saying," he rasped. "This… this…."

Edward scowled, his forehead growing red. "Get your perspective of the world realigned some other time, Mullins. Right now we've got work to do."

"But don't you want to hear the reason—" Everybody wanted to hear the reason a demon became a demon. It was often their last and most painful link to the human they had been.

Edward's eyes, green and clear as glass, bored through Mullins's façade. In that moment, Mullins could believe Edward Youngblood saw him exactly as he'd been 300 years ago, and loved him for all his tragedy and flaws.

"You'll tell me in time," he said. "Right now, my love is plenty. Now here's the list of ingredients, and here's the column for possible substitutions. Now see this column here?"

Mullins nodded dumbly.

"This column is the most important. This column here is for what we think the first ingredient does. Do you understand?"

"What do you mean, what it does?"

Edward grinned. "It's brilliant. Trust me. Harry and Francis—they don't look like a brain trust, but sometimes they'll surprise you. Here—this is what we need to do."

DEMON STEW

REMEMBERING THE orgy was a mistake.

Edward firmly believed in consensual sexual experimentation. He saw no morality or immorality attached to a consensual act, and as he figured it, he'd been blessed enough to appreciate all sexes, so he happily took advantage of that attraction.

But that particular moment had been so intense, so sexually charged—his intention had been to forget his grief in its entirety, and he'd almost managed it. He'd orgasmed, the experience so raw he felt like he'd blown his humanity out his cock, leaving his interior clean, antiseptic, unsusceptible to the vulnerabilities of love ever again.

Right up until he'd felt Mullins's arms around him, heard his voice, low, rough, civilized, in his ears. Mullins might have thought Edward forgot about standing under the spray of the shower wrapped in Mullins's embrace, but he hadn't.

Mullins's upper thighs, groin, torso, and upper arms were all those of a man.

For a few moments, Edward had closed his eyes and pretended he was in the arms of a lover, and when he'd opened them again, he knew that someday it would be true.

After mourning for Dorothy, he stayed celibate for many, many years, and his lovers in the past fifty or so had been mostly casual. Those moments, Mullins holding him, their skin bare, his soul stripped of all pretense, was enough to sustain him.

Someday they would be together.

Edward would not be deterred.

But remembering that moment, their bodies together, made Edward's body hungry for Mullins in a way Mullins wasn't ready to be yet.

Edward could see the man—the beast was but a thin overlay, a transparency made to blur his features, but Edward saw him true enough. He knew that if he reached over and put his hand on Mullins's hoof, they would lace fingers, and the itch to do just that was almost overwhelming.

But he would follow that touch with a cupping of his jaw, and then he'd close his eyes to the blurriness and follow that with a kiss.

Mullins's body was fully functional.

The kissing would lead to lovemaking, and that would be…

Premature.

Mullins had no hope now. As far as Edward could tell, the man he and his brothers were risking everything for was humoring them.

Edward wanted him to hope. Sex now would be like goodbye.

"So," Mullins said, breaking into Edward's contemplation of the summer blue of his human eyes, "what ingredients did the original have?"

Edward grimaced and went back to copying the list onto the legal pad, finishing with a flourish.

"Come see."

Spell for reversing a demon's curse—
Magic user makes up his own spell verse

"Ugh," Mullins muttered. "Poetry—not our best."

"I'm going to hope they mean blank verse and leave it at that," Edward agreed. "And I'll be working on it as we go, so don't despair. Keep going."

THE SPIT of the lying tongue, a traitor of the Chameleon people, after he has lied and before the spit has dried.

Edward produced the baby food jar full of Harry's spit. "I think we can do better than this," he admitted. "But since Harry lied to me to trap me and force me to accept his help, I'm going to just set this here and stop carrying my brother's saliva in my backpack."

TEARS OF one untouched by lust, by the arousal of the flesh, one whose passions stir not with desire but with love.

"A virgin's tears—" Mullins began, but Edward cut him off.

"Not necessarily. Untouched by lust could mean a lot of things. There's plenty of people out there whose sexuality doesn't include sex."

Mullins blinked at him. "Asexuality has been around for a very long time," he said, looking embarrassed. "That one should have been easy."

Edward shrugged. "Everybody makes assumptions—but see? An open mind can't hurt. And it doesn't say we have to torture anybody. I mean, I know a couple of people—I could just take them out to a sad movie, buy them popcorn, and have them bottle their tears. This one's a sinecure."

The pointed horn of the ibex of the Pyrenees.

"Now that one is extinct," Mullins muttered, glaring at him. "How on earth—"

"Now here's where we get really tricky," Edward said. "We can find the horn of some of other ibex, but before we go chopping the horns off the poor creatures, let's look at *why* we need them. Demons lie, and their shapes are deliberately changed and distorted—the shapeshifter betrayer's tongue must be a way to access that, to reach that part of the magic. So as gross as it is, Harry's spit really might be what we need. The tears of someone untouched by lust—isn't hell ripe and chock full of lust?"

Mullins looked away, distinctly uncomfortable. "Many demons fornicate regularly, often with the unwilling," he murmured.

"So what they really needed was an element of purity, of true platonic affection, to cleanse the… the sordidness of the sex from the demon at hand. So our solution would work there too. Now what do you think about the ibex?"

"Well, we all have horns," Mullins said, his artist's finger going immediately to the rams' horns sprouting from behind his ears. "But not all of them are the same."

"So, a Pyrenees ibex would be a horned animal adept at… what? Jumping a lot? Climbing…." Edward paused, the answer coming to him. "Climbing! So we need a thing that climbs—and sheds its horns. You know, maybe the horns that look like yours—"

"Why an animal that climbs?" Mullins asked, seemingly caught up in the mental exercise if not the hope.

"Because you're climbing out of darkness!" Edward felt the thrill of solving a puzzle rush through his veins, and it did nothing to quiet the underlying thrum of desire that ran there as well.

"Oh!" Mullins grinned at him, caught up in the same rush, apparently. "Good, then. We'll find an animal that does that—let's put an R here for research, yes?"

"Excellent. Now, the next thing on the list is going to need you and Suriel to get a grip and spill," Edward said soberly. "Because we know there must be such a thing because the two of you are so damned cagey about it."

THREE STRANDS of hair from an elven king.

"Nnnnnnnnnggg...." Mullins's noise was not promising. "Edward, that one really is—"

"Don't lie to me, Mullins," Edward snapped. "Harry, Francis, and I kept brownies in our rooms for ten years after Dorothy died as an experiment of sorts. Harry came up with it to lift my spirits. We left out beer, and it disappeared and our rooms got clean, and we kept giving them beer and crumbs of Emma's best home-baked bread, and we didn't have to clean our own toilets or change our own sheets or so much as sweep the corners of the room—ten years!"

"You have no proof of—" Mullins began primly, but Edward cut him off.

"We saw them. Harry brought them pie once, fresh blackberry pie, and they got drunk off it. One minute we were watching the thing just disappear, tiny bite by tiny bite, and the next there were all these brown-pelted spider-shaped creatures, about two feet tall, lounging about our room in a stupor. Harry and I had to tackle Francis so he didn't turn into a cat and chase them, and we realized that now that we *knew* what they looked like, it would really be best for us if we did our own chores."

Mullins laughed delightedly, the sound curling low and hot in Edward's stomach. "You three never told us that!"

"We never told Suriel, either," Edward said, brows knit. "Or Emma and Leonard. Because every time we tried to mention the fey to you, it was all, 'Uhm, you know....' Same with the vampires and shapeshifters—yes, we know about the vampires. That shit that went down in Redding two years ago—the club leveled to the ground, the blood everywhere but no bodies? Everybody in Emma's witch's circle knew something huge had gone down, but nobody knew what it was. I'm telling you, Mullins, it's starting to hurt our goddamned feelings is what it's doing."

Mullins inhaled harshly. "It's... well, it's not your fault," he murmured. "But.... See, there was a terrible quarrel between God and Goddess about two millennia ago—"

"Convenient timing," Edward said dryly.

"We're not going there," Mullins returned, voice no bullshit. "Anyway, afterwards, all of God's creatures were supposed to ignore the fact that Goddess and her get existed, and that included God's supernatural creatures too. But... but there's something weird going on down south—that's all I can tell you. The last five or so years have just been... odd. Like Goddess has a champion and her brood are all joining under one umbrella, which is ridiculous, of course, but—"

"Why ridiculous?" Edward was fascinated. They'd studied for 140 years, but this was a whole new world.

"Because vampires and werewolves, yes—they have a symbiotic relationship. Vampires drink their blood and werewolves protect them when they're dead to the world. But elves and vampires? Who's ever heard of such a thing?"

Edward rolled his eyes. "Witches and ex-demons? Familiars and angels? Familiars and demons? Come on, Mullins—I know you've been operating from a base of fear for the past few hundred years, but use your imagination!"

Mullins sighed. "Okay. Yes. Fine. I'll put some feelers out. But you boys are going to have to do the final contact. I have no idea what would happen if God magic and Goddess magic collided to that extent."

"What kind of magic are familiars?" Edward asked curiously.

Mullins shifted a little on his buttcheeks, which Edward found unbearably cute. "You are not, strictly speaking, supposed to know this, but when Emma calls on Hecate and Juno and Venus and Artemis and Brigit—"

"They all relate to Goddess," Edward figured dryly. "Damn, Mullins—does Emma know this?"

Mullins grimaced. "She figured it out long before she fell in love with Leonard. Frankly, I think it's why she was bold enough to summon angels and demons. She had a feeling she had a more direct connection to a higher power."

Edward chuckled, impressed. "Emma is nobody to mess with or deceive," he said with some satisfaction. "I'm surprised she didn't rip yours and Suriel's ears off for the deception."

"It's not necessarily deception from Suriel," Mullins admitted. "It's more... what's that sci-fi term? Doublethink. Where on the one hand he knows, but he's not supposed to know and it's not supposed to exist, so on the other hand he knows nothing."

"Oh my God," Edward muttered. "Enough. You two will need to talk and give us some places to ask so we can go make a very odd request of a complete stranger, no matter how powerful they might be. And, for the record, unbelievable. Just… unbelievable. Okay, moving on to the next ingredients on the list—what?"

Mullins was tapping his lower lip with his forefinger—which looked much better *with* a forefinger than it had when all Edward could see were his hooves.

"We should probably figure out why we need that," he said, thinking. "I mean… we can get it, but I think you're right. Figuring out the significance to the spell is going to be important. It may even help us build the wording—in rhyme or not."

"Well, what does an elven king represent to you?" Edward asked, curious. "You barely admit there *was* one."

Mullins blew out a breath. "Well… who do you think my boss is?"

Edward raised his eyebrows. "Uh, the… you know… uh… de… vil?" It sounded superstitious to even say it, and the skeptical rise to Mullins's eyebrow indicated this wasn't the right answer by a long shot.

"Simply? No. My boss in hell is other demons—demons who've traded their soul to the other for… well, for an immortal life, or power, or some sort of 'get out of jail free' card, yes?"

Edward nodded. "So we've always assumed."

"Edward—there are no human souls down there."

Edward's eyebrows went straight up. "I'm sorry?"

"Everybody in hell is a demon, and all the demons are tasked with torturing other demons. Hell is peopled with either the monstrously evil—people who have already traded themselves and just don't care—or the monstrously desperate and afraid. The man who ruined his life by shooting a clerk in a 7-Eleven isn't there. He's in the other place, learning the full extent of the damage he's done and grieving for every soul he's hurt. That's his hell right there—and I wouldn't want it for all the years of torture I've lived. My boss isn't a mythical devil—it's the terrible things people make of themselves when they're truly evil, or truly desperate and unable to cope with the natural laws of God and man."

"But… but who takes your soul?" Edward asked, appalled.

"It's supposed to be the other—but that's not really how it happens."

"Who?"

"Well…." Mullins sighed. "This is the thing nobody learns," he said quietly. "This is the lore nobody believes. But… I think it explains why you need to go introduce yourself to a strange elf and steal his hair."

Edward braced himself. "Shoot."

"Fine." Moodily, Mullins laced his fingers and rested his chin on them. "The legend is, there were three. The God, the Goddess, and the other. We don't capitalize his name—he doesn't really have a… codex or anything. He's just… you know. The other one. Anyway, God created the world—and it was very orderly. And Goddess wanted to create too, and together they came up with the perfect harmony of the cosmos. The way plants give us oxygen and then food, the perfect symmetry of science, you understand?"

Edward nodded. "Yes. It's a lovely story."

"Well, according to the story, at first, the other wasn't… wasn't characterized as evil. He was just… you know. Asymmetry. Leaps in evolution. The way gasses and magnetic fields create the aurora borealis. The scattering of stars as they appear in the sky. Chaos."

Edward thought about that. "Fields of flowers, schools of fish, kittens in a clowder—also lovely."

Mullins sat up straighter and nodded. "Agreed. But then… well, God's creatures procreated. And the Goddess got in there and realized procreation could be fun—not just a drive to copulate, you understand, but…."

Under the ever-thinning mask, Edward saw a dark crescent of heat stain Mullins's cheeks. "Pleasurable," he supplied, a wave of want washing his own body. His neck prickled with heat.

"Yes." Absently, Mullins chewed on a cuticle. "And she played with the creatures, taking their shapes and then giving birth—"

"Shapeshifters?" Edward gasped.

"You're very quick," Mullins said, smiling that proud paternal smile he often used when the boys were in lessons.

"But they're supposed to be a myth—"

"There is no bible with this story, Edward," Mullins said primly.

"But… but that explains it! And the vampires—"

Mullins's expression closed down so fast it was like a wall. Even his mask dropped in place. "Don't make me tell the story of the vampires," he begged softly. "It… it ravages the heart."

"Sure, beloved—"

Mullins pulled in a breath. "That's their word too."

Oh, this was a surprise. "Beloved?"

"Yes. See, the Goddess—"

"The one that's never mentioned."

"She's mentioned, just not, you know, where certain people can hear. Anyway, she was… not promiscuous so much as adventuresome. God produced the angels, beings like in power but… but not of this world, you understand? They were of the aether. I would imagine Suriel had to choose a gender before he came down to speak to Emma. Harry is just very lucky that gender was male. Anyway—she and the other were like beings, and the other enjoyed the pleasures of the creatures in the world. They, uh…." A series of vague gestures with hooves that now very clearly were hooves.

"Went clog dancing with mountain goats," Edward supplied dryly.

Mullins thunked his beastly head on the table. "Fuck off," he said pitifully, and Edward burst out laughing.

"Gracious, Mullins—that could be the second time I've ever heard you swear."

"Fuck off twice," he whimpered, and Edward took pity on him, squeezing his shoulder and leaning over to whisper in his ear.

"The words you are looking for is made love, Mullins. Goddess and the other made love."

Mullins shook his head—and his goatlike ear. "No. They had sex. And enjoyed it. But you see—it… I see humans do this all the time. Their bodies do great things in coitus, and they play with them and go *whee!* Like a child learning how to do a flip off a diving board into the water. But that's not what God meant for bodies to *do*. Sex was his greatest invention— particularly among the sentient. It bonded in body and soul. So Goddess bore a successive brood of children from the other—not as powerful as angels, but beautiful, some of them. Some of them…." He smiled, and even on his beast's face the look was beautiful. "Some of them were like two-foot-long spiders with six opposable furry arms."

Edward blinked. "Chaos. Goddess and chaos."

"Yes."

"Elves. Fairies. Sprites."

"Yes."

"But why is there no… no myth—"

"God did not approve. He… he wanted to be the one for the Goddess, and she had loved him from the first. They were together and they bore a son—"

"I know this story," Edward said, awe curling in his stomach.

"Yes. And you know the end. When the great quarrel happened. And God turned his back on all his lover's other children, and she devoted her life to keeping them secret from his followers' misguided wrath."

Edward took a big breath and rested his forehead on his fist. "Emma and Leonard come from a whole different mythology," he said. "Emma created us with elemental forces. We're not anything like the shapeshifters I've heard of."

"Yes."

"It makes so much sense. So there are elves!"

"Yes."

"Excellent. Wait until I tell Harry and Francis. And you really don't know where they are?"

Mullins grunted. "I… I don't. And I don't think anybody in hell does either. They're not of hell. The elves dislike the ugliness of hell—and I think even the other is repulsed by the chaos. About the only thing I can think of is… maybe creating chaos? Not the terrible kind—no explosions or fires or anything. Like… fields of flowers, I guess."

"Beautiful chaos," Edward said brightly.

"Yes. That exactly. If I can cause some beautiful chaos, with a shapeshifting cat by my side…."

"Someone might lead you to elves."

Mullins nodded. "Indeed."

"Excellent. So, we can put an M next that one—"

"An M?"

"For mission," Edward said gravely. "This one is going to take all of us."

"No it won't. Just me and you and the chaotic event and some investigation and—"

Edward just waited for him to peter to a halt.

"What?" Mullins asked.

"If we see elves and fairies and Harry, Francis, and Beltane do not, what do you think will happen?"

Mullins grunted. "Chaos."

"And there will be nothing beautiful about it. So M for mission. Now what's next on the list?"

A SINGLE red grain of sand on a beach of black.

"Oh, that's going to be fun," Mullins muttered.

"It depends on the company," Edward told him. Then he frowned. "But... but we may be able to make a substitution if we stumble upon one, yes?"

"How?"

"Well...." Edward smiled gently, "I know the why of this one already. It speaks of rarity. You understand? All the demons, screaming in hell, and maybe one in a million of them has the soul of a man who can be raised out of the masses. A single red grain of sand, yes. But also a blue rose on a branch of white ones. Or a multihued butterfly in a swarm of orange. Or a four-leaf clover in a field of thousands. This is the easiest thing on the list."

"Do you think that should tell you something?" Mullins grumbled.

"You complain a lot. Were you this pessimistic as a human? Because that should be fun for us. I worry and you predict doom."

Mullins thought about that for a moment. "No," he said. "I was... I was the one who could always find a way to win." He smiled faintly, and Edward hung on his every facial twitch. "I... I used to be brave."

Edward nodded. "You've been brave all the time I've known you," he said softly. "You've defied hell a hundred times for us. Can you do no less for yourself?"

"I'm here, right?" he said with some irritation. "But we don't have much more time."

"Okay—I'll list the rest and you memorize the list and think about some of the less obvious ones, yes?"

Mullins nodded, looking exhausted. Edward had never been clear on the physics of summoning, but he'd always gathered that a demon's price for leaving his prison was a great expenditure of energy. Mullins had grown stronger with each passing year in their service. Edward had hopes that he could be strong for them until the end, when he could finally leave hell for good.

"So," Mullins said heavily, "what's the rest of the list?"

DEMON BLOOD, shed in a righteous cause.

"At least it doesn't say last mortal drop," Edward muttered.

"It's implied," Mullins said darkly.

A CROSS that won't burn the flesh of a demon.

"There's a fun experiment!" Mullins rolled his eyes.

"We'll line them up," Edward told him. "You can run across them like a firewalker—we'll cheer you on."

"Your tongue—"

"Is going to lick all over your body someday, so be nice."

"Nungh."

A MIRROR so pure a vampire may see his soul.

"I actually had one of those," Edward said, shaking his head in disgust.

"But you just asked me about vampires!"

"Well I didn't see any vampires! But I bought it from a very reputable vendor on the desert plain."

"If you want me dead, Edward, just say so. There's no reason to risk my life by using Ktarkech's cut-rate supplies."

"Just think about why we need it, dammit!" But Edward knew the answer to this one. If a vampire could see his soul, then a demon could surely see his worth. Mullins didn't need Ktarkech's cut-rate supplies, really. He needed a way he could see that he still had a soul.

LIQUOR SO pure it burns to the heart.

"Please tell me you're not going to get me drunk," Mullins muttered.

"I don't know, after this list of items, I think you could use a drink."

And so on. In the end, there were over forty items on the list of the spell for demon redemption and recovery—but it was the last one that made them both pause.

Mullins grimaced. "This one…."

Edward nodded.

ESSENCE OF one passed down the line of what was once the demon's kind.

"Nice," Edward said with a sigh. "This was one of few items I didn't have in the minivan when it blew up."

"Wait a moment!" Mullins protested. "You… you had most of the ingredients in the minivan before it blew up?"

"Yes. Yes, I did. And then we all went on a mission without Harry and they spotted us and were completely on our tail with guns and Emma pulled us out of the minivan with that boomerang thing she does in her sleep, and the minivan was sailing through the air like an unmanned cruise missile. Are you happy?"

"But… but you were doing this before? Without my knowledge? Edward—*why*?"

"Because I wanted it all done before we told you!" Edward exclaimed. "I wanted to offer it—and I know it's silly and simplistic and sad—but I wanted to offer it, like a courting gift, and say, 'Mullins, I've loved you forever. Will you leave hell for me?' And then everything I'd collected went kaboom and…." Edward's shoulders slumped. "Harry and Suriel were separated. And I know we told you about it afterward, but… but I thought I was going to lose my brother, Mullins. And I was terrified. So I gave up the search until Suriel was released from heaven, and now—"

"Now you're ready to search again." Mullins bowed his head. "Edward, you have nothing to be ashamed about. You should have asked me first—"

"So you could say no?" Edward demanded.

Mullins shook his head, eyes focused on Edward's loopy scrawl. "I wouldn't have said no," he whispered. "Not to you."

And Edward had to grin, his heart warming in his chest. "And that is the best thing I've heard all day. But about that last thing—"

"I'll search for it," Mullins told him soberly. "But sometime—not now—I think I'm going to have to tell you the story about how one young cotsman became a demon."

"I'm waiting to hear it," Edward whispered. "Mullins, you're growing thin. Let me kiss you, and you can wear my love under your skin, to protect you until it's time again."

Growing thin was the expression Francis had coined for the transparency Mullins formed around the edges before Mullins asked for the words that would banish him back to hell.

"Kiss—"

Edward ignored him, turned his head, and cupped his jaw. His fingers slid through the façade of the beast like a photo projection on the wall, and he could feel the faint bristle of day-old beard abrade his palm. "I can see you, this close, Mullins. I know who I'm kissing. You are a very beautiful man."

He found Mullins's mouth unerringly, and Mullins's gasp of surprise told Edward the touch was alien, and not unpleasant.

Edward breathed softly and found the seam of Mullins's lips with the tip of his tongue, and Mullins's breathy little moan sent wildfire ripping through Edward's blood.

He slid his fingers along the back of Mullins's round, human skull and plundered.

So many years of depending on this steady, practical demon. So many years wanting to escape the strictures of courtesy and magic that bound them.

And now Edward was *tasting* him, and he tasted rich, sweet, exotic— Turkish coffee and cinnamon.

Mullins groaned and lifted his hand to Edward's temple—

And sliced his skin with the sharp edge of his hoof.

Edward gasped and Mullins jerked back, turning away and shrinking inward.

"Let me go," he murmured, like the last hour of them working together, partnering as though they had a future, had never happened.

"Never."

Edward reached for his chin and found it—still human under his fingers. He gave a little pull and Mullins reluctantly turned toward him. Edward couldn't see him anymore, but he could feel him under his fingers. "That kiss is my vow to you, Mullins. I fell in love bit by bit, you understand? For the last fifty years, it's been you, just you, in my heart, but that doesn't mean you haven't been there from the very first. You and me, we have things to do together. This isn't the end. I may let you return to your cell, to gain strength, to think about the challenges we have together, but trust me, I'll be summoning you again. And if you don't come, I'll know you've been taken, and thanks to you, I've got a plan—"

"What's the—"

"Enough. Enough of the plan." Edward smiled and tapped his forehead, calling up his brother's mantra when things got really hairy. "It's all up here," he said.

Mullins didn't smile back. "You're right," he said quietly. "I do have a soul. But if you get hurt before we can make this come true, you'll break my heart."

Edward nodded, suddenly sober. "Understood. I'll say the words to let you go, and I swear I'll call you back again." A drop of blood dripped over Edward's forehead from the cut Mullins had left, and before Edward knew how to react Mullins leaned forward and lapped.

The buzz of magic that passed through the room left them both breathless.

"What the—"

"I'm sorry!" Mullins muttered. "I'm sorry, I don't know why I did that—"

Edward's cockiest grin took him by surprise. "I do. You locked that promise in blood, you clever boy. I'm sworn to it for real now—written right in the annals of hell, isn't that how the blood oath goes?"

Mullins shut his eyes. "It was unconscionable—"

"It was *heroic*!" Edward crowed. "And I owe you the same sort of heart. I'll get you out of there, beloved. Just hang on, understand?"

To his relief Mullins nodded, and Edward reached out and touched his face tenderly. "Get thee gone, demon," he said, voice choking on the old words. "Return only when summoned, harm none in this house, harm none at my hearth. Get thee gone."

And Mullins disappeared, fading into the air, leaving only the heat of his body and his hope behind.

At that moment, Edward felt a telepathic tap on his shoulder from Harry.

What?

Did you make any headway?

We only talked about half the list, but yes.

Fair enough. Get your ass to Mom's house—we've got a rescue to make. We can hash out the rest of the list while I drive.

Edward half laughed. *On it. Taking the truck.* As he tucked his legal pad and his sulfur and his chalk and thyme into his backpack, he recognized the ache in his heart and knew nothing could make up for watching Mullins fade from his home, from his life, one more time.

But going out to kick a little ass with his brothers helped.

UNDER A ROCK

OVER THE years, Mullins's cell had come to offer a certain comfort. It was a stretch of cot—Emma had given him bedding for it—simple, human, and permeable through the dimensional wall that separated hell from the surface of earth—and somehow it had escaped notice or censure of the other demons. The surrounding walls had not worn one molecule more comfortable or smooth in the hundreds of years since his incarceration, but every bit of flesh or drop of blood seemed to have rendered the cell into something Mullins had never known before his time in hell:

A thing uniquely his.

Disconsolately, he sat down, patting the plain cotton bedding.

Edward's kiss buzzed like wine beneath his skin.

Freedom.

Edward promised him freedom.

Typically, he had not asked Mullins if he wanted such a thing—he had simply assumed it would be reasonable that Mullins would not want to linger in hell.

Did Mullins want to linger in hell?

Alone, without Edward there to disappoint, to hurt, Mullins thought carefully about why he'd ended up there in the first place.

"Clyde! Clyde! Come look!"

"Ruth—wait!"

Clyde's little sister was always so fast! *He ran, tired—he'd snuck out the night before, because the smithy's boy had beckoned, with wicked eyes and forward hands. Rutting with women had never appealed to Clyde, but the things Clyde and James did when no eyes pried were magical.*

"But can you see him? It's the man! The red man!"

A shiver raced up Clyde's spine. "No red men, Ruthie—do you not learn your scripture?"

"But he's not evil—he's kind! See?"

She crouched at the split base of an old oak tree that had once been riven by lightning, poking at the offerings.

An odd sort of flower, with stiff white petals and a cluster in the center the color of blood, sat in the crevice, along with a tiny sweet, wrapped in parchment.

Clyde stared at the offerings for a moment, undecided.

"The sweet may not be—"

But Ruthie had already popped it in her mouth, and she sucked on it with a look of bliss. "See, Clyde? He's not evil. He's my friend."

Clyde shuddered. Nobody in the family had seen this "red man." When asked to elaborate on "red," she'd pointed to their mother's faded washday skirt. "That red—but brighter."

Not a human red.

Clyde had kept the conversations to himself—there had been a witch burning not five leagues from their village the year before. His little sister was kind to feral cats, sang to the chickens as she fed them, mourned the slaughter of every pig for the winter. Clyde didn't see how his sister, little more than an infant, really, could be under the sway of devils, real or imaginary.

He wouldn't turn their village on her for all the gold in England.

"Ruthie," he said hesitantly. "Ruthie, your friend may be made of nothing more evil than dead leaves and wind, but when the wind stirs up dead leaves, people often cry ghost. Please, little one, for me, don't call attention to this red man."

"Fine," Ruthie huffed. "I'll be quiet. But he comes to my window at night—how do the others not see him?"

Clyde shuddered. Their cottage had two rooms for sleeping—and four daughters and one son. Clyde spent his nights in the front room, on a pallet by the fire. If the red man was coming to her window, Ruthie had to walk over a lot of bodies to talk to him there.

"Ruthie—be careful! You shouldn't ought to—"

"I'm being careful," she assured him, so winsome and so prim at the same time, Clyde didn't have the heart to reprimand her.

He sank to a crouch before her. "You make me smile, little one. Please—we don't know who this red man is. There's plenty of evil men out there who might fancy a sweet little maid in braids."

Ruthie nodded soberly, biting her lip. "I'll ask him to meet you, the next time he comes," she told him. "That way you don't have to worry...."

"Mullins!" Renotly's voice shrilled, breaking into his reverie. "Where have you been?"

"Summoning," Mullins answered, keeping his voice dead, when the vision of his sister was still very much alive behind his eyes. "Can you not smell the spell?"

It was a taunt. Renotly was magic blind in the worst way. Most summoning spells left a trace in the air that even the most inexperienced demon could detect—but not Edward's or, in fact, any of the family. But saying the smell of sulfur and meadowsweet and blood lingered in the air when Renotly couldn't detect it was both cruel and a safety precaution. Renotly wouldn't admit he couldn't sense it, and nobody had to know Mullins went mostly willingly when he was supposed to have been compelled.

"Of course," Renotly said smoothly, customary horrible grimace deepening. "Anybody can smell it. You were just gone a long time."

"They needed something complex," Mullins told him. "Unfortunately it was for completely unselfish reasons—not a soul on my roster today." He barely contained the lilt in his voice celebrating the fact, but Renotly rolled his narrow eyes anyway.

"You haven't taken one soul," he sneered. "Not in nearly four hundred years. You're fooling nobody, you know. You're soft and weak—not one soul, not one person lured to their doom—you just sit and scribe and scribe. It's like you're not even in hell."

"And yet, here you are. Was there something you needed?"

"Vanth," Renotly muttered. "Have you seen him? Menoch claimed to smell him around your chamber, but I don't sense it." Renotly sniffed wetly. "Although I do smell... wine? Like champagne...." For a moment Renotly flickered, and Mullins got a view of an elegant young man wearing an Art Deco style suit—with a self-inflicted hole in his temple. "Ah, I miss champagne...." Mullins watched sadly as the person Renotly had been before he'd given himself over took a sip of champagne and a shot of opium and embraced his father's pistol. He'd heard the story of the young wastrel who'd sold his soul to replace his family's coffers, but seeing it enacted in front of him, as the young man's sweetheart ran across the room to stop him, was absurdly affecting.

"I've never tasted it," Mullins told him gently. He'd been a demon long before champagne had become a delicacy among the emerging middle class of England. "But I'm glad the smell brings you joy."

Renotly shook himself, and the vision of him as a human disappeared. "Vanth," he said, holding on to the mewling tone in his voice with what sounded to be quite an effort. "Champagne," he whispered, his association so strong Mullins had a moment to wonder what it was he smelled.

"No," Mullins lied, pulling his attention away. "Haven't seen the nasty buzzing thing. Where was he last stationed?"

"The Market." Renotly lowered his head conspiratorially, shaking himself back into the game. "We got a line on your old mentor, my boy. Menoch has the perfect plan to lure him back into hell."

Mullins raised his bristly eyebrows, keeping his face and body neutral. He couldn't afford to kill Renotly—the replacement they sent probably *would* be able to sense some of the things Mullins had been up to. "Unlikely. Leonard had to sacrifice many things in order to escape. Why would he come running back now?"

Renotly's grotesque features had relaxed somewhat—not the stunning young man, but not the contorted demon. In this moment Mullins could see them both—how ugly the stunning young man became when his only expression for a hundred years was contempt.

"Because that get of his is coming close to mortal peril—that's what I've heard… the whole Market is buzzing about it—searching for illicit things…."

"Everybody searches for illicit things in the Market," Mullins said, as though bored. "I understand Balaam ejaculates into shot glasses so Ktarkech can sell it for gold."

Renotly's eyes widened. "Do people buy it?"

Mullins had many years in which to learn to keep his features schooled and blank. "By the wagonload," he said.

"If you see Menoch, tell him I'm looking for Vanth in the Market," Renotly hissed, disappearing in short order.

Mullins waited an entire minute, sitting primly on his bed, eyes staring blankly ahead, before he allowed himself to breathe.

In his head, he summoned his stylus, but instead of writing on the earth, he envisioned the rearview mirror in the old truck the family used on their property. In his head he wrote *The market is compromised* on the mirror, and got a good look at Edward's eyes growing large as he saw the writing.

Another breath, the stylus disappeared, and Mullins was back in his chamber, summoning an old-fashioned fountain pen and white paper with which to write.

By the time Menoch found him, he was immersed wholly in his work of transcription, and the smell of spellwork had disappeared.

"Vanth…." Menoch mumbled. "I smell… wine?"

"I smell neither," Mullins lied. He'd thoroughly disinfected the area of Vanth—that at least he didn't have to worry about. But the wine—again? That was… troubling.

"I don't smell Vanth." Menoch crossed his stubby arms. "What are you doing here in the dark?"

"My job," Mullins told him shortly. "I've always worked in my cell." This was truth—he'd started when Leonard told him there were no rules against it. For some reason, Menoch would rather bitch about the lack of rules than go to his superior to figure out how to make one.

"Why?" Menoch did that thing where he made his snout touch his upper lip. It was repulsive.

"Why what?"

"Why do you smell like wine and why do you work in your cell?"

"I don't smell like wine, and I work in my cell because, if I can escape the usual round of fornications and murders on the scribe floor, I alone can finish all the work you need done that allows that to happen." This was only partially true. Mullins and Leonard combined used to be able to knock out the "work" the scribes were supposed to do. Mullins alone managed about half of it—but one demon doing the work of 333 wasn't bad.

Menoch's snout and upper lip maintained contact. "It still doesn't excuse the wine."

Mullins stood, still bored, and began to strip out of his clothes.

"What are you doing?" Menoch demanded, aghast.

"Were you going to scourge me for smelling like wine? Because if so we need to do it now before you get behind."

"No! Hells no!" Menoch turned and stalked toward the entrance in a fit of disgust. "No! Just do your fucking job!" he snarled, and Mullins waited until the stench of rotting flesh receded before he flopped back onto his cot.

Hells.

He tried to be horrified—he really did. He smelled like wine, and apparently every demon in hell could tell something was amok.

But he couldn't be horrified. Edward's kiss had not stopped buzzing under his skin, had not stopped bubbling, like carbonation, in his veins. Ah, gods—so sweet. Edward looked like a young man, but he kissed like a master, and in spite of that, some innocence and a whole lot of hope permeated his every touch.

Mullins could taste the boy he'd seen on Leonard's hearth that first night, could taste the man that both loss and triumph had shaped, and the results on his tongue, in his *human* mouth, were *glorious*.

Mullins had not felt like this since… since….

Oh hells… must he remember?

"You need to go!" Clyde whispered. "It's not fitting a grown man should visit the window of a child."

"But she's lovely!" the man at the window said, laughing. "Who would harm such a charming little girl?"

He wasn't red tonight, he was blue, as though a perfectly ordinary—if extraordinarily beautiful—man had been suffused with indigo.

"Anyone who thought she was trafficking with spirits!" Clyde told him indignantly. "You're blue*!"*

The "red" man flashed a white smile. And his color—barely distinguishable in the midsummer sunset—changed to a rich orange-gold. "And now I'm not." He blinked, his almond-shaped eyes growing sleepy. "And you too are a charming child—but a fully grown one." He extended a finger through the opened window and tilted Clyde's chin up. "And you like my form?" He smiled prettily, his lush mouth tilting at the corners. "Mm… not this one?"

In a breath he was female, with a softer jaw and more delicate chin, face a perfect oval. Lush yellow hair spilled over bare shoulders, and Clyde felt the spell woven by the man fade.

"No," Clyde said, leaning back from the soft fingertip at his chin. He'd had to walk over his sisters in their beds when Ruthie had hissed at him. "I'm sorry. My sister is innocent, and you are… fey?"

The other changed forms again, to a man this time—naturally colored. Skin a medium clay color, not cochineal red, hair a lush straight spill of black past his shoulders, chest a smooth expanse of touchable muscle.

He was wearing a loincloth and nothing else.

"Not fey," the man purred. "Father of fey." His hooded gaze raked Clyde up and down. "Perhaps you are one of my many times removed great-grandchildren. I don't smell fey on you or your sister, but...." He closed his eyes and inhaled sensually. "Still delicious."

Clyde swallowed. "You need to go away and not eat us," he said seriously. Behind him, Ruthie giggled.

"Like porridge?"

"No, little one. That's not how he meant." The man pinned Clyde with a rather stern expression. "Your sister is too young. She does not need to be here for this."

Clyde gasped, turning toward Ruthie, suddenly afraid. She yawned, looking confused, and fell backward onto her thin pillow, snoring softly.

"What did you—"

"Just put her to sleep. She will wake in the morning, thinking this is a dream."

"She thinks you're her friend!" Clyde couldn't contain his outrage.

"I am!" A white smile flashed, and Clyde's stomach quivered. His groin tingled as though it had been touched. "Some days, I play with the friends who like sweets and poppets and daisy chains." That finger moved to Clyde's lower lip. "Some days, I play with the friends who have delicious pricks and juicy holes."

Clyde swallowed, the crudity not repelling him at the least. "My parents are asleep in the next room," he said, his throat dry. The practical thought helped ground him. "And I... I frolic with another—"

"The smithy's boy? Mm... whom do you think taught him about goose grease, young cotter's son? Imagine the things I might teach you."

Clyde shuddered sensually, but he knew his duty. "You put my family in danger every moment you stay," he said softly. "You should leave us to our ordinary lives."

"Then we shall go somewhere else," the man said easily. "And you will be back in your bed by morning, with a story to tell the smithy's lad and a body that's been well used."

Mullins swallowed hard on his little cot in hell, his face working painfully as he fought tears. Oh, they said the road to hell was paved with good intentions, but his had been paved with the worst. He didn't remember much of his time with the other, but he certainly remembered the aftermath. Jonathan, the boy he'd loved—yes, he could say that now, he'd once loved—had not been entertained by his story in the morning. In fact he'd been so damned hurt, he'd told the entire village of the terrible creature who snuck into young people's beds and seduced them in a field of flowers, no single bloom the same.

"Clyde!" Ruthie screamed, tripping on a rut in the road. "Clyde! Where are we going!"

"To hide!" he said, scrambling around brush. Oh God. Oh God—they'd set their house on fire. His mother and father and sisters had been held back, shouting their names as the villagers had chased after them in the night. He still remembered the shocked hurt on Jonathan's face as his confrontation in front of the town square grew wildly out of hand.

He'd cried, "Clyde, I'm sorry!" as the house had gone up, but Clyde and Ruthie had been on the run, so Clyde hadn't been able to reply.

They were going to catch Ruthie. Jonathan had been yelling at Clyde about sporting with demons when Ruthie had cried out, "But he's not a demon! He's my friend!"

And that had been it. The end. Their fates sealed. If their own village didn't kill them, they'd die of starvation, exiled from all the villages for miles around. But Clyde couldn't think that way, couldn't think of abandoning his sister—he just had to get them past—

"Clyde—they're behind us," Ruthie wailed, and Clyde had had enough.

He dragged Ruthie into the underbrush by the river and cautioned her to lay low. "If they catch me I'll say I drowned you," he whispered. "But hide. Don't let them see you!"

"But Clyde!"

"Love you, little sister."

And then he'd started to wade into the river, calling at the top of his lungs.

"Demons and devils, whoever seduced me, come out! Come out! I have a bargain to make, damn you all! Come out!"

A hideous creature appeared then, with bulging skin and sparse green hair and the stench of a thousand tortures, and for a moment, Clyde recoiled.

"No!" he cried to the creature hovering over the water that he stood waist-deep in. "I don't want you!"

"What you want is immaterial," the creature hissed. "You called on demons and I'm a demon—now tell me your bargain!"

"My sister!" Clyde's voice trembled and his eyes burned. "Save her—" And oh, he knew the stories of the crossroads demons! "Save her, let her live a long, happy life, with children who live long, happy lives and so on for as many generations as there are down the road. Save her and...."

"I know the rest," the creature purred, holding up a gleaming golden parchment and a sharpened quill, rusty and black at the end.

Clyde quailed at the sight of that quill, closing his eyes and saying a brief prayer. Oh, whoever that man had been, the one at his window, who had seduced him in a bed of flowers, no two the same—why couldn't he come to offer Clyde a millennia of servitude?

"They're coming," the creature wheedled. "Sign for Menoch, yes? I won't hurt you... that badly."

Clyde looked away, and then, involuntarily, he looked to Ruthie, crouched in the underbrush, terrified. She didn't deserve this. Oh God—she didn't.

He seized the quill from Menoch's pudgy hand and plunged it into the vein in his wrist, then signed his name on the line the way he'd learned at his father's knee.

Menoch gave a howl of laughter—and in that moment, the other man appeared.

He took in the scene—Clyde, Ruthie, Menoch, the signed contract—and then, over Clyde's shoulder, he saw the villagers.

To Clyde's surprise, his face filled with sorrow.

"You couldn't have wait—"

"There he is!" someone cried from the distance.

"No, I suppose not," the man sighed. "I'm so sorry, my boy. This is not the kind of chaos I'd envisioned the two of us wreaking."

"Help me!" Clyde wailed as Menoch seized his hand. "Oh please— make sure they don't hurt Ruthie—"

"Your sister, I can help," he said, pausing to, of all things, rub his thumb along Clyde's lower lip. "But you, boy—I'm sorry. All things considered, I really don't care for demons."

At that moment the villagers crested the levee leading down to the river, screaming with rage as they caught sight of Clyde.

"I'll save her, boy."

And Menoch gave his arm a hideous wrench, parting his shoulder from its socket, and blackness washed over his vision.

When he awoke, he was in hell, and Leonard was setting his shoulder, telling him how to keep hold of his sanity.

Mullins had nearly 400 years to keep his emotions in check, to hide his grief, to hide his fear, to hide, even, his humanity, which he was painfully aware had never deserted him as it seemed to have left his peers.

But as the memories rolled over him, he could smell the sweet liquor of Edward's love buzzing just under his skin, and thought of the moment he'd have to tell Edward that his crime had been being a faithless lover, an easy target for the other, a willing participant in a careless seduction.

He'd put his entire family in jeopardy to have sex in a field of wildflowers, no two blooms alike.

Objectively he knew his crime was minor—he'd seen murderers in these jagged stone caves, rapists, narcissists who toyed with the emotions of the people they claimed to love until that person committed suicide out of desperation.

But hell was not built with bricks of objectivity. It was thrown together haphazardly with the bitter, razor sharp stones of self-blame.

Not even Menoch could stop his beast's face from contorting as he shed bitter tears.

THE YOUNGBLOODS GO ON QUEST

"SO THE message just appeared?" Harry asked, jouncing down the driveway in the family minivan.

"In the rearview mirror of the truck last night," Edward confirmed. "And I could...." Ugh. This sounded so personal. "I could smell him—Mullins, I mean. It was from him."

"I don't doubt you," Harry said mildly, swerving to avoid a pothole. Leonard had been promising to re-gravel the driveway for months. "I'm just saying, that's a fun spell. Since we can't use telepathy when he's in hell and all."

Mullins had very carefully explained to them that just as a summoning could be detected by the denizens of hell, so too could any connective magic. It was why they were so careful about calling him, even when things got crazy. It was why Edward had been so surprised to see him in that hotel room in Vegas, when he and Francis had been losing their minds.

"I'm not sure if I can return the favor," Edward said, depressed. He'd kissed Mullins—had savored it, had wanted more. But they had what? Two more months? Four more months? Before they saw each other again?

Once, they'd gone four years.

It felt like a lifetime, and Edward wasn't ready to wait a lifetime, not when he'd just decided to be with Mullins *now*!

"Probably not," Harry said practically. "But maybe, if we use a little, I dunno, *magic*, we can make it easier to fix a mirror to be ready for him. So, you know, like buying a phone so he can text us."

Edward looked at his brother in admiration. "That's really a good idea! So, like, things of Mullins that will make the mirror more accessible." Edward had a few things. Thread from the frayed cuff of his customary suit. A whisker that he'd shed over fifty years ago, that Edward had tucked in his pocket for luck. Once, when they'd been practicing spellwork outside, Mullins had looked in fascination at some California poppies and told Edward that, where he came from, they were much bigger, lusher blooms. Edward had plucked one—it hadn't been illegal then—and presented it to

Mullins in jest, in a sad effort to flirt, and told him that these flowers were for his memories of the Youngbloods alone.

Mullins had inhaled the scent delicately and then handed the flower back to Edward with his customary faint smile.

"That's kind, my boy, but I shall have to trust it to you for safekeeping. It wouldn't do well in my cell."

Edward had kept that too—had kept all of the small mementos of Mullins in a carefully hand-carved box made for him by Paul, the first lover he'd dared to take long term.

He'd asked himself, once, if it was fitting to keep the mementos of one man in the keepsake of another, and in the end, he'd decided that it was. He and Paul had spoken a few times about Edward's long life, and Paul had mourned more for Edward than for himself. He'd wanted Edward to find lasting happiness—and had worried, rightly, at how hard the grieving would be on Edward's heart.

The box was a promise of sorts, that Edward would more than love again. He would eventually find love eternal.

If he were to truly honor his first love, he would trust Paul to safeguard the treasures of his heart.

Edward pulled the thing from a hidden pocket of his canvas rucksack and dug some more for one of three mirrors he kept for various scrywork.

"A pink compact," Harry said dryly. "Very stylish."

"The compact keeps it safe," Edward said mildly. This particular compact also had a little compartment in the back—meant for a makeup sponge or a tissue, Edward assumed. He opened that and added three of his Mullins treasures. Then he put the rest back into Paul's box before fitting it into the pocket.

Then he closed his eyes, summoned his stylus, and focused his will. *Speak and your words will show.*

He gave a little push of will, his words became permanent on the oak gall and parchment, and the compact glowed for a moment—as, hopefully, did the one Edward knew for a fact Mullins carried in his pocket for use in spellcasting.

Edward opened it up to look in the mirror and gasped.

He could see.

"Oh my God, Harry, look!"

Harry braked hard, just as they came to the exit from the Youngblood property to the seafront highway that would take them to the next step in their quest.

"Ouch!" Suriel gasped from the seat behind them. Beltane and Francis—who were in the far back seat—yelped and mrowled. Harry looked back apologetically.

"Sorry, guys, but Edward said 'Look!' and I didn't want to drive us off a cliff!"

"Of course," Suriel told him. "It would never be intentional."

"I'm going to vomit," Edward muttered. "Harry, are you looking?"

Harry looked over his shoulder and gasped. "Oh... Mullins."

Mullins didn't discuss the bowels of hell often. In fact, he had a number of verbal tricks to neatly dodge the subject should it ever come up. But there, reflected in the glass, was an image none of them could escape.

Mullins, cross-legged on a clean white bed, in a tiny cave, the rocks that made up the walls jutting out like razors. The darkness around him was choking—even through the small mirror he was apparently holding up to look at—and his discomfort could be felt through the image itself. Edward wasn't sure if it was a real, physical thing, or if it was simply the psychic residue of so much pain in such a place, but the razored rocks around him seemed to be dripping and crawling with blood.

Slowly, as though alerted by a sound, Mullins went from squinting at the mirror in puzzlement and gazing straight into Edward's eyes. Edward bit his lip. He looked so vulnerable—so lonely.

Across the mirror came a stately cursive. *Very clever.* The words disappeared, to be replaced with *It grew warm in my pocket. Handy.* Those words disappeared after a moment, replaced by *I'll check in on your progress when I can.*

Edward summoned his own stylus, and across the mirror, in Edward's blocky print, appeared *I will try to show you beauty.*

Mullins's eyes widened in surprise, and then he gave a beast's grimace. *Someone's coming.*

Edward shut the mirror quickly and shoved it in his rucksack.

"Can I go now?" Harry asked after a moment of Edward trying to control his breathing.

"He looked... awful," Edward said, although there had been no mark upon him. It was hard to read past the pig's snout and the horse's forehead and the ram's horns—but even the darkness of hell, the beastly features, and the distance of magic couldn't obscure the fact that Edward could still see the human eyes.

"Tired," Harry said softly, surprising him.

"How could you see that?" For a moment, Edward felt betrayed—Mullins had always been Edward's.

"Edward, do you love Suriel?"

Edward blinked. "Of course." Suriel had been a beloved family member, a much older brother or a young uncle.

"Does seeing him without his wings pain you?"

Oh. He had to close his eyes and swallow. In the months since Suriel had slid through the fabric of time and space from heaven into Harry's bedroom, back bleeding from the lashes of heaven, the scars of his absent wings still healing, none of them had been able to see the lack of that vast chaperone behind Suriel without feeling an empty wound.

"Of course."

"We all love him. You just want to…."

Edward had to laugh. Harry's face—oh, his brother didn't blush often, but it was almost worth the price of admission.

"For which I'm reassured," Edward said dryly. "Okay. So I get it. You're not just doing this for me."

"Nope. The sooner you and Mullins have your own cabin on the property, wafting bursts of sulfur and wine, the happier I'll be. Our friend is in hell, Edward."

"Let's get him back."

Harry held his hand out for a fist bump, and Edward didn't leave him hanging.

"Okay, here we go. Everybody ready for the boomerang?" Harry had been practicing sending more than one person—or a large object—including himself, into space for the last two months while Edward had been sneaking off to go on his hunt. Harry did have his own little ways of preparing for a challenge.

Beltane whimpered and Francis hissed, and Edward closed his eyes. "Let us know when we're on the ground, okay? You sure you know where we're going?"

"Of course I do—you remember that stretch of highway near Coos Bay?"

"The one with the blackberry bushes almost completely obscuring the road?" On the one hand, it was brilliant—if the minivan just appeared on a deserted country road, odds were good the van could just keep going on the road with no problems whatsoever.

On the other hand, it was madness, because what if someone *was* there. You'd just drop out of the heavens onto their car or their horse or their bare-assed crunchy skull!

"Yeah, that's the one." Harry checked the rearview mirror and sighed when he saw lights. "Dammit! What's the use of leaving at o-dark-thirty when fucking tourists are going to dog me?"

"But Harry, how do you know someone won't be there!" This stretch of road had been deserted even in the daylight until twenty years ago. Now the cows that fed there were frequently disturbed by cars driving too damned fast.

"Because I've taken precautions," Harry muttered, glowering as the car geared up to pass them. Harry had pulled back on the speed to force this maneuver, but Edward was pretty sure that irritated him too.

Harry didn't like to lose.

"Precautions." Oh Lord. That could be anything, from a spell dissuading any traveler from lingering in the area to a dragon who would eat them if they did.

"Oh my God, you're a worrier princess!" Harry burst out. "Just sit there, shut up, close your eyes, and hold on!"

There was a collective grunt as the entire car was encompassed in a wave of vertigo, and then a thump, like they'd just gone over a speed bump. The car swerved hard, and Edward opened his eyes to see Harry wrestling with the wheel, struggling valiantly to keep the car on a properly deserted road.

"Edward!" Harry gasped as they went up on two wheels around a particularly sharp curve. "If you could maybe—"

Edward centered himself and muttered *Grow ever on and on* in Latin, and two things happened.

The first was that the road spread before them, wider, straighter, better paved than any stretch of it for a hundred miles.

The second was that the blackberry bramble began to spiral out of control, like Jack's beanstalk except more inimical to the paintjob on Emma's brand new Honda Odyssey.

"Dammit!" Edward burst out, trying to control the road before it spread off the side of the cliff they were heading for. "Francis, a little help with the fucking bush!"

A bubble of space appeared around the car—fortunately not under the wheels—and as Harry rocked the car back to a smooth passage on the road, Edward managed to make both the sudden advance of tarmac and the writhing bushes themselves recede.

"Whew," Edward said, feeling the panic sweat seep through the pit of his sweatshirt.

"Bloody marvelous!" Harry cackled. "I can't believe that worked!"

"What did you do!" Edward couldn't see a car in either direction for maybe ten miles.

"Oh—that? I put out detour signs and illusions of road construction that just bypassed a good ten-mile stretch of road. Looped right around some pot farmer's territory and gave us room. It was the landing I was worried about, but you two just stepped right up! Good job!"

Edward let out a groan, and behind him Francis did the same.

"I'm going to kill him," Francis said, in that frighteningly alert way he had when he was about to pounce on someone in human form.

"You can't," Edward told him practically. "For one thing, he's driving. For another, he's the only one with that damned spell. If we don't go bouncing around the planet in this damned minivan, this quest will take us years!"

"Years?" Beltane said, sounding as though he'd been awakened from a sound sleep. "That's no good. Mum said I have to go back to Oxford in two months!"

Francis let out an unhappy grunt, and Edward didn't have to look into the back seat to know he'd changed form.

"It's not going to take years," Harry muttered. "I don't think it can."

"What do you mean?"

Harry settled into the driver's seat now that the car wasn't going to buck them off the twisting highway and into the pounding surf below.

"Okay—you went to talk to Mullins, and I'm sure it was all very tortured and him trying to be noble and you trying to be practical and both of you thinking you want sex and neither of you actually saying anything—"

"Oh God—get out of my head, you pervert, it's like you were there!"

Harry rolled his eyes. "I know you, brother. Deal with it. But the thing is, neither of you talked about the demon we had to chase from the Market, and I'm pretty sure he wouldn't mention it if he had to kill the thing and bury what was left."

Edward thought of the times he was pretty sure Mullins had gone above and beyond in his attempts to protect the brothers and murmured, "I'm pretty sure he wouldn't either."

"Well, see? That only proves what I'm trying to tell you. Hell could be positively buzzing with where the demon went, and we don't know if the fucker told anybody what he'd seen, and frankly, Mullins has a hard enough time keeping his head down as it is."

Edward nodded glumly. This wasn't news. Leonard spoke sparingly of his time in hell, but when he did speak, there was always a punishment involved for dodging out on the commands. They couldn't kill a demon for refusing to kill or seduce somebody—but they sure could torture them.

Leonard said frankly that he'd given in for a span of years.

But he had held firm again when Mullins came to hell. He'd never said why, but Edward had always figured it was because Mullins had been cheated into hell—every bit of lore he'd read spoke of slick-tongued demons who would trap a human with even their purest emotions.

"I have the feeling he's hurt a lot," Edward rasped, hating that.

Harry's hand on his shoulder reassured him. Suriel had endured his share of torture to visit the Youngbloods as well—watching someone suffer for your love was about the hardest thing to endure.

"Me too. But see? That only proves my point—they don't like him already. Either that little bug spy spilled the beans or Mullins got him first, but either way, they're going to be more suspicious than usual. We need to keep the mirror trick to once a day—at the most—or he's going to get caught looking for us, and not only will *he* have to suffer the consequences, but *we* will be contending with the hosts of hell and we won't be able to help him."

Edward swallowed. "Do we have a time? A limit? A—"

"Jesus, stop it. I can't quantify fucking hurry, and neither should you! We go as fast as we can and be as careful as we can and contact Mullins as little as we can—"

"Maybe I should just throw the mirror away!" Edward began to search his rucksack, appalled, as both Harry and Suriel snapped, "No!"

Edward stopped. "Why not?"

"It gives you both hope," Suriel said softly. "Oh, Edward. You had a front row seat to Harry and I. You must assuredly know how important hope can be."

Something in Edward's chest settled then. "Hope," he said quietly.

"Yes, hope."

Okay. Edward could hope.

TWO HOURS later, he was *hoping* he didn't fall to his death.

"What are we getting here again?" Harry called up to him, one hand clasped firmly around Edward's wrist while the other scrabbled for purchase on a cliff face over the Oregon coast.

Edward was hanging upside down from his knees so he had a better grip on Harry's arm, and he had to concentrate over the blood rushing in his head.

"An eggshell from a black oystercatcher's nest on a cliff," he yelled.

"Why a cliff?" Bel called from his place securing Edward's legs so he didn't fall.

"Because...." Edward clapped both hands around Harry's wrist as Harry tried to find his footing. "The spell called for *a thing of seabird in the air, an old thing from the young, one who watches over instead of dwells in the crowd.*" Edward practically had the poetry memorized by now. "These birds make their nests down among the rocks!"

"Not this one," Harry muttered with grim satisfaction. "Let go, Edward, I'm going to need both my hands."

"Secure your piton," Edward gritted.

"Do you really think—"

"Secure yourself, idiot! My head's gonna explode!"

"Fine." Harry took his hand back and pulled his piton and his hammer out, then slung the rope at his waist through the carabiner on the piton, and then wrapped the end around his arm. Thus secured, he grunted at Edward, who allowed Beltane to hoist him, feet first, up over the cliff.

Of course Bel let him dangle for a minute once he had Edward to a safe patch of grass.

"Nice, dumbass," Edward grumbled, arms extended so he could catch his fall on his hands. "You're a foot taller than all of us. Must be nice to be born in the twentieth century."

"Twenty-first," Bel said happily, setting Edward down so he could execute a neat tumble. "I mean, it's close enough. In a couple thousand years, who's going to care about such a pittance?"

"Is Harry back?" Suriel asked, turning from a cat as he walked with Francis at his heels. They'd been on watch for any other visitors to the overlook—or at least that's where Harry had asked him to serve. Edward was pretty sure it had been a ruse to keep the two of them from seeing the dumb-shit thing the three of them had just done.

Francis, at least, was not fooled. He hissed, pulled himself upright, and spat.

"Did you think we wouldn't see that? Not one of you thought to learn how to fly?"

Bel and Edward exchanged looks. "We can't fly," Bel said logically. "There's whole texts about how wizards and witches don't have the power to fly. Sorceresses, yes. Wizards, no. I'm not sure why."

Suriel looked carefully, neutrally, over Edward's shoulder, and Edward narrowed his eyes.

"This is one of those God/Goddess things, isn't it?" he asked. "And other. There's a rule here we don't know about. Like, God's children can't fly but Goddess's can?"

"Hm, I'm going to go check on Harry," Suriel said, as though he hadn't heard.

"I can fly," Francis said, because couldn't everybody?

"Really?" Bel didn't sound jealous, even a little. "Show us! Then you can go help Harry."

Francis took a deep breath and held his arms out as though to balance, and then ascended slowly into the air. "It doesn't feel like other magic," he hollered, his white-blond hair a furious tornado around his head.

Edward stared, both impressed and appalled, and Bel whooped. "That's amazing! I'm so jealous! Now go somewhere!"

They were so entranced that nobody heard Harry behind them, struggling to hoist his body up the cliff—but they all heard his reaction.

"Fucking Jesus, Francis—why didn't you just say you could fucking fly!"

Francis set himself down and smiled smugly. "Now you know," he said, and turned cat again to trot away.

"Where's he going?" Edward asked, and Bel shrugged.

"It's gorgeous up here. Let's go kill seagulls!" And then Beltane turned into a big blond dog, woofing ecstatically and chasing the wind.

Harry and Edward watched them go, shaking their heads. "I'm...." Edward made helpless gestures with his hands.

"Yeah. Me too." Finally Harry shrugged and held out a small ziplock bag. "Here—put that in your scary freaky little drawer organizer with the number system, and we can eat the lunch Suriel's going to make and I'll tell you about the next run."

Edward took the bag on automatic and was heading for the piece of luggage Francis had crafted him, which they kept in the minivan before the rest of what Harry said caught up with him.

"Okay—so first off, how did you know I even number the compart—"

"Oh my God!" Harry threw his hands in the air. "Could you not even? What? Have I been stupid for the last hundred and fifty years?"

Edward felt a little shame. "No, brother. You're just not great at planning."

Harry stared at him impassively, and Edward's remorse increased.

"Okay, okay, fine. You're good at planning, just not great at... I don't know. Schematicking."

Suriel, who had been looking from one of them to the other, tilted his head. "That's not a word," he said, and given Suriel spoke every language known to man *and* beast, he would know.

"It's an Edward word, beloved," Harry said, his grim mouth twisted a little at the ends. "As in 'go schematic yourself' or whatever. But what was the other thing?"

Edward shifted uncomfortably. "You, uh, have plans for the next thing on the list?" Because he had a few for a few items, but he had no idea Harry had already prepared.

Harry smiled, the picture of feline smugness. "Go schematic, Edward. I'll show you *my* list after lunch. I'm going to go keep those two from chasing the oystercatchers. They're a protected species, you know." And then Harry turned cat and scampered off, leaving Edward to stomp to the minivan, Suriel at his heels.

"You're not going to go with them?" Edward asked, trying to keep the surliness from his voice.

"Why are you angry?" Suriel asked, his voice kind.

Edward paused in the act of unlatching the back of the minivan and sighed. "Not angry," he said truthfully, remembering that Suriel had been their wise and compassionate counselor for many, many years before he'd been Harry's lover. "Just... he makes me feel inadequate," he confessed with a sigh.

"How?" To his credit, Suriel sounded genuinely puzzled, and Edward looked at him with fondness.

"He's very good at everything," Edward said with a little laugh.

"So are you."

"But... but he's the leader. I thought, you know. I'd be leading this one, because... because—"

"Because Mullins is yours?" Suriel asked perceptively.

Edward sighed and started working the case with the little number compartments out of the back.

"Yes," he admitted after a moment. It sounded even weaker as he said it.

"Well, I was Harry's, but that didn't stop you all from summoning *me* when he was....". Suriel's voice dropped. "Bleeding," he finished with a swallow. Harry had been dying—but had been too stubborn to summon Suriel because of the personal cost to Suriel every time he left heaven. "Everybody needs help sometimes." Suriel's voice strengthened. "Even Emma and Leonard needed Mullins and I, remember?"

Edward smiled and put the ziplock bag from Harry into the numbered slot in the case. "I was there," he said mildly.

"I know you were. It's my understanding you followed Harry's plan in that instance too."

And nothing had gone as planned—but everything had turned out better than their wildest dreams.

"We did," Edward acknowledged. But then, the painful truth. "But Francis and I got... we got left behind, you know. That's why Francis was so out of it. Because Cass caught up with us while we were trying to find Harry."

"Ah." Suriel stood there, back straight, head tilted. Edward missed the wings that used to hover over his shoulders, but he could, in fact, almost see them, even though they'd been stripped away when Suriel had chosen to return to earth and Harry's arms.

"What?" Edward could almost hear the words. But not quite.

"It's why you fuss so much," Suriel said. "About having three backup plans to Harry's one. It's a good system." His full mouth flashed a quiet smile. "Just remember—Harry learned from that too. And he doesn't ever want to let you down again."

Edward swallowed and zipped up the case, replaced it in the back of the car, and pulled out the ice chest.

"Here," Suriel offered. "Let me get that. You close the hatch."

Which probably meant Suriel had prepped the ice chest. Cooking seemed to be one of his passions, and as often as he cooked for Emma and Leonard for their family dinners, Edward couldn't object.

"He's never let me down," Edward said after a moment as they headed for the picnic table.

"He'll be glad to hear it."

Edward smiled a little. Suriel's implicit, eternal faith in Harry was a little nauseating—but it was not, in fact, misplaced. Edward needed to remember that.

Suriel opened the ice chest and proceeded to make five outstanding sandwiches with the grace of a dancer. Edward dressed them on paper plates and added chips and sodas around the table, and they finished up just as their rogue familiars trotted toward them.

"I hope you're hungry," Edward called, "Suriel's outdone hims— goddammit, Francis!"

Francis hissed and spat out bird feathers, then had the gall to look surprised as they floated around his head. He turned human just so he could appear innocent and said, "I have no idea what you're talking about. There's feathers everywhere. They stuck to my fur is all."

Harry spat and changed form. "Of course they stuck to your fur— you *ripped them off some poor bird*. Oh my God, Francis—not even an oystercatcher—a seagull. Ew!"

Francis spat another feather and grimaced. "He did taste sort of like a garbage bird. Huh."

Beltane wagged his tail once and then stood, engulfing Francis in a protective, over the shoulder hug. "And what does a garbage bird taste like?" he asked, his human ears practically perking up.

"Like chicken nuggets," Francis said decisively. "I've seen birds eat those, you know, which just proves that they're not real food."

Edward and Harry stared at each other, mouths opening and closing helplessly.

"Wash up," Edward said finally. "All of you. Spigot's behind the van. Suriel made damned good sandwiches, and we can fit in another stop today."

Harry got back first, of course, and stood on tiptoes to kiss Suriel's cheek. "They look wonderful," he said. "Thank you for making lunch, belo—"

"Beloved my ass," Suriel snapped. "Now that we know Francis can fly, can you maybe not dangle from a cliff next time? Good grief, Harry."

Harry twisted his mouth. "Still, uh, upset—"

Suriel stared at him, earth brown eyes alight with irritation, until Harry bent his head. "Of course, Suriel. I shall be ever careful of my own mortal frame. I completely apologize."

"Thank you, Harry. Sit down—yours is the one with hummus instead of mayonnaise."

Harry grinned irrepressibly. "Does that mean you're done being mad?" he asked, mischief in his tone.

Suriel and Edward had a rather panicked conversation over his head.

"That depends," Edward said after Suriel gave an imperious nod. "Exactly what's next on the agenda?"

Harry cackled and reached into the pocket of his jeans to pull out a battered paper map. "Did we bring our waffle stompers and leather kneepads?"

"Why—are we going clubbing in LA?" Edward asked.

Harry let out a snort of exasperation. "Oh, Bel and Francis wish. I swear, if they're going to be this obvious they need to make a family announcement and deal. But no. No clubbing. In fact, no lights, no air conditioning, no electricity—"

"We're going to the desert, aren't we?" Edward asked, shuddering.

"Oh, not just the desert, brother. We're going to the *Badlands*."

"Oh hells. No. No—can't we go to a museum? For God's sake—that's what I did last time. I just broke into a museum, stole a toenail, and took off before the alarm sounded!"

"Well, your spell would have been damned shitty," Harry said hotly. "Because you didn't look at what that passage meant."

"*Great beast of old, stripped to bone, roar again in the sands of home. Help your demon find the sands of home*," Edward recited from memory. "So we bring a little sand with—"

"No. You don't get it. It's about reviving something on its home dirt. It's about unearthing the past and letting it breathe in the present. Pulling that bone from a museum is like showing a made-for-TV historical romance of Mullins's past. Digging one up in the heat and the grit of the desert is going to give power to the thing. Mullins isn't getting out of hell unless he airs his dirt, Edward, and we can't cheat on the items any more than we can cheat on the spell. Now *you* deal."

With that Harry took a massive bite of his sandwich, letting out an appreciative sigh. He swallowed and hollered, "Beltane! Francis! Whatever the hell you're doing back there, stop it and come eat! Did I mention we need to hurry?"

Bel and Francis appeared, looking suspiciously innocent, and Harry rolled his eyes and went back to his sandwich.

"This is really excellent, Suriel. Like I said, thank you."

Suriel preened, and Edward let out a grunt.

"He's only irritating because he's right," Suriel said, all serenity.

"He's only irritating because he's my freaking brother," Edward growled. But then he sat down and took a bite of his sandwich and calmed down.

God, he was luckier than he deserved, and he knew it.

THE BADLANDS of South Dakota really were as bad as advertised. The decomposed granite under their feet had hardened to cement—cement with little crystals in it that tore through a kitty's paws and could easily rip through denim.

The four of them outfitted themselves in their stoutest clothes while Harry had Francis scry for the bones of a long-dead beast.

Their first try turned up a rotting coyote, and Harry and Edward refined the spell to bones of stone of a creature that roared, and Francis gave it another go.

Another two miles of hiking and they ended up at a long-abandoned excavation site, while Francis gave them instructions for how and where to dig so they didn't disturb more bones than necessary.

Beltane was the one who actually unearthed the bone, using a shovel to carve through the hardened soil with a lunge and a heave. Then he bent to wipe the thing down with a cloth until they could see the petrified ends.

Edward stood back and took it in, his great broad-chested brother kneeling in the magenta and orange of the sunset. He felt his pocket, where the mirror was warm and vibrant in his hands, and opened the compact.

He saw Mullins, staring into the mirror avidly, and smiled, giving a thumbs-up. Then he panned the mirror around, showing everything: the stark hollowed-out shapes of eroded hills, the layers of soil exposed by the wind, the stunning vibrancy of the lowering sun.

He finished up with the silhouettes of his brothers, oohing and ahhing over Bel and Francis's discovery. The guys saw the mirror aimed at them and smiled, thumbs up, as though taking a selfie, and then Edward turned the mirror back to himself.

We found item 13, he printed.

Well done. Thank them for me. The words faded, and then: *It really is beautiful there.*

Edward took a moment to appreciate the scenery, as he hadn't when they'd been so driven to search. He didn't see the heat or the discomfort or the savagery of the wind. He just saw the shadows, the sunset, and his brothers' dusty triumph.

Some day you shall join us, he sent, sighing when Mullins's picture went dark.

They packed up and got back into the minivan, where Harry exhaustedly boomeranged them to a campsite, and they all settled down in their animal forms for the night.

When Edward woke up the next morning, he checked the mirror again, and while the picture was still dark, Mullins sent a message.

Someday I shall.

Hope. Dammit, Harry really was right a lot, wasn't he!

WHEN HELL IS NOT HELL

MULLINS HAD been born 300 years before the idea of a television had even been conceived. He'd never known the illicit joy that came with watching grown-up cartoons when parents thought their sweet little boy was watching SpongeBob, or of going to a friend's house to see horror movies that had been expressly forbidden.

But working in hell, doing what he always did, which was laying low, and sneaking glimpses through Edward's portal mirror, taught him that sometimes, watching something on a little screen could be just as absorbing as living it himself.

It wasn't that Mullins was unaware of the peril he was in.

Vanth had never been found, and the buzz over where he'd been before he'd gone missing occupied the halls of hell for many weeks. Mullins was keenly aware that one trip to the Marketplace and somebody would place Vanth with the Youngbloods, and the jig would be up.

His only hope was to keep his countenance as serene as it had been since Leonard had left, his face as impassive, his emotions as tightly under lock and key as always.

At first he was terrified.

Menoch was dressing down the scribes of hell, choosing his daily victim, and Mullins—who knew logically that he must fall under the lash at least every eighteen months—was taken by surprise by the pounding of his heart, the sweat under his suit.

It was like unlocking his heart to hope, to the taste of Edward's passion, had unlocked him to the fear that Leonard had helped him stomp to death in his first month in hell.

Fear only made the pain worse. The demon who was unafraid was the demon who would never truly sacrifice his soul.

So as he stood in line, trying desperately not to attract Menoch's eye and knowing that desperation had its own stench that would draw Menoch even faster, he found himself remembering Edward's hunting the day before.

The night in the desert had been beautiful—Mullins had been truly captured by that moment, but he hadn't expected another that lovely.

The next day he'd been surprised to get a vista of pounding surf against black volcanic sand through the opening of a cave. The tide would eventually rise, blocking the entrance, but for that moment, he could see his family, even Suriel, searching about the sand very deliberately, on hands and knees, sifting every grain.

It was Harry who burst out in a characteristic temper. "Dammit, does anyone have a really ripping illumination spell that will help us find this goddamned grain of red sand before we go blind or drown or both?"

Suriel had stood as Harry was ranting, and spread his arms. Mullins had never really known what to think of Suriel, largely because he'd never been sure what Suriel thought of *him*. The two had only ever known *of* each other—until Suriel had fought for his own freedom from heaven, he and Mullins had never actually been in the same room.

It was the stories from the boys that gave them their grudging respect of the other. Harry always spoke so glowingly of Suriel to Mullins, and, Mullins was beginning to suspect, Edward had only spoken of the good of Mullins to Suriel. Over the past century and a half, the two beings who had never met had learned to trust each other as allies because they'd learned that the other one shared their singular devotion to the Youngblood family, one member in particular.

Fortunately, it had been a different favorite, or a terrible celestial conflict might have ensued—or even just hurt feelings and bitterness when the boys' lives hinged on every family member working in concert.

So seeing Suriel in action these days, watching him quietly and competently taking care of things such as food, sleep, making sure everybody was wearing a jacket when it was cold or had water when it was warm, had given Mullins the same sort of protective feelings over Suriel that he'd developed for Beltane after he'd been born.

Not quite as deep as for the three original Youngblood boys, but that was only because he hadn't known them as long.

In this particular instance, as Suriel stood apart from the boys, arms spread, Mullins was confronted with Suriel's lack of… wings.

Suriel needed wings.

He'd known that Suriel had allowed them to be ripped off his back as penance for leaving the duties of bondage he'd given himself to for millennia, but the loss had been… intellectual for Mullins.

Now that he saw what appeared to mortals as a very beautiful man with long fire-gold hair spreading his arms as though to embrace all of humanity with compassion, he recognized the loss of wings on a gut-deep level and mourned, just as Edward had.

And then he gasped, because apparently, while the wings had been ripped away, not all of Suriel's powers had suffered the same fate.

Suriel began to glow.

Subtly at first, and the quality of the light that came from his body made everything else in the cave as clear as cut crystal.

Every rock formation in the ceiling was revealed, some of them grotesque and some of them a tracery of limestone and lava. Every grain of sand was revealed, the obsidian black of them thrown into rainbow relief.

The boys all took the hint immediately and turned toward the sand, sifting through it as fast as they could until Beltane shouted "*Stop!*"

All activity ceased as he scooped up a handful of sand and dusted it, a few grains at a time, from his palm.

"Guys, come here! Come here and look! It's gorgeous!"

Edward had apparently propped the mirror on a rock so he could see the adventure, and now he picked it up and aimed it toward the few grains of sand left in Bel's massive palm.

One of them—though seemingly made of the same obsidian—had captured brilliant garnet colors in its depths.

Item #25! Scrawled across the mirror.

Hurray! Tell Suriel he's brilliant and I see why Harry adores him.

Edward turned the mirror to himself and smiled boldly, and for a moment, Mullins let himself fall into his boy's eyes.

Clear green, the green of bottle glass or a lake in the summer, the antidote to all of the drab and bitter things in hell.

That had been the night before.

Now, Mullins stood in that miserable line of groveling flunkies and felt that hope again. His breathing calmed down, his heart rate slowed, and he breathed out his anxiety as hope filled him. His boy's eyes were green, and they could see Clyde, the cottager's son, brother to Ruthie, Sarah, Mary, and Elizabeth.

The boy who had traded his soul to hell to save his sister's life.

That boy had been bold once.

That boy hadn't known vengeance or resignation.

That boy could stand impassively, mind on a faraway beach with sand of obsidian, looking at a miracle through the lighted glow of an angel's love.

That boy didn't flinch when Menoch's lash fell on the demon next to him, who let out a piercing shriek and wet himself. Mullins simply fell out with the other ranks of demons and went back to his cell, where a fragment of mirror sat in his pocket, ready to grow rich with heat, ready to show him wonders once more.

TWO WEEKS after their first triumph with the oystercatcher's eggshell, Mullins was frowning into the mirror, trying to figure out what in the hell they were doing.

He and Edward had started to experiment—it turned out that if Edward left the mirror open and nearby, it would capture the entire adventure as though from Edward's point of view. Mullins could watch it at his leisure, like a human might watch his favorite television show—except humans were not often in mortal peril from their favorite TV shows.

This particular show was... confusing.

He studied where they were, what they were doing, hoping for Edward's usually pithy commentary to scrawl across the mirror to clarify.

The boys were combing through the African underbrush, by a nearly empty watering hole, tracking buzzards the size of small cars.

Harry wasn't looking well.

It was one of the first things Mullins had noticed in the last few days. He was pale and had lost weight, even in the fortnight since the adventure began. The spell he was using to transport them was very powerful. Mullins knew Emma saved it for big events, and he was wondering if boomeranging a minivan full of wizards wasn't having a terrible effect on his health.

He kept his back straight, though, and poured himself into every adventure, and here on the savannah he started gesticulating wildly to get everybody's attention. The lot of them—all dressed in cargo shorts and hiking boots, even Suriel—went running for a corpse that had nearly been picked clean.

A rhinoceros corpse—but judging from the tatters of skin left on it, not an ordinary rhinoceros.

We asked local game wardens if they had any albino rhinos recently dead. We were lucky—we killed six poachers just trying to find it. That horn is big medicine.

Killed?

You killed them? It sounded so cold-blooded from his boys.

Edward's disgust dripped off every letter of his response. *Trust me— just as satisfying as killing human traffickers. No regrets.*

Mullins thought about it, about the cold-bloodedness needed to kill a stunning creature of the veldt and hack through its flesh. These were people who wouldn't hesitate to kill or sell anything—human, animal, anything.

He was pretty sure the paving stones of hell were built on the bones of poachers.

Understood. But I don't understand—

OMG!

The image jostled, and Mullins found himself watching Edward's boots kicking backward as Edward took off for his brothers, who were suddenly in the center of some *very* rough-looking men wielding guns and surrounding the dead rhino's corpse.

He couldn't hear anything—he *couldn't hear anything*! It was terrifying, watching the boys in the center, hands out, while Edward— always the best at languages—tried to negotiate with men who very much wanted what the boys had.

Then Harry cast a spell.

It must have been him—the mirror threw a sort of glow around anyone who used magic as it was. Bel's was gold, Francis silver, Edward green, and Harry's was amber. Now it grew strong and stronger, while around them—

Mullins squinted at the mirror, and then squinted again, and then had to clap a hoof across his mouth to keep silent.

About 200 snakes were undulating through the air, all of them coming from different directions, in different postures, as though Harry had simply cast a spell calling all snakes and then making them fly.

Beltane literally grabbed Francis around the middle as he leaped into the air to do battle with them, and Edward looked decidedly uncomfortable as the creatures passed overhead. Cobras, anacondas—poisonous and non—the snakes continued their way suspended in the air as they might have through the tall grasses or in their underground abodes.

And then abruptly dropped on the poachers' heads.

Mullins would forever be grateful he couldn't hear their screams, because few things in hell rivaled the mayhem that followed. Each man got more than a man's share of deadly venom from multiple sources, and the snakes themselves were not happy with each other as they landed. Edward's solid blue shield appeared around the boys as Mother Nature and some of her most toxic creatures struggled to balance the scales.

It felt like it took them an absurdly long time to die, thrashing, extremities blackened with toxin, tongues protruding, eyes leaking blood. Edward spoke sharply to Harry, and the snakes suddenly rose again to be catapulted a good mile away—some place where they could hash out their differences away from human or animal eyes.

Only one remained—a giant white anaconda, perhaps twenty feet across and a foot around.

He was shedding his skin as they watched.

Edward dropped the shield, and the boys looked at each other and then at the snake, and Edward pulled out the much-weathered list of things on the long-ago-written sheet of yellow legal paper and consulted. His face wore a look of intense disbelief.

Well, it should have. That snake was at least a hundred miles from its rightful home in the jungle—and Mullins was pretty sure it only shed during the rains.

Not only that but, according to the list in front of them, they needed it?

No.

No no no no no—

Impossible.

Mullins had been over that list with a fine-toothed comb. He'd helped Emma assemble the ingredients the first time around with Leonard, and he'd known it. This time, his job had been to determine which things on the list could be substituted by things with similar magical and metaphorical properties—he knew that list in his sleep.

There *was* no call for anaconda's skin or rhinoceros's horn—there just wasn't!

There was no reason on earth—*literally* on earth—for the lot of them to be there, watching an impossible creature shed its skin.

Eventually the snake was done, and Francis and Bel were given the job of rolling the skin up carefully while Harry and Suriel very gently disengaged the dead rhino's horn from its skull. Edward strode forward to retrieve the mirror, and he visibly flinched from Mullins's message.

What in the bloody hell are you doing?

They're on the list! Edward added a wild gesticulation to the thought, and in other circumstances Mullins might have been amused.

No they're not! They weren't on it for Leonard and Emma, and they shouldn't be on it for me!

Edward held his list up to the mirror, and Mullins squinted. It *looked* like Edward's handwriting, and it was definitely in the right place in the poem.

Albino skin of one that slithers, horn of one that thunders the earth, fit together, sword and sheath, use the wand to find your ease.

BUT MULLINS *knew* he hadn't written it.

That is not an ingredient I know!

Edward huffed with exasperation.

I don't know what to do about that!

What does it mean, wand?

I have no—

All of the Youngbloods ducked, and Mullins suppressed a groan. More bullets! Damn this family, why were there always more bullets?

Later! Edward finished, and the mirror went black.

BLUE EARTH, RED SKY

HARRY BARELY boomeranged them in time.

The original group of poachers—the ones rotting from snakebite on the savannah—were apparently an advance guard. The Youngbloods had stalked the watering hole for two days, trying to make sure the gamesmen who'd been watching the rhino be reclaimed by the wild weren't going to jump out and get them.

If the Youngbloods hadn't been hunting poachers to help the gamesmen, they would have.

So having a group of freaked-out poachers, replete with automatic weapons, jump out of nowhere to take off their heads was a bit of a shock. Harry's mastery of the teleportation spell was commendable. Not even Emma could have gotten them out of danger faster.

The only problem was—

"Where in the hell are we?" Edward asked, looking around him in confusion.

"A cornfield in Kansas?" Francis hazarded. "Where the corn is the size of a small child. And blue."

"An MC Escher painting?" Bel was poking one of the stalks of—grain?—tentatively, and they were all relieved when it didn't wiggle like an alien embryo pod.

"An alternative plane of existence with oxygen and water," Harry muttered weakly. They all turned to him in time to watch him topple over, a red stain spreading on his shoulder.

"Seriously?" Edward muttered, as Suriel caught Harry before he hit the ground.

"It's not bad," Harry assured them—and given the number of times he'd been injured, he should know. "Blood loss. Edward, you can doctor it. Beloved, any healing would help, but don't feel obligated—"

"Harry, for fuck's sake, shut up," Francis snapped. He fell to his knees by his brother's side, put his hand on Harry's shoulder, and muttered a few words.

The area around Harry's shoulder glowed brightly, and Harry gave a yelp of pain. "Jesus, Francis—" He hissed then, and his eyes rolled back in his head as he passed out.

"Francis?" Beltane asked, concerned. "You didn't kill him, did you?"

"No." Francis scowled at everybody. "My power's different. 'S weird. But the wound's closed. Bullet's out. Let him sleep."

And then he turned into a cat, leaving the three *conscious* adults to stare at each other. But the mystery of Francis was no clearer now than it ever had been, and they had other things to do.

"How is he?" Edward asked Suriel.

"Like Francis said," Suriel murmured, looking thoughtfully at Francis as he insouciantly licked his paw. "The bullet was pushed out." With one hand, Suriel scrabbled in the earth—the *blue*-colored earth—beneath Harry's shoulder and came back with the small bit of lead, still steeped in blood. "The bleeding is stopped. He's just…." Suriel tilted his head and listened for his breath. "Just sleeping to heal."

Edward and Beltane exchanged glances. "Uh," Edward began.

"You think…?" Beltane tried, and Suriel rolled his eyes.

"No, we're not going to wake him early. We have granola bars and water," he said sharply. "We can wait two or three hours, right here, while he sleeps off whatever healing Francis gave him. He's exhausted as it is from using the boomerang nonstop in the past two weeks. Imagine what would happen if he tried to pull us back to earth, weak as he is? That thing in your pocket might pull us halfway to hell, Edward, and your yearning for Mullins might take us the rest of the way."

Edward and Beltane looked at each other shamefaced, and Edward let out a sigh.

"The sky is creeping me out," he confessed. Bloodred, with a moon of glowing black.

"The earth is creeping me out," Beltane admitted. "And I keep expecting those ears of whatthehellever to open up and eat us."

Edward held his finger to his lips. "Sh! They might hear!"

Beltane nodded and held his hands out in a shrug. Francis jumped right into his arms and started licking his blond-stubbled chin.

"Thanks, Francis."

Francis rubbed whiskers against Bel's cheeks, and Bel sat back on the weird blue dirt and made out with his boy in cat form, leaving Suriel and Edward alone, as it were, with an unconscious Harry.

"What were you arguing with Mullins about?" Suriel asked quietly, holding Harry's head in his lap and brushing his hair back from his brow. He looked awful, almost gray, and gaunt, and Edward's heart pinged. He'd been driving himself damned hard.

Edward frowned. "It was weird. Suriel, he said that the things we were looking for—the horn, the snakeskin—they weren't on our list."

Suriel's eyes opened wide, and he frowned and then did that searching thing with his eyes in his head that people did when they lost their glasses.

"Is he sure?"

Edward had to laugh.

"Little bit, yeah. He's sure. I mean, he helped Leonard and Emma, right?"

Suriel sat up a little straighter, careful not to disturb Harry as he did so. "So did I," he said softly. "Edward, let me see your list."

Edward handed it to him, three pages of dirty, rumpled legal paper, painstakingly graphed and copied into Edward's phone as well.

"These things I remember," he said, tracing an elegant finger down each page. "I remember the ones we altered for Leonard—"

"You altered the spell for Leonard? Why didn't you tell—"

Suriel shrugged. "You didn't ask. Also, Emma didn't sit around and have a discussion circle." His full angel's mouth twisted up. "She gave a lot of orders in those days—particularly after Leonard got captured and tortured in Mullins's stead. I think it took Emma about three hundred years of knocking about the world on her own to understand how much she hungered for company, Edward. You three learned it in about twenty years. Not bad for a learning curve."

Edward rolled his eyes, frustrated. This alternative plane of existence smelled like barbecued potato chips, spoiled salsa, and dead lilies. He really wanted to go home.

"I still can't do a boomerang spell," he muttered.

"Well, she didn't get really good at it until you four started getting into danger," Suriel reminded him. Then he frowned again. "Mullins is right. These items—they're not… they're… fuzzy."

Edward looked over Suriel's shoulder. "They're clear to *me*," he said. "I mean, Jesus, Suriel—I wouldn't have just sent us all into that sort of danger for kicks, would I?"

Suriel shook his head and stroked Harry's brow again. "Of course not. If nothing else, none of us is thrilled to see this happen again."

"We were lucky it wasn't us," Edward admitted, squeezing Harry's uninjured shoulder.

"It's like he's a magnet," Suriel muttered. "I'm… there is something *so odd* about this writing here. I can see the bit of verse you copied, and then the notes about what you think it means, but… but it's giving me a headache. I don't think you wrote those words at all."

Edward shivered. "But who would alter the spell?" he asked, feeling a hint of desperation. "Seriously, Suriel—what purpose would it serve to change the damned thing? This only has consequences for Mullins and me—"

"And those of us who love you both," Suriel interjected. "You should already know it's no easy thing to see a brother suffer."

"Understood." It was a brief word—a brief way—to underscore Edward's appreciation and love, but they needed to think about other things now! "But we don't know if the purpose there is friendly or not friendly or even where it came from!"

"Well," Suriel said, tapping his lip with a finger. "I think there's one way to find out. Beltane, do you have the—"

"No," Edward said, feeling panic settle in his bones.

"No what?"

"No, whatever you're going to do here that you seem to think is so logical. Suriel, I don't even know *when* we are. I mean, I want to get Mullins out as quickly as possible too, but we're not going to get back any quicker if we try some sort of fucked-up spell here where the barbecued corn chip lilies bloom!"

Suriel inhaled deeply and grimaced. "Ugh. Yes. I understand. If nothing else, the snakeskin and rhinoceros are both dead things. I can't imagine it, but the spell could even get worse."

Edward smiled slightly and squeezed Harry's shoulder again. "A few hours?" he said, to make sure.

"I promise. Whatever magic Francis used, it was good stuff. He'll be hungry and thirsty when he wakes up, *so leave him some provisions!*" That last was aimed at Beltane, who looked up from the granola bar he was shoving in his mouth and pointed to the satchel at his hip, indicating more. "And then he should be able to get us back home."

Edward nodded and yawned, and Suriel pointed to his shoulder. "You used to fall asleep when you were doing lessons too."

"Not Harry?"

"No." Suriel leaned forward and kissed his beloved's brow. "Harry was like a torch, the entire time. Never wanted to waste a second."

Edward swallowed. He wanted to see Mullins again, for real, where he could touch, and maybe lace fingers, and feel his body's heat.

He wanted it so badly his lungs labored under it. So badly his stomach cramped.

They had two more things to get, but first it was time to go home.

ACCORDING TO Suriel's prediction, Harry woke up in a few hours, ate all the granola bars, apologized profusely for getting shot, and agreed that while peaceful, wherever they were was creepy as hell, and he was more than ready to go back.

Which meant he was feeling well enough to boomerang them back to the minivan, still parked on the savannah.

It was infested with lions. They'd eaten most of the upholstery—but they'd left Edward's carry-case of spell articles alone.

The five of them stood, staring at the beleaguered automobile, heads cocked. Suriel supported Harry with an arm about his waist, because the boomerang had taken it out of him after a trying day, and as Harry made helpless gestures toward their one method of transportation, Suriel kissed him on the temple.

"We need to get that carry case," Edward said rather grimly. "We *can't* go through all that again."

"Wait," Harry muttered, holding up a finger. "I've got a plan."

"Against lions? What are you going to do, catapult them to where the snakes went?"

Harry squinted at Edward and Edward squinted back. "No, idiot. I'm going to boomerang the damned case. It's got your blood, sweat, and tears in it—literally."

"Francis made it—use his. I did not cry over the damned case." Oh, but he had.

"Bullshit." Harry let out a sigh and dragged his hand through his hair, sending it flurrying in every direction. "Look, Edward, we're worried too. We were careless with that last run. It's why we got caught flat-footed. I'm sorry we had to take a detour to big-corn-land, but trust me. And come here and spit in a bottle."

"Nice." But Edward got it. Harry was going to boomerang something dear to Edward—so he was going to use a little essence-o-Edward to start the spell.

"Shut up, pull out a few hairs, spit, and if you can shed a tear or two—or even some blood, that would be helpful too."

Harry reached into his pocket and pulled out one of the baby food jars they'd all started carrying around just in case. You never knew when you were going to step over a white snail with seven chambers to its shell, did you? Or see a green ladybug. You never knew what part of the spell was just going to be there, looking you in the eye, so you had a sample bottle there—they all did.

Looking half-asleep, he opened the jar and grimaced.

"Ugh," Edward agreed, taking the jar from his bloodied hand. Yes, the wound had closed—but all that blood he'd lost had dripped right down his arm. Edward put his own samples in the jar, and Harry reached into his other pocket and pulled out the keys to the car.

"Let's just see if this still works here," he hazarded, and with a little click, the back hatch opened slowly, as one of the puzzled male lions stuck his head out. Harry stared at the case, which sat under the totaled ice chest, and closed his eyes. Suriel wrapped both arms around his shoulders, obviously sustaining him in the most basic way possible, and after a moment or two, Harry took a few steps away.

"Here goes nothing," he said. Then he stopped himself. "We only need the two things in addition to what we retrieved today—"

"I need to talk to you about those…." Edward grimaced, and Harry rolled his eyes.

"Later?" He showed his teeth.

Of course. "Yes, later. And yes, the snakeskin and the rhino horn are the last two things we can get now, and Francis and Beltane have them."

"Well, then—let's send the case back to Emma and Leonard, and then we can trudge down the road until we find a place to sleep, and when we wake up, the rest of us can join it."

Harry's face was white and sweating, and Edward realized what a cost this was to his brother. For the umpteenth time, he got angry at whoever had fucked with their list and sent them off on a wild goose chase to the African savannah.

"Fair deal," Edward said. He frowned. "Does anybody have charge in their phone?"

"I do," Beltane said smugly. "Because I brought a battery."

Edward rolled his eyes, unimpressed. "Because you are 200 pounds of mostly muscle, Bel. A battery doesn't make a dent in your trousers. If any of *us* tried to carry that thing about, it would drag our pants to our knees."

Bel grinned. "I have my uses."

Edward smiled weakly back. Beltane—the three familiars had loved him from the moment he was born. It was hard to stay irritated, even if irritation was what was keeping you upright when you'd had a hell of a day.

"Okay," Harry said, sounding resolved. "Gonna do this, then gonna run like hell. We all ready?"

"Ready, Harry," Bel said.

"Ready, Harry." Francis was human—which said he was as serious as the rest of them.

"Good luck, brother," Edward told him, and Suriel trailed worried fingers over the nape of his neck.

Harry closed his eyes, mumbled his spell and….

Disappeared.

Or not disappeared per se—more like he got *dragged* by an unseen hand, past the brothers, out of Suriel's arms, and straight for the minivan full of lions. He hit the trunk at full speed, and nobody was more surprised than Edward when he had the presence of mind to grab the case by the strap before he blurred out of sight again, disappearing before he hit the horizon.

Ping.

No more Harry.

No more case.

Gone.

The lions roared experimentally, obviously as surprised as the humans, but then they went back to gnawing on the headrests and the lid to the ice chest, because flying humans were just too much of a bother.

"The actual fuck," Edward swore, his voice cracking sharply. His brother and all their hard work—just gone?

"He must have gotten some blood in the jar," Suriel said practically. Then, "Oh, sweet heavens… Harry!"

At that point Bel—who was standing, jaw as dropped as the rest of them—reached into his pocket looking bemused.

"Mum?" He paused. "He's okay, right?" Bel grimaced and held the phone away from his ear. "He showed up home," he said over his mother's screeching.

"Great," Edward said, meaning it. "And the case?"

Bel stuck his tongue out at Edward and then pulled the phone to his ear. "Uhm, Mum, was he carrying anything when he showed up on death's door?"

More screeching, but Beltane brightened as he held the phone away from his ear. "Yes—totally intact," he said happily.

"Great!" Edward felt the tension dissolve from his body so fast, he actually sagged against Suriel. "He's okay," he said to nobody in particular. "Does she say anything about—"

At that moment they all felt the stomach-lurching displacement of a boomerang done by a truly irritated witch, and the savannah fell away.

When the world stopped spinning beneath their feet, they all collapsed to their knees in the front room of what had been their home for the past 140 years.

Emma stood in front of them in a bathrobe, hair crackling about her head and escaping from its customary braid, and Leonard stood next to her.

"Who shot Harry?" she demanded. "That's all I want to know. Who shot him, and are they dead?"

"Oh, Mum," Bel said, sounding beleaguered. "That was three crises ago. For all we know they were eaten by snakes. Speaking of which, is there anything to eat around here?" He scrambled to his feet. "We've been living off PowerBars for the last three days. I'm famished."

She glared at her youngest, the child she and Leonard had given a great deal of their power and some of their immortality to bear. "There's leftovers in the fridge," she said, voice cold but civil. "So you *didn't* kill the person who shot him?" She glared at Suriel. "Seriously?"

"We were surprised," Suriel said simply. "Harry pulled us out of the ambush. Can I see him? Where is he?"

"The bathroom," she said with a huff. "Where all of you are going, I hope. Dear Hecate—the stench coming off the five of you could crumble this house to its foundations. When was the last time you even—"

"Hawaii," Francis said, standing up with Bel's helping hand. "We all swam in the ocean. It was lovely. Then we almost fell in a volcano. Edward saved us. That was scary. I mean, I can fly, but I would have fallen in if everybody else was going to. Fish? Do you have tuna?"

"Always, Francis," Emma said absently. "Did he say he could fly?"

"Don't ask us," Edward told her bluntly. "He just started flying on the first day. It's come in handy more than once but…." He grimaced. "Emma, Leonard, we have a *lot* to talk about—"

"Like what in the holy hell you were doing on the savannah!" Leonard burst out. "I don't remember anything there being on the list!"

Edward and Suriel met eyes. "Like that. Look—can we just… just…." He felt the mirror in his pocket grow warm. "Can we get some food, shower—"

"Burn those clothes," Emma said direly.

"Do that," Edward agreed. "And even nap. And then meet back here tomorrow morning?"

It was the sort of thing Harry would have done—and it took a bigger act of will than Edward knew he had.

But Leonard and Emma responded surprisingly well. "Fine, son," Leonard told him, nodding. "Suriel, you may need to go help Harry in the shower. We'll bring a tray of food to Harry's room for when you're done. You too, Edward." There were four bathrooms in the house in Mendocino now, when there used to be one room and an outhouse. "Bel and Francis are apparently going to eat the refrigerator before they bathe, but yes. That's a plan." Leonard met Edward's eyes then. "I'll speak to you when you're done with your shower."

"And Francis," Emma cautioned, "you and I need to have a little talk."

Francis rolled his eyes, and Emma held up her hand.

"And if you think you're getting out of it by turning cat, remember, I can put a stop to that."

Francis glowered. Emma had only done it once, but she *could* pull Francis's familiar powers. Francis could be incredibly intractable about facing things as a human being.

"Fine," he said shortly, shoving a forkful of tuna into his mouth. "After food and bath."

"Agreed," she said. "Bel, you need to be elsewhere when we have this conversation."

"Whatever," Beltane grunted. He'd apparently found steak, and nothing was going to turn him from his purpose.

"Edward, you're standing there stenching up my nice living room. It was a great plan. Make it so."

Edward nodded meekly and trudged off toward the guest bathroom, Suriel at his heels. Suriel split off at the hallway to the bath that adjoined Harry's and Edward's rooms, and he paused in the hallway.

"What?" Edward asked, weary to his bones.

"It's good to come back home from something like that," he said, sounding contemplative. "All those years, I wondered how you boys left home to go on your adventures. I had no idea that it was the coming *back* home that gave you your strength."

Edward smiled faintly. "I want Mullins to come back to this someday," he said, and then hated himself because the tears spilled over.

"He will," Suriel told him soberly. "Believe it."

AFTER THE shower, Edward curled up on his bed with one of several ham sandwiches and a giant glass of milk that had been waiting for him when he was done. While he was eating, he checked his mirror. Scrawled across the front was *Please tell me you're okay.*

We're fine. We're home. Harry got shot again, but we hope he'll be okay after some food and a good night's rest. We have all the ingredients. We just have to figure out who dicked with the list.

It was a lot to fit onto the mirror. Edward looked into the glass and said, "I miss you, beloved," and then folded up the battered compact and put it on the table.

He felt weariness in every bone, every sinew, every corpuscle. He must have dozed off, because when he startled, Leonard was in his room, sitting by his bed.

"Sorry," Edward yawned, and Leonard gestured to the half-finished sandwich on his plate.

"Don't be sorry. Eat. Be full."

Edward sat up and picked up the sandwich. "Harry?"

Leonard gave a resigned shrug. "We will always worry about Harry. Apparently he got a few flakes of blood into the sample jar, so when he cast a spell asking for blood sweat and tears to be taken to safety…."

Edward snorted. "Oh, heavens. That's… that's…." He couldn't help it. "Poor Harry!"

Leonard chuckled softly. "Well, yes. He did some very creative swearing when he landed here. And some bleeding. The trip was rough."

Edward groaned. "This was supposed to be my quest!"

"You would deprive your brothers of all the fun?" Leonard asked, laughing. "Seriously, Edward—Emma and I are just so pleased the four of you enjoy doing things together still." He sobered. "We… for those first years, we couldn't even hope you'd all stay with us. I'd been alone in hell, Mullins and I, clinging to each other's hands, you understand? So afraid of betrayal on every side. So many years. And then I had a family. The way you and your brothers looked to us—"

"We were terrible!" Edward remembered every petty rebellion, every resentment to the two people trying to raise them when he and Harry had been making a living on their knees for years. He'd complained bitterly to Harry at every turn about how Emma and Leonard kept giving them orders, and why did they need to clean their rooms anyway?

"You were boys," Leonard said kindly. "And you were ours. And we would go to sleep at night praying that you'd let us parent you just one more day, because you needed us. And every day you woke up and you did. Emma and I used to rack our brains coming up with spellwork that you'd enjoy—that wasn't dangerous—to make it worth your time to stay. So desperate. And then you brought that girl home. We had a mission—and a worthy one. It's still worthy. But you all forged yourself into our family." Leonard reached out and ruffled Edward's hair—a rare physical gesture from a man who had learned restraint in the bowels of hell. "And now I can't imagine our lives any differently."

Edward smiled a little, warmed. "I've really only followed Harry's lead," he confessed sadly. His brother had worked so hard. It hadn't been until he'd stood to cast that final boomerang that Edward had realized what a toll the past two weeks had taken on him. He remembered those dark days when they'd feared that Harry would lose himself, die pining for Suriel, whom he'd been sure he could never be with. He'd thought his brother was the most self-centered asshole on the planet then, but that hadn't been it at all.

Harry had taught him, with everything in his fighting heart, what it was to love someone more than yourself. He'd loved Suriel more than his own life. He'd loved his brothers more than his pain.

When he'd thrown himself into Edward's quest, Edward's secret relief, his joy at working with his brothers for the duration, had been a palpable thing.

It had been the thing that gave him the courage to kiss Mullins, to launch into their quest with hope.

Leonard snorted. "Oh, that's a load of crap and you know it. Boy, I'm not sure which two boys *you've* been watching for over a century, but you and Harry function very well as a team. Yes, Harry always has the first plan of attack, but you've often got the one that saves everybody's ass. You want to know what my happiest moment in the last year was?"

"When Suriel came back and they got to be together?" Because Mullins was still just a hope, and Edward's relief that his brother's lover would be with their family had been acute.

"Besides that," Leonard conceded. "It's been a big year. But no— when you asked if you could build your cabin on the property too. Because that meant that our family would get bigger, and it would change—but it wouldn't disappear."

Edward nodded. That thought had occurred to him too. "Who knew you were never too old to need your parents," he said with a smile.

"Mm." Leonard nodded, and his expression grew stern. "So, were you and Harry ever going to tell us about Bel and Francis?"

Edward and Harry had learned how to lie fluently in their childhood at the Golden Child. It had been their only way to survive. "What about them?" he said, making his green eyes big and smiling prettily.

Leonard cocked his head and raised an eyebrow. "That was amazing. Try again."

Edward let out a sigh. "Suriel saw it first," he said. "He didn't seem… concerned. Harry and I lost our shit all over each other, of course, but… but they're… you know. Them. They've been inseparable since Bel's birth, you know? This just seems like they've… grown into it, I guess."

"Mm." Leonard pursed his lips. "Your brother…." He caught himself with a twist of his lips. "*Francis*," he elaborated, "has never taken a lover. Did you know that?"

Edward nodded, biting his lip. "Over two human lifetimes. It's a long time."

"Yes—yes it is. And we... I guess maybe it was inevitable. I guess we just thought they'd... you know. Learn what the rest of the world had to offer. You did. Harry did. Even if he never settled on a mortal lover, he knew what he was walking away from." He sounded resigned.

"I guess *our* fear is that if it didn't work out, we'd never see Francis again," Edward said, and it felt good to say it. "He'd turn into a cat for eternity, which is great to keep down the vermin, but sometimes it's nice when he's our brother."

Leonard let out a laugh. "Your mother would not allow that," he said soberly. "Five years, maximum, before we took away his cat power and made him be human for a while. But you're right. He's... peculiar, your little brother. He doesn't react to emotions in a predictable human way."

Edward bit his lip. "Uh.... Mullins speculated that he might be... uh... fey," he said delicately. "And the flying thing—not so much human, you know?"

Leonard raised both eyebrows. "No. No it is not. How does he fly? Does he change shape? Cast a spell? Use elemental forces to—"

"Put his arms out to balance and levitate into the air?" Edward finished for him. It hadn't been any less unnerving the fifteenth time they'd seen him do it as it had been the first. "He's getting better, but you can tell there's a learning curve." He'd gotten over 200 feet up *twice*, and Edward had needed to throw a levitation spell at him to make sure he didn't hit the ground. The second time, Bel had barked at him for ten minutes and then sulked for a good part of the afternoon, muzzle on paws, tail not thumping once. Francis had promised he wouldn't go that high again until he got better.

"That's terrifying," Leonard announced after careful consideration. "Lucky, you and Harry getting to help him through that."

Edward let out a careful breath. "So, *so* lucky."

Leonard winked, all compassion. "Well, luck in our family is a double-edged sword." He gave a nod and got down to business. "So, we suspect Francis is fey and we know he and Bel are no longer brothers. And that could be both troubling and wonderful—but ultimately there's nothing to *do* about it. They're both adults. Technically, Francis is more than an adult, but we both know Bel's the oldest in that relationship, so we won't split hairs. If they're not putting themselves in danger—"

Edward glared.

"—any more than usual," Leonard acknowledged, "what's to do? It would be wonderful if they made an announcement. 'Mum, Dad, we're married. Or seeing each other. Or need one of the bigger bedrooms with a king-sized.' Emma and I aren't particular. But until that moment, and even afterward, they're ours. They will never not *be* ours, so we need to table that subject. Now tell me about the whole African savannah thing, because I find that *fascinating*."

Edward nodded and handed him the list, which he'd set on his bed stand. "Look at the last items."

Leonard ignored him and skimmed the other pages. "Aren't you clever. The substitutions are perfect, by the way. Emma had to do substitutions for my hex bags as well—but she… well, putting them on the list and changing things just never occurred to her. It's one of the problems of genius, I think. You don't understand why the world can't read your mind. Anyway, all this looks normal—and your interpretations of why the ingredients are needed will help you write your own spell. Didn't know you needed that, did you?"

Edward looked uncomfortable. "No. We didn't hear Emma cast one out loud."

"All up in her pretty little head, my boy. *Never* underestimate your mother's mind. Anyway—you and Mullins will need to have a long talk about what you'll need to…." He lowered his voice. "It's not a spell, really."

He just let that hang there, and Edward stared at him expectantly.

"And?"

"Son, you… of the four of my children, you will know best what it needs to be. Harry was Harry—he picked his one path and charted a straight course. Bel and Francis were simply… themselves. But *you* have loved and lost. You know what it is to have something important taken from you." Leonard's eyes grew shiny. "Losing Dorothy, so soon? We all suffered then, but of course, you most of all. So you'll know what it needs to be when the time comes to say it. But it's not a spell. Not really. I heard Emma's words in my heart of hearts. They're written there for eternity, in fire and blood. Call it a spell if you have to—but know that it's more."

Edward nodded and swallowed. All the things he wanted to say, all the things he'd thought for so long—those were weighty things, painful, minutely revealed truths about what it was to bind one person to another. He could not say them out loud, not if he had an eternity.

But he could say them in his heart, and that, apparently, was what needed to be done.

"So," he said after a heartbeat. "About the elven king—"

Leonard gave a brief smile. "That, son, is your mother's story. She had those three hairs with her when we met, and I was not allowed to ask. But she'll tell the lot of you tomorrow, I'm pretty sure. What really troubles me is these new ingredients. They're... they're here deliberately. And they... they don't fit into the spell, exactly."

"Well, they're both rare things," Edward said, but there was something nagging him about that too.

"Yes, but not *that* rare. I mean, they exist in nature, a few every generation. Pretty much everything else on this list is bloody impossible, unless you've got four wizards and an angel on your side, you think?"

Edward had to nod. "Yes... and these things don't have anything to do with being a demon, do they?"

"That's it!" Leonard half leaped out of his chair and then settled back down. "I am not young anymore," he muttered. He and Emma presented themselves as being in their forties—apparently just when humans began to realize their bodies would not be young eternally. "But no. They don't. But they do seem to fit together. Both rare animals, and... I know this is odd, but I keep thinking sword and sheath. Staff of power, thing to hold it. Something along those lines. The rhinoceros is the warrior—always has been. But the snake is stealth, feminine logic, calculation."

"Oh Jesus," Edward burst out. "It's a... a joke? A message? For me!"

"I'm sorry?"

"Harry always calls me a worrier princess. It's... it's like this thing is... a gift?" No. There was nothing about this that said "gift," was there? Except the word kept ringing in his head. "It's a gift for me," he said softly. "That's got to be it. Who would give me a gift of magic artifacts that we almost get killed hunting down?"

"I don't know," Leonard said softly. "Maybe Mullins would."

Edward grunted and rubbed his temples. "I seriously doubt it—he was the one who told me they weren't on the list." And he'd been pretty freaked out about it too. "My head hurts," he said grumpily. He'd finished his sandwiches—it wasn't hunger. "What time is it?" They'd been kiting around the globe—and beyond—and Edward had no idea how long it had been since they'd last slept.

Leonard rolled his eyes and took the tray from him. "Sleep, son," he said, his voice vibrating with the slightest, oldest magic in the world.

Edward toppled to the bed before he could even get angry.

WANDERFUL

MULLINS SAT in his cell, not even pretending to work, and stared hungrily at the little mirror in his hand.

The first message that had scrawled across it had been, "Do you want us to summon you?"

Of course he did.

He *yearned* to be summoned. Over the past 140 years, being summoned to the Youngblood living room had kept him sane, reminded him repeatedly that under the trappings of a beast beat the heart of a human being.

Seeing Edward had started as a bonus, at first. A pretty young man, intelligent, easy to talk to. Intense. Kind. Sober.

And then, that moment after Dorothy, when Edward had seen him truly, had touched him, had told him that there wouldn't be another mortal lover. Edward was holding out for Mullins himself.

And Edward had become more than a "bonus." He'd been Mullins's reason to keep existing in hell.

Some demons—the ones who refused to find glee in inflicting pain—simply shorted out. Mullins had seen it happen. They subsisted, day after day, resigned to the next beating, to the next order, to the next painful act of defiance that would keep their soul their own, and then they just....

Pfft.

Disappeared.

Soul and all.

Nobody even noticed they were gone.

Mullins had taken to scratching their names on the various outcropping rocks in his cell, just because *somebody* should remember them.

He'd started when he first arrived, when Leonard had told him, sotto voce, not to say anything—Leonard had scars on his back to this day from the one time he had.

Leonard had started taking down the names of the ones he'd seen so that Mullins had a more accurate count.

For the months after he'd helped Leonard and before his first summoning, the only thing that had kept Mullins from becoming one of the truly damned had been the knowledge that if he disappeared, nobody would even scratch his name on the stones.

So yes—oh God *yes*—Mullins wanted to be summoned.

But they were close. So close. And demons still wandered past his cell, sniffing, saying things like, "Merlot? No—chardonnay! No… pinot noir…."

Edward's love had settled under his skin, become part of his blood, even. One more trip to the Youngblood's living room and Mullins would never be able to return to hell, and unless they were ready to go, had the hex bags in his knapsack, he feared bringing the hosts of hell on his heels and into the Youngblood home.

Not yet, he replied on the mirror. *Just keep me in the loop.*

Can you cast a spell to listen?

Oh. That was…. Mullins closed his eyes and thought, writing the spell, erasing it, again and again, to make it perfect, silent, like a set of magic earbuds, listening to the movie on the little mirror.

Done.

"Okay, he can hear us," Edward said, his voice in sync with his mouth as he set the mirror on a window ledge. He set up a couple of mirrors feeding into the mirror so that Mullins had a panoramic view of the Youngblood living room.

Very clever, Mullins scrawled across the mirror, and Edward looked directly at him and grinned, then bowed with a flourish.

Oh gods, Mullins missed him.

"You know he's the cleverest," Harry said, and Mullins spared a glance for Edward's brother.

Harry looks like hell. Will he have time to rest?

Harry rolled his eyes and tried to sit up a little straighter. He looked pale and thin, as though boomeranging around the world was a heavy-duty spell that even Emma took time out to rest from, and he'd been doing it several times a day. "If this little search party ends up on a faerie hill, I'll sleep in the bloody car," he snapped. "No way I'm missing that!"

Mullins fought a smile, and Edward winked at him. "Told you," he said mildly.

Have Emma teach you to boomerang.

Edward's face fell. "Not for this mission," he said, obviously put out. "Everybody's afraid the mirror will pull me toward you. But once we get you back, I'll make it a priority. Now we need to make this quick, because you don't have that much time. Leonard, do you want to tell him what we talked about?"

Leonard stood up then and moved to the center of the room so Mullins could have a good look at him. Gah! Middle-aged fatherhood looked good on his old friend and protector. Mullins had seen it many times in the past century and a half, but now, as he grew sharp and purposeful and brilliant, Mullins blessed his luck that he'd fallen under the protective wing of the one decent demon in hell.

"So," Leonard said with a little smile, "we have almost everything on the list—including a couple of things that weren't there originally. We're short the three hairs from the elven king—and Emma will talk about that shortly, but first, let's talk about the things that got added."

Who added them?

The question had been bothering Mullins like an abscessed tooth.

"We haven't the slightest," Edward said, sounding irritated. "But given that was the mission that got Harry shot, I'd like to have a few words."

"So would I," Suriel said, and for once he sounded far from serene.

"I'm fine." Harry glanced over at Beltane then, who was sitting cross-legged, Francis purring in his lap. "You two, go fetch those last two items. You're the ones who had them with you when we landed."

Bel nodded, and Francis spilled out of his lap. Together they sauntered off toward the bedroom.

"And don't dawdle!" Edward called after them, and everybody exchanged uncomfortable glances as "dawdle" assumed a completely different meaning.

"Good idea," Leonard said quietly, and Emma just shook her head.

"So Leonard and I were trying to figure out why these two items," Edward continued. "And the conclusion we came to was that they don't have anything to do with the demon potion, but they *do* have some sort of significance."

"We think they become a wand," Leonard told him shortly, and Mullins wasn't sure his expression could convey his surprise.

I'm sorry?

"Here, son—give me that."

Beltane came back from the hallway and handed his father the snakeskin, looking so virtuous, Mullins wondered if they'd had time to have sex in the brief moments they'd been out of the room. Francis came right behind him and was reaching into a satchel, pulling out the horn as Leonard took the skin.

"So what we have here is a sword and sheath," Leonard said, "Male and female, staff and cover—"

Francis and Beltane burst into laughter, and Leonard pinned them with a dad-glare.

"Say it," he told them, sounding bored. "Come on—your inner twelve-year-olds are dying to say it."

Their laughter faded abruptly.

"Not if you're going to take the fun out of it," Beltane muttered resentfully.

"It was really much funnier before he said that," Francis agreed.

Leonard gave Mullins one of those equal-to-equal, long-suffering looks, straight through the mirror, and Mullins didn't even try to fight his smile. God, he loved them. All of them. So much. He wanted with all his heart to be in that room.

"And what we figured," Leonard continued, working hard to keep the corners of his mouth from turning up, "was that we'd let the items function as intended."

"Really?" Bel perked up. "You're going to have hard-core rhino-anaconda coitus, right here in this very living room?"

Francis burst into laughter, rolling on his back, and every other adult in the room looked horrified.

Right up until Harry gave a tired snicker. "Oh my God—I'm glad someone else said it."

"You are so immature," Edward snapped, but he was fighting not to grin too.

"Fine," Leonard told them, obviously disgruntled. "Oh, baby, baby, do it like that, make me feel good, put the rubber on the staff and wield it!"

All of them collapsed—all. Suriel, Harry, Edward—even Emma smirked and hid it behind her hand. It didn't help that Leonard was rolling the snakeskin over the horn—all nine or ten inches of it—as he spoke. He made a few suggestive thrusts and finished covering the "sword" with the "sheath."

Abruptly, the rhino horn and the snakeskin ceased to be.

In their place was a staff, stiff and unyielding, but covered with the soft, silkily plated skin and flesh of a truly magnificent albino snake.

Leonard stared at it, and the rest of the family stopped their own antics, attention firmly on the relic in front of them.

"Ouch!" Leonard dropped it suddenly, shaking his hand.

"Please tell me it didn't bite," Edward said, drawing closer.

He extended his hand tentatively, as though drawn to the thing, and Mullins felt a wave of outright need swamp his body. He reached to the mirror, feeling the staff pulsing through the glass.

"No," Leonard replied. "It just got... hot. Uncomfortable. Is it hot for you?"

The family's attentiveness to this new development could be measured by how not a soul in the room laughed at the easy bait.

"No," Edward said thoughtfully, taking the thing by the middle. He tossed it lightly from hand to hand, frowning in concentration. "It feels... living. Like it has a will of its own," he murmured. "Like there's power just pulsing under the... skin."

"Well, those were pretty powerful artifacts," Harry cautioned. "But if it wants you to hold it, I'm not going to argue. Anything else it wants you to do? Conjure a new minivan? Order takeout? Can it do a boomerang for us?"

What happened to the minivan? Mullins scrawled. *Dear God, Emma— will you be able to get a new one? Edward?*

Edward was pointing the staff directly at the mirror. "What will happen," he mumbled. "What will happen if I...."

And then the end of the staff bridged the gap between hell and earth, and popped out of Mullins's mirror and tapped him on the chest.

Mullins grabbed it in sheer surprise, and Edward gave a shout and yanked.

Mullins kept hold of the mirror with all his strength in one hand and clung to the staff with the other, and Edward used a thing that should not be to turn reality inside out.

Mullins slid through the mirror like coming through a waterfall, ending up on the Youngblood's living room floor and dropping the mirror to the rug.

"Oh Good Lord," Leonard breathed. "Mullins, is that you?"

Mullins squinted at him in confusion, and then Edward, his boy, launched himself into Mullins's arms. "Mullins!" he sobbed. "Oh Lord. I missed you so bad!"

Mullins wrapped shaky arms around Edward's shoulders and bent to kiss his forehead.

His very human lips made contact, and for the first time he tasted the sweetness of Edward's skin without disguise or magic between them.

"Sweet," he croaked, shaking. "So sweet. Everything I dreamed it would be."

Then Edward raised his face and Mullins took his mouth, falling into the taste of the man he loved.

It was glorious.

THE KISS had to end—it had to. But for a few brief moments, Mullins remembered… *everything*. Human emotions. Love without fear. The joys of unfettered flesh. He moaned slightly, his groin tingling, growing heavy, and that attention made him aware of one more thing.

He pulled back and grimaced.

"What?" Edward asked, sounding dazed. His green eyes were heavy-lidded, his pupils blown with passion, and his cheeks blotched, freckles standing out clearly against the pale patches. With his mouth—plush pink lips—swollen and red, he was all that was gorgeous about lust.

"I still have a tail," he mumbled, embarrassed, and to his intense discomfort, the entire family walked around him to check out his posterior.

"I had no idea you had one before," Harry said, sounding as delighted as a child. "Is that why the trousers?"

"What's it look like?" Francis asked. "Can we see?"

"No you can't see!" Mullins found he was laughing even as he felt the appendage through his the seat of his eighteenth-century pants. He was as delighted to be in the center of his family, no runes, no protective spells, no formality of the summoning circle, as he'd always imagined. "It's… it's short with a little tuft at the end—like a boar's."

"Could be worse," Beltane said seriously. "It could be corkscrewed, like a piglet's." He giggled. "We'd totally make you show us that, you know."

Mullins fought the urge to cuff the brat playfully. God, he loved these people.

"I'm afraid not," he said shortly, some of the giddiness fading. "I think it's there as a…." He frowned, feeling his demon magic pulsing under his skin. Leonard had been reborn with no magic at all. Emma had needed to gift him with some of her immortality, which was why she'd needed to put her power in the boys as familiars. Those sorts of spells tended to take everything, if there wasn't some of it in a "bank." Leonard had learned more since, and his knowledge from his time in hell was impressive, but he'd never reclaim the amount of power he'd had as a demon.

Mullins still had that power. And he still had his tail.

"It's not over," he said, feeling the beat of little minds searching for him even as he stood with Edward in the circle of his arms. "We need to finish the hex bags, complete the ceremony. This is… a reprieve, I guess. I'm not sure why or how, but someone wanted me to spend some time as a human being before I…." He thought about his cell, the constant fear, the screams that never got less awful. "Before I ret—"

"You're not going back!" Edward snapped, and Mullins looked… not down. Mullins the demon was about a foot taller than Edward. Perhaps it was the beastly head.

"We're the same height," he said in wonder, not wanting to think about his life if Edward was wrong.

"Lucky bastard," Harry muttered—Suriel was nearly a foot taller than him, still. "Edward, I know he's yours, but let us all hug him before we do anything else. God, Mullins." Harry's voice cracked a little. "Edward's a lucky boy—you're damned pretty as a human."

Mullins smiled at him, affection beating against his chest. He opened his arms, and Harry, Francis, and Beltane surrounded him, Suriel coming a little more slowly.

Like that, he went from being alone, to having his boy in his arms, to being in a circle of brothers. For that moment all uncertainty, all terror of going back, all fear of never holding Edward in his arms like a man—all of it disappeared.

For a moment he let joy glut his skin and the family he'd seen from a summoning circle claim him as their own.

IT WAS Suriel who felt Harry wobble, backing from the group hug to scoop him up in his arms.

"Dammit, Suriel!" Harry muttered, struggling to stand.

"You need to sit," Suriel said implacably. "You need to rest. I'm excited Mullins is here too, but we're going to sit down and finish this conversation so they can spend time together and you can sleep."

Harry scowled at his beloved. "This is so not fair—"

Emma walked by and casually swatted him on the back of the head, even as he sat on Suriel's lap. "Shut up," she snapped. "You'd think I'd worry more about the one in love with the demon, but no. You're still the one making me old before my time. Edward, Mullins, take a seat—Suriel is right. We need to talk about elves."

"We have a plan," Edward said excitedly—*not* sitting down and *not* releasing his hold on Mullins. "We thought about this—Mullins said that the fey were the children of the Goddess and the other—he's the force of chaos. So we figured we'd go...." Well, they hadn't really finalized this plan. "We'd go create chaos," he said, deflating a little. "And see if we could attract their attention."

Leonard and Emma stared at him. Leonard spoke first.

"God, he's pretty. Don't you think he's pretty, Emma? I think our son is pretty."

"So pretty," she said, without even the trace of a smile on her face. "I'm just glad he can rely on his looks when so many resources seem to have failed him, aren't you?"

Mullins felt the heat of Edward's face as he pushed against his throat. "Maybe that wasn't the best thought out thing we've ever done," he admitted.

Mullins kissed his temple. "I don't know—I've been watching you five going on this scavenger hunt for weeks now—you'd think if we were going to attract the attention of chaos, that would have done it."

"Oh hell," Emma muttered, and next to her Leonard smacked his forehead with his palm.

Mullins could barely spare them a look. "What?"

"Don't worry, we'll get to it," Emma said dryly. "First, sit. Mullins, can I get you anything to eat or drink? We all had breakfast before we... you know, called you into the living room, I guess. Do you need anything?"

Mullins thought carefully. "I'm not fully... human yet," he said after he took a moment to monitor his functions. "I think I can eat, but it's not necessary?"

Emma harrumphed. "I'll be back with food," she muttered. "Boys. Why boys? A girl would be like, 'Starving, thanks!' Boys think they can reform the world on a granola bar."

"Harry would like something too," Suriel said politely.

"I would no—"

"Harry, shut up," Emma muttered. "I'll be back."

Mullins felt Edward shift and looked around for the couch. The two of them sat, and Mullins said, "Did she just leave the room so she didn't have to talk about elves?"

Leonard allowed his mouth to twist up fondly. "She was a couple of hundred years old when she found me," he said, "but she still likes to pretend that I'm her first."

All four of the boys—Edward included—struggled upright.

"We did not just hear that," Edward said, horrified. "Did we just hear that, Harry?"

"No, brother, we did not. Bel, Francis? Did we just hear that?"

"Christ no," Bel said, prompt and resolute. "Francis?"

"Fuck no."

As a unit they turned to Leonard. "You understand"—Harry spoke for all of them—"we did not hear that."

"Of course," Leonard said mildly. "Just saying that makes it so."

Mullins didn't like Edward sitting so far from him. He wrapped his arms around his waist and hauled him back, his very human warmth sinking into Mullins's flesh, seeping into his sinews.

"How very possessive," Edward murmured. "I had no idea."

"You… I need to feel all of you," Mullins whispered next to his ear. "I had forgotten—being human. How much you crave touch and warmth."

"You," Edward whispered, turning his head.

Mullins moved forward, ready to claim his mouth again, regardless of the onlookers, when Emma bustled back into the room with sandwiches on plates. She made sure Mullins and Harry were served first, but there was plenty for everybody, and given how short a time she'd taken to prepare them, Mullins had to wonder if magic hadn't been involved.

"So," she said, as though the pause had never happened. "Since we know running around attracting chaos doesn't attract elves—"

Leonard cleared his throat.

"—and we'll discuss what it attracted in a moment, let's talk about elves."

"Yes, dearest," Leonard said wickedly. "Let us discuss elves."

Emma cast him an arch look. "We were not together when that happened," she murmured.

"No—and even if we had been, I wouldn't have stopped it," Leonard said surprisingly. "There are consequences for meddling with the will of the Goddess, and this is one of them."

"Oh great," Edward muttered. "*Now* they tell us about the Goddess."

Emma ignored him. "I assume Mullins has briefed you—as far as he knows."

Edward nodded—of course he'd briefed Harry and the others. "The whole thing sounds like a big ugly adolescent fight," he said crossly. "God's children do magic *this* way, Goddess's *that way*, and he's not speaking to *her*, and she's going out of her way to avoid *him*, and all because…." He couldn't finish that sentence while being sardonic—he just couldn't.

"All because he wanted to make a blood sacrifice of their child to protect his people, and she refused." Emma's voice was firm. "It's not a black or white issue, Edward—faith and sacrifice rarely are. But it's not our job to debate the politics of the God and the Goddess—it's our job to talk about elves." Her face washed bright with color for no reason Mullins could think of. "We're here to talk about Green."

"The color?" Beltane asked blankly.

"No. Green the elf. They tend to have…." Emma smiled sweetly. "They tend to have names that reflect who they are. Green is simply growing and kind. He's warmth and gentleness and the strength of an oak tree—or a lime tree. Green is his name—and it's who he is."

"Is he a king?" Edward asked eagerly, and she held out her palm.

"You need to listen," she said, meeting his eyes. "This is important. Elves had one king, in England. For all I know, Oberon is still there, and his court is…." She shuddered. "Unhealthy. Green was fleeing from him, oh, about twenty years before I met Leonard—which was about twenty-five years before you boys came into our lives."

Edward shifted in Mullins's arms. "Eighteen fifty?"

"Mm-hm. Thereabouts. He had just come from England—and he brought with him two things. One was a shipment of fruit trees that he kept alive in the hold via pure fucking magic, as far as I could tell. He sold them for land and supplies, keeping a few to plant so he could sell fruit in the hard land. The other was a vampire—although I don't think he'd been a vampire when Green met him. I think the young man chose that way of life so he could stay alive for Green."

"So… immortal?" Harry asked.

Emma shrugged, her expression sad. "Ageless," she corrected. "I… I understand that Adrian passed in battle, maybe five years ago. They loved each other fiercely—I can only hope Green survived."

"Wait a minute," Beltane burst out, surprising them all. "Elves? Vampires? You've spent our entire lives schooling us in magic and the arcane—how is it you've never once mentioned these things?"

Emma's mouth quirked up. "I don't know," she said with a shrug. "Maybe because when I was young there was so much superstition around them, they were built up to be evil. As the ages passed, they were brushed off as child's stories. They weren't my field of study—I just didn't feel as though I knew enough to verse you in them."

"And she didn't want you to know she spent a magic night with an elf," Leonard said dryly.

"But I thought he loved a vampire?" Francis said, in a rare moment of curiosity. He hadn't touched his tuna sandwich—he'd been listening to Emma's story in rapt attention.

"He did," she said with a quiet smile. "Elves aren't often monogamous. They are, in fact, highly polyamorous—although I believe there are a few exceptions, Green couldn't afford to be one of them. See…." She let out a sigh. "I met him in Sacramento, during the gold rush, and he was… well, so very bright and so very clever, but so out of his depth. He'd needed to leave Adrian behind on his mountain to guard it. By then, they had sort of an enclave of shapeshifters and a few vampires looking for peace and quiet, and even some local Goddess's get and a few ex-pats, following in Green's footsteps. He was, in fact, a little frantic. There were thirty or so people living on his hill, and some sort of land-rights bill had just been passed. He'd bought his land fair and square, but suddenly he had to file paperwork on it. He'd apparently seduced the first three assayers who came by to try to tell him the government wanted his hill, and he was a fair hand at fixing things—but he just didn't understand the American hierarchy, was all."

"Did he tell you all this?" Harry asked, puzzled. "I mean, he saw you were a witch and—"

She shook her head and bit her lip shyly. "I saw the ears," she said, trying to mask a delighted smile. "He was wearing glamour. I was apparently the only person in the room who could see his ears, and the faint peach and green cast to his skin, and the way his eyes were too big and too wide set for a human's. We were sitting in a pub, and one moment I was fending off advances, and the next moment I was looking on a dazzling man with long yellow hair who was most assuredly not human. He caught my gaze and smiled—it was a grand smile."

Mullins looked around and saw that Emma's sons had all put their hands in front of their mouths, hiding fond grins of their own.

"I helped him with the paperwork," she continued, her eyes far away. "And we… talked." She said it simply, like it surprised her. "I mean, there was the other thing—but that's private. Mostly we just talked, and he was… kind. Very worried for his people—he already thought of them that way. His people. I looked at him and saw all of the dedication he had to keeping his lover, those people on his hill safe, and I told him he was already a king of the new world. And he got this… this odd smile on his face. Before I left the next day, he pulled three hairs off his head and wrapped them in a complicated knot, tied with thread. He told me since I was a witch, he knew things like this showed up in spells every so often, and he was grateful for the help. When it came time to free your father, I had them ready in my pocket."

"So he wasn't a king?" Edward said, like he was trying to keep things straight.

"Oh, but he was," Emma said confidently. "His kingdom was very small at the time, but he was definitely someone who took care of his people. Someone who would sacrifice anything to keep them safe." Her smile went nostalgic. "He was, in short, everything a good leader should be—if anyone could make themselves king by virtue alone, it would be Green."

Edward, Harry, and Francis all snickered at the same time.

"I'm sorry?" Emma asked, affronted.

They shook their heads, still trying not to laugh. "It's not you," Edward said, trying hard to keep himself under control. I swear it's not you. It's…." He glared at his little brother. "Francis, you snot—how could you project that!"

"I was thinking it too!" Harry howled.

Emma tilted her head. "Boys?"

Beltane shrugged at his mother. "I'm sorry, Mum. I heard what Francis thought at them, but I don't understand what he meant."

"Well, what did he say?" she asked, humor quirking at her mouth.

"It's a spell," Bel told her, still staring at the boy convulsing with laughter on his lap. "But I don't get it. He said, *May your many arms have enough work to amuse you, may you go somewhere you find no fear. May you inhabit a kingdom that values your worth, you furry brown drinkers of beer.*"

Mullins's eyes popped open.

He knew this. Edward had told him this story.

For once he was not the stranger called into the circle. For once he was in the circle, looking out.

Helplessly, he dissolved into laughter, Edward in his arms, as Emma and Leonard rolled their eyes and Beltane and Suriel demanded to be in the know.

Eventually the story poured out—Edward, Harry, and Francis all taking a sentence or two in the telling—and Emma closed her eyes and pinched the bridge of her nose.

Mullins knew from experience that never made anything go away.

"So, you sent the brownies to Green's," she said seriously.

"Can you think of anywhere else they'd go?" Edward asked, just as serious.

"No, no. I'm just… I'm impressed, is all. You didn't even know who he was."

"But we knew they looked to *somebody*," Edward responded. "They wanted things to do. I mean… ten years, we didn't have to clean a damned thing. I almost forgot how to hang up my own jacket."

"And you little shits couldn't have sent them to the kitchen *once*?"

"Sorry, Emma," Francis mumbled.

"Sorry," Edward seconded. They all looked to Harry, but in the space of a heartbeat, he'd fallen asleep.

Suriel stood, and all traces of laughter fell away. "So," he said, situating Harry tenderly, head against his shoulder, in a way that belied the tremendous strength that apparently had not been stripped away with his wings. "Emma, I take it you know where this Green might live?"

"I do," she said, eyes gentle on Harry.

"Two days," he murmured, kissing Harry's forehead. "Mullins, do you think we have that long?"

Mullins moved from Edward's side and bent to pick the forgotten mirror up off the floor. In its frame, he could see his old cell, as still, quiet, and unchanging as it always had been. Nobody knew he'd gone. It hadn't been a summoning; there hadn't been a spell. He'd been simply scooped up, and the remaining demon trace of him was probably as faint as the last mark of it on his skin.

His tail twitched slowly—but it didn't tingle.

"I think so," he said, hoping this wasn't just wishful thinking. "I... if you have wards, I suggest you set them up—"

Her soft laugh indicated the place had been warded since its inception. "Every drop of sweat, every tear, every bit of blood shed here, Mullins. Do not worry about our land—it's wired to our flesh. If anything tries to get in, I can boomerang you and Edward where you need to go."

"And us!" Francis demanded, sitting up suddenly from his perpetual sprawl over Bel.

"All of you," she conceded. "I do understand that sending any but the full complement of Youngbloods will start a family crisis. But I think two days will be fine before you all drive there. If nothing else, it will give us time to purchase a new—" She sighed. "—minivan. Anyway, Edward. The original cabin, yes? Since yours isn't close to finished?"

Edward sat up and clutched Mullins's hand. "Is it provisioned?"

"It will be by the time you get there," she said sweetly, and Leonard assumed the faraway look he often got when practicing his own magic. She came forward then, and blessed them both with a kiss on the forehead. "Make the most of your time," she cautioned. "Mullins, I think you're right. I think this is far from over. I have an idea of who gave us this chance for you and Edward to know each other, but I do not know why. Take nothing for granted, my children, are we clear?"

"Yes, Emma," Edward said, sober and practical as always.

She smiled faintly and ruffled his hair, motherhood written in every line of her face. "Maybe get some sleep," she told them. "If you can find the time."

She made to take a step back, but before her foot even landed, Mullins and Edward were deposited, without ceremony, in the front room of the small cabin where Edward had first kissed him, less than a month before.

THE TIME WE STOLE

EDWARD TOOK a breath and yawned to make his ears pop.

"I am going to have to learn that damned spell," he muttered, looking around the little cabin. It hadn't changed much since he and Mullins had met there to plan. He was pretty sure Emma had it cleaned every so often—maybe if they left out beer and forwent the blackberry pie, they could lure the brownies back.

"Why haven't you?" Mullins asked, and Edward spared a moment to smile at him. He was still so beautiful—his eyes were that lovely lake blue, his mouth soft and sweet. His hair—dark and chestnut—fell across a poet's brow, and he had a tendency to bite his lower lip as a man, which was something he'd not done as a beast.

"It makes no sense," Edward murmured. "It relies on instinct and partial guesswork, and Harry keeps trying to teach me that, but I don't understand." They were standing still in the circle of each other's arms. They'd not stopped touching since Mullins had shown up in the living room, surprised and desperately happy to be there. Edward had felt every emotion radiating from him—incredulity, joy, surprise.

And now, as Edward took in his very human face and body, shyness.

Edward took a step in to touch him again when Mullins said, "I must wash."

"I'm... okay, why?"

Mullins shook his head. "I smell like hell," he said, twisting his lips. "Don't tell me you can't smell it."

Sulfur, brimstone—things that Mullins had always worn on his skin.

What would he smell like when they'd been washed away?

"Let me help you," Edward said, thinking of the intimate possibilities.

But Mullins shook his head, his expression serious and sad. "Please, Edward—I was barely starting to hope, and now this. Let me feel myself as a man and not a beast. That way I can remember how to please you as a man. Please?"

Edward nodded, understanding. He took a step in and captured Mullins's chin. "You cannot wash away four hundred years there," he cautioned. "You can't wash away who you are. Soap your hair, your tight spaces—I'll be in bed, waiting."

This Mullins had fair skin, and a heated flush spread along his cheekbones. "I don't want to… to spread my hell to your bed," he said, pulling his dignity around him.

Edward leaned forward and took his mouth hard, relieved when Mullins opened to him on a soft gasp.

He tasted like wine—a dark red—and like chocolate, and Edward could have gotten drunk on his kisses alone. He pressed the kiss, pushing Mullins back from the center of the room, toward the bed in the corner, and he was disappointed but not surprised when Mullins stopped and made a stand.

"Please," he panted, hands on Edward's shoulders, fingers kneading as much as his palms were keeping Edward back. "Please let me do this for you." He looked to the side, his mouth twisted bitterly. "You're literally bailing me out of hell," he said softly. "Can I just not bring it into our bed?"

"Five minutes," Edward told him, jaw set. "You won't be any cleaner in thirty than you will be in five. My arms ache for you, Mullins. For years I've barely dared to dream and now here's my dream—and he's got a pressing need to go shower. Five minutes." Edward took a step back, reminding himself that if Mullins was not comfortable, what they were about to do wouldn't be comfortable. "Please," he whispered, running his fingertips along Mullins's jawline. "Think of me out here, waiting for you, naked. Make it quick."

Mullins made a desperate sound and turned and fled. Edward made good to his word and stripped down to his skin, and then slid between the covers. He reached into the drawer and pulled out a bottle of lubricant that he personally had stocked the place with after their last meeting, hoping for this exact moment.

Edward liked to be prepared.

He lay there, cotton quilt protecting him from the worst of the dampness and the cold of the room, his hand traveling up and down his body, sensitizing his skin, making himself ready. His fingers found his own nipples in anticipation, and he pinched softly, then harder, as he gave himself over to pleasure.

This new Mullins, this human man, was younger than Edward had expected—he must have been achingly vulnerable when seduced into the world of hell. His smile was shy and a little bit needy, and Edward wanted to give in to his every need.

Shelter him from anything that might hurt him.

He closed his eyes and ran his hand down his abdomen, his cock swelling heavy against his thigh as he did so. As if in a trance, he heard the bathroom door open, and he inhaled lightly, taking in the scent of Emma's specially made family body wash—lavender and leather, clean and light and incongruously male.

"Starting without me?" Mullins asked, sounding a little hurt, and Edward rolled to his back, pulling back the covers.

"Acquainting myself with the equipment," he said soberly, grasping his cock in his palm and squeezing. "It's been a while."

"Has it been 400 years?" Mullins asked archly, and Edward smiled at him. He'd wrapped a towel around his waist, and his skin was flushed pink from the hot water.

"You're the one who had to shower." Edward's playful expression softened. "Is the smell completely gone?" he asked.

Mullins closed his eyes and shook his head. "I might always smell a little bit of hell," he confessed. "I'm not good enough for my boy."

Edward sat up, reaching for him and pulling him close to the bed by his fingertips on Mullins's backside. "Can I touch it?" he asked, feeling the restless swish of the thing by his knuckles.

"Not now," Mullins begged. "Do you want me to drop my towel?"

Edward met his eyes. "I'll die if you don't."

The towel was gone. Edward closed his eyes, kissing his naked thigh, the space under his navel, his hipbone.

Clean, bare skin met his lips—but no beastly fur. No magic guise. No shifting between what was under his hands and lips and reality. Mullins knotted human fingers in his hair and tilted his head up.

"All that about losing the towel…," he joked.

Edward grinned. "Get down here in bed with me," he ordered, scooting back and turning to his side.

"Fine," Mullins said, obeying. "What are we doing?"

Edward grinned at him, shivering. "Me. *I'm* doing. I'm touching you. Your male human body. I want to celebrate it." He cupped Mullins's shoulder in wonder, ran his palm down a developed tricep, around his elbow, to the tips of his long artist's fingers. "Look at that. Hands. We really are a marvel of design." He pulled Mullins's hand to his mouth and proceeded to take each finger, one by one, between his lips, where he sucked on it and released it with a nibble at the end.

Mullins let out a little groan, hips wiggling, as Edward scraped the pad of his thumb with sharp teeth. Perfect.

Edward wanted to pleasure him, making him so comfortable in his human body that his soul couldn't even conceive of being trapped in hell again.

"I want to touch you... oh!" Edward moved closer, nibbling his chin, his jaw, his neck. All that skin—soft and human—so forbidden, so hidden from sight for so long, touching it with his lips and tongue was the most erotic of acts.

Mullins slid his hands along Edward's arms, shuddering at their nakedness, Edward was sure.

It was why every touch made *him* tremble.

He pulled a nipple into his mouth and suckled, the taste of wine and chocolate suffusing his senses. Mullins cried out, arching his hips against Edward, and came without warning, his semen scalding Edward's stomach as he pulled.

Edward ignored it.

Edward had been abstinent for five years—his body was primed and ready.

Mullins had been void of human touch in time that could be measured in centuries. His skin was an organ ripe for the playing, and every touch would produce a new note.

"Edward!" Mullins panted. "I... oh hells... oh... oh gods! Augh! Again!"

This time his entire body convulsed as his cock spat come, and Edward pulled away and licked a lazy circle around a pink areola.

"How you doing?" he asked, his body on high alert just from bringing Mullins off. "You have a few more of those in you?"

He gave the nipple a pull and started to lick his way down Mullins's belly, pausing when he came to patches of semen. He licked them up, almost laughing when they tasted like merlot and chocolate too.

"You have words yet?" he asked, peering up to see Mullins's expression.

"No words," Mullins choked. "What are you—oh!"

Edward took him into his mouth, cleaning him off with happy abandon. Ah! He'd forgotten how good a man tasted on his palate, the joy of that presence stretching his mouth. He pushed forward, taking Mullins deeper and deeper into his throat, aware of the tug of Mullins's fingers in his hair as he sucked hard, once, twice, again—

"Augh!"

Sweet.

The taste of a man's spend, hot and salty, spilling down his throat. Mullins cried out again and again, his entire body spasming as he lost control and gave in to human touch for the first time in centuries.

Finally he battered weakly at Edward's shoulders, and Edward scooted up in bed so he could rest his head on Mullins's chest. He stayed there for a moment, soothing, patting Mullins's abdomen, quieting him as he shuddered the last of the orgasm out.

"Oh heavens," Mullins mumbled. "I'm so weak. I had… I had no idea. Every touch, it's magnified a thousand times. I could come again just by stroking your hair."

Edward rolled slightly to the side and traced his mouth with a gentle finger. "Is that bad?" he asked, biting his lip with joy.

"I… you're not getting much out of it."

Edward sobered. "Oh, my love. I'm getting to touch you. The real you. I'm getting to hear your sounds and taste you. This is a prelude—this is getting the awkwardness out of the way. I'm going to drape myself all over your body until you get used to the idea of wearing me like a shirt. When every touch doesn't send you into a spiral of orgasm, *then* I'm going to show you what it feels like when you can control yourself, when you can let the passion take over."

Mullins looked away. "Honestly, I'm sort of in this position because that's what I did."

Edward rolled over to prop himself up on his elbows. "Really? That's wonderful! You went to hell for lust?"

Mullins shook his head, a small smile twisting at his sober mouth. "No. I went to hell for…." He sighed, and Edward's heart ached. "The consequences of perfidy," he said at last. "I went to hell because an otherworldly being showed up at my window and I thought that gave me leave to betray a lover who truly cared for me. He… he was hurt. He told the entire town the devil showed up at my window, and…." He shuddered. "They burned down my house and chased me and my sister into the night. I called on the forces of hell to save my sister, since it was my own weakness that put her in danger."

"Ah."

Mullins turned back to him. "I… I put off telling you that," he confessed. "I… there you were, going to all that trouble to get me out, and I might not be a good bet as a lover. Now you know."

"Know that you were young and confused and frightened?" Edward asked softly. "I'd already guessed that."

"I was unfaithful, Edward," Mullins said baldly. "I—"

"Will you be faithful to me?" Edward asked, knowing the simplicity of the question was what Mullins needed to calm his fears.

"I'd die before I hurt you," he answered, as though honestly shocked. "I can't… I'd die." And something in his brow relaxed then, his chest, his neck, as though he'd been holding on to the last of the tension a good climax should relieve. "I'd die before I hurt you," he said again, and Edward moved up so he could pull his lover into his chest and let him weep softly, for the sins he'd committed long ago and still held tight to his heart.

"Mullins," Edward whispered after his quiet sobs had stilled. "I'm falling asleep."

"Me too."

"Good. Sleep. I trust you in my bed, naked next to me. We'll have more lessons when we wake."

"Lessons?" Mullins struggled back to gaze up at Edward with tear-reddened eyes.

Edward wiped traces of brine from his cheek. "Human lessons," he said, popping his thumb in his mouth to savor the salt. "This was only the beginning of lovemaking. This was the glory of touch. There is so much more. But sleep for now. Heal. Know you're cared for." Edward closed his eyes and carefully set up every ward and protection Emma had ever taught him. "Know we're safe here. There is so much for us to share together before we finish this quest. Don't fear, don't ever fear, that I'll be done with you."

Mullins nodded weakly, and Edward sheltered him again in the haven of his arms. His body was tingling with unfinished release, and his cock throbbed against his thigh. These were small prices to pay, though, for knowing his lover was safe, was replete, and was learning how to be human again so they might share their more than mortal lifetimes together.

They were hardly payments at all.

HE AWAKENED to Mullins's touch, featherlight, over his chest, and kept his eyes closed so as to not startle him.

"I know you're awake," Mullins murmured, kissing his shoulder.

"Pretend I'm asleep," Edward told him, his lips quirking up.

"Why?"

"So you won't be afraid to touch me just a wee bit harder. You're going to tickle."

Mullins let out a grunt that should have been a laugh, and Edward realized that he *had* heard his laugh that day, when talking about the brownies—and that it had been the first time.

He opened his eyes and returned Mullins's caress along the curve of his jaw. "Laugh more," he whispered.

Mullins ducked his head behind his bicep. "There is no laughter—no good, pure laughter—in hell."

"You're here now."

Mullins sobered. "For how long—"

"Don't," Edward said, his chest suddenly aching. "Don't... don't assume this will end. Hope. I begged you to hope when we went looking for the list—did you?"

A shy smile tugged at Mullins's lips. "Not at first," he admitted. "But hells, Edward—the things you five did for me! Dinosaur toes and red grains of sand and... just everything! I... I was a part of it, I guess. I saw it. All of you. They love you so much, and... and...."

"And I love you," Edward prompted. It could not be said enough. "I forgot, you know. That they'd do anything for me. It wasn't until I started artifact hunting and Harry called me to task that I remembered. Getting Harry and Suriel together was a full-family project too."

Mullins met his eyes soberly. "You were so worried."

"Oh yes." Edward nodded. "And they were worried about me and you. And they still are. You were in hell for four hundred years for infidelity, Mullins. Can you come out long enough to remember why to be faithful?"

"I am out!" He ducked his head again, and Edward brushed the chestnut strands from his forehead.

"Kiss me," he whispered. "Kiss me until our bodies forget the fear."

Mullins looked up, searching Edward's eyes with his own, and pushed up, claiming Edward's mouth this time, taking his advantage.

Edward relaxed back against the pillows, taking Mullins's tongue into his mouth, letting him pillage, inviting his plunder. Mullins's light touch grew firmer, strong, his palm and fingers mapping all the skin they could find.

Mullins stopped with a gasp when he found a scar across Edward's ribs. "I remember this," he said, moving so he could kiss it. "You damned kids didn't wait for me. You summoned me and went in first and...." He mouthed the scar, and Edward bucked up, remembering how angry Mullins had been when Harry had carried Edward out of the melee where they'd just broken up a child pornography operation. No man had been left to stop them, but Edward had needed Suriel's healing that time.

Mullins had stayed by Edward's side until Suriel's glow became overwhelming. They hadn't known what would happen if both of them were summoned at the same time—but Edward remembered the anguish on his face as he'd faded.

"I'm fine," Edward whispered, threading fingers through his hair. Mullins moved up to take Edward's nipple into his mouth, and Edward gasped. "I'm even better than fine."

Mullins didn't answer, just suckled as Edward had, until Edward cried out and tugged hard at his hair.

"You like that?" Mullins whispered.

"Very much. But it's not what you want to do to me."

"It's not *all* I want to do to you," Mullins agreed, moving unerringly toward Edward's thickened, dripping cock.

He moaned as he took it into his mouth, and Edward threw his head back, eyes fluttering closed. Oh! Yes—somebody had taught Mullins how to do this and do it well. He teased the head with his tongue, he teased the frenulum, he stroked with his fist.

"Good?" Edward asked on a moan. "Do you like that?"

"It's a beginning," Mullins said, in complete seriousness before he went down again.

He was shifting, though, shoving himself between Edward's thighs. He released Edward's cock with a soft little pop and moved his palms to Edward's ass.

"This," Mullins said. "This here. I watched you in that orgy. I saw you getting fucked. And all I could think—besides easing your pain—was that I wanted to possess this. I wanted to be the one stretching you. I wanted to be the one who left my spend inside."

"You want that, right?" Edward asked as Mullins parted his cheeks and breathed softly on his tender hole. "You want to be the one to possess that?"

"Yes!" Mullins punctuated that with a lunge forward. He buried his tongue between Edward's cheeks and licked hard, relentlessly, until Edward had to clench his stomach to keep from spewing come.

"Then take it!" Edward cried. "Take it! Take *me*. Possess *me*. I want to be fucked and taken and used by you, Mullins. I want to be *claimed*."

"Slick!" Mullins demanded between licks. "Spit isn't good enough!"

Edward was in a raw mood—spit would be just enough to let him slip in, and that would be *great*. But Mullins wanted to care for him, and that would be glorious too. Edward fumbled with the bottle and dumped some lubricant on his fingers, then shoved them past Mullins's tongue, coating his asshole and shoving both fingers inside.

Mullins yanked them out and replaced them with his own. "*Mine!*" he roared, scissoring two fingers while Edward shook with need beneath him.

"More," he demanded simply.

Mullins added another finger, and Edward let out a little whine as the stretch took over his body. Needed—it was needed—because Mullins was well endowed—but everything behind Edward's eyes became a ring of fire on a background of black velvet. He needed so much.

"Take me," he ordered from a throat gone rusty with moaning. "I need it—I need you. I need you inside me, Mullins—*take me!*"

His fingers disappeared and Edward grunted with yearning.

"Turn over," Mullins told him, and Edward, blind with wanting, shaking with emptiness, would have done anything he asked. He rolled over to his hands and knees and waited.

Mullins leaned over his back, capturing his throat with the vee of his finger and thumb. "Mine," he said again. "Forever. I won't take this back, Edward."

"I won't give it," Edward snarled. "*Fuck me!*"

Hard and huge, he thrust in, not without pain, but the pain was worth it. He seated himself completely, and Edward buried his face in the covers and screamed, flush and full with him, not sure he could breathe if Mullins ever went away.

"Good?" Mullins asked, his sweating, shaking hand against Edward's throat telling him everything about self-control.

Edward took his thumb into his mouth and sucked hard, nipping as he let it go. "Fuck me," he demanded again. *"Fuck me!"*

Mullins pulled out, slowly, slowly, slowly, until Edward buried his face in the quilt and howled, just as Mullins slammed back in again. *"Yes!"*

Edward knew he screamed—his throat was raw with it—but he heard Mullins behind him, saying it hoarsely as he thrust in to the hilt, and Edward pounded the bed with his fist. "So good," he panted. "More."

Again and again, every thrust exploding inside Edward's body like they were reforming his insides to take his forever lover, to hold him, cradle him for all time.

But Mullins couldn't last long—not this time—and too soon he stopped, deep inside Edward's body, and started the mini-thrusts that signaled his climax. Edward wasn't done yet, wasn't ready, and he grabbed his cock, stroking hard, hoping to make it soon enough to send Mullins over but—

"Augh!"

And Edward could feel it, deep inside, hot and full. He buried his face in the sheets and groaned as Mullins softened, still not full, still not—"Oh!"

Mullins didn't collapse on him, didn't roll over. Instead he pulled out and licked Edward again, his tongue probing the slack, tender entrance while Edward stroked himself hard and harder, and then Mullins's fingers took over, four of them this time, and Edward screamed as his climax destroyed him.

He fell to the bed, limbs useless, Mullins's fingers still buried inside him, thrusting.

"No more," he whispered. "Done. Please."

The fingers disappeared, and Edward collapsed against the mattress, melting against the sheets.

He barely hit consciousness when Mullins started kissing his shoulder gently, whispering soft things in his ear.

Finally, the syllables became words, and Edward could find words to respond.

"Good?" Mullins asked uncertainly.

"I'm dead," Edward mumbled back. "Annihilated. Destroyed."

"So that's good?"

Edward turned his head, relieved when Mullins took his mouth without making him move too much. "You know some good tricks," he mumbled. "Where did you learn all that?"

"Later," Mullins whispered. "Right now I just want to kiss you."

Edward smiled dreamily. "Kiss the man who did that to me just now? My pleasure. I can't imagine kissing anyone else."

Mullins's mouth on his felt right, dominant, taking charge. Perhaps Edward would take him next time—or perhaps not. Right now it was enough that they'd possessed each other, that he could feel Mullins's come trickling down the back of his thigh, taste some of it on Mullins's tongue.

"Mm...." Kissing. It went on and on and on, until Edward grew hard again, rolling over to his back and spreading his legs in invitation. Mullins took him again, holding his legs up, slamming into him with suppressed violence, until Edward—tender and primed—went off again from his own hand on his cock.

This time Edward saw Mullins's face as he climaxed, saw his jaw grow slack, his eyes roll back, his mouth contort.

Saw him lose himself trustingly as he spent inside Edward one more time and collapsed forward into his arms.

SOMETIME IN the middle of the night, Edward turned cat and curled up against his chest. It wasn't conscious—mostly habit. All three of the brothers did it—four, if they counted Beltane's dog form, a gift from Leonard, who had dabbled in old magic before he'd become a demon.

He woke up to Mullins stroking along his back, paying particular attention to the base of his tail. Edward purred and kneaded his chest, enjoying the comfort.

"I didn't realize how much you three used your forms still," Mullins said softly. "Bel does it to stay with Francis. Why do the three of you do it so much?"

Edward licked a paw, because part of the beauty of being a cat was that he didn't have to answer shit.

Mullins grunted—but he kept scratching his ass.

"So you do it to feel safe," Mullins said, because asked and answered. "I wish I had a form that would make me feel safe."

Edward started licking his face with a rough tongue, proud when Mullins smiled.

"So your form will make me safe?" Mullins asked, but Edward could hear the melancholy in his voice, and it needed to be answered like a man.

He changed, suddenly face-to-face and intimate, Mullins's slow blink the only proof that he was surprised. "I only spent a few years in hell," he said softly. "But I was a child. We were all children. The cat was like a gift—an easy escape from hell. I… I can take you out of your hell, Mullins, but I can't give you an easy way to leave it in your mind. I… I think you may need to ask Leonard how he did it. Just know you're not alone."

Mullins's lower lip wobbled a little. "That's the worst part," he rasped. "It's the only reason I haven't… haven't given my soul up. It's the only reason I haven't despaired. Leonard held my hand for three hundred years. His family held my heart for the last century and a half. But this last month, watching you boys go off and adventure, I suddenly saw what I'd lost, what I'd *missed*, by not giving in sooner. Oh, Edward… I have… I have been so alone."

Edward's turn to soothe. Edward's turn to comfort, to hold.

He only hoped he was as good at it as the people who had taught him—Emma, Leonard, and Mullins himself. Holding his lover and whispering him out of hell was the only currency he had.

JOY AND CHAOS

MULLINS AWOKE to the smell of breakfast—bacon, toast, and fruit—and stretched, yawning.

Somehow, he and Edward had managed to make love when they should have been eating the night before, and his stomach rumbled fiercely—but his body?

His body felt newly made.

He rolled out of bed, naked, and reached quickly for a pair of boxers from the chest of drawers near the bed. His old sulfur-infused eighteenth century clothing wasn't practical, now that he wore a man's shape and was no longer subject to being summoned back to hell. He was rather looking forward to dressing as the boys did—jeans and T-shirts and hooded sweatshirts—all worn and comfortable and casual.

"Suriel wears a leather jacket," he pondered, sliding on a pair of jeans that could have fit any one of the Youngblood boys except Bel.

"I wake you up with breakfast and you're wondering about Suriel?" Edward asked from the kitchen side of the cabin.

Mullins found his grin came easier and easier with practice.

"He wears a leather jacket. Why is that? Even Beltane wears sweatshirts."

Edward rolled his eyes. "Pure vanity," he responded. "Harry once told him he liked James Dean, the actor, and Suriel showed up for the next fifty years wearing a leather jacket and jeans."

Oh! Mullins slid the sweatshirt he'd claimed from the drawer over his head, then held his hand to his chest, suddenly conscious of the softer emotions and how much he treasured each one.

"They're very dear," he said, and Edward's sardonic expression softened.

"They are. I popped into Harry's head today—he's miffed because Suriel's serious about bed rest being actual rest, but he says he feels much better."

Mullins's mouth twisted. "You don't believe him?"

Edward held out a hand and tilted it both ways. "Maybe yes maybe no? He's a really excellent liar when it comes to his own health. By the way, that was cleverly done."

"What?" But Mullins never could lie worth a damn. It was why he'd chosen to tell the truth to Jonathan rather than mislead him about his time with the red man.

"You hid your tail. We made love four times by my count last night, and not once did I get to see your ass."

Oh damn. Mullins couldn't fight the flush taking over his body, so he gave up trying.

"Is it because you don't like to be penetrated," Edward asked, raising his eyebrows mockingly, "or because—"

"Not when you can see my tail," Mullins bit out, not wanting to be this cranky, but… *tail*!

"Mm…." Edward took the few paces to cross from the kitchen to the sleeping area and stopped in front of him. "I think tails are cool," he proclaimed, and it was Mullins's turn to roll his eyes.

"I think mine means I might still end up in hell," he responded shortly, and then his irritation faded. "And I'd rather you not think of me like that."

"We won't let that happen." Edward wrapped his arms around Mullins's shoulders and kissed him.

Oh, Mullins wanted to believe him. With every fiber in his being—except, presumably, the flesh invested in the damned tail—he wanted to believe in Edward's power to overcome every obstacle in his path.

But he'd spent 400 years watching the young and innocent being deceived and watching the older and wiser succumb to the need for power. He'd seen people corrupted by greed, corrupted by lust, by addiction, by despair.

He'd seen people with the same hope Edward had, that of overcoming old power. He'd seen them ground into the dust.

"You're so young," he whispered. Then, before Edward could repeat that he was over 150 years old, because that didn't seem to matter in the youth and naivety of the Youngbloods, he kissed him to stave off the argument. They all just had such a dreadfully strong belief in themselves, in their lovers, in the power of love to change the world.

Edward grinned cheekily and turned toward the kitchen, dragging Mullins along with him.

"That reminds me. Harry and I talked about when you transform completely—we're going to need to do some spellcasting, you realize."

Mullins frowned. "Why? What do you mean?"

"Well, Emma stored a great deal of her power in us, and then spilled the balance into Leonard and back into herself. She took what was probably a two or three millennium lifespan and spread it out among the five of us, you understand?"

Oh. "I knew that," Mullins said, nodding. "I wasn't there, but yes. She told me."

"Well of course. So, Francis, Harry, and I have all been building power back, and Emma and Leonard have been building their own. We are, in fact, significantly stronger now as a family than Emma was by herself all those years ago—and we have Beltane and Suriel as well. Suriel came with his own power—shapeshifting, healing, telepathy. Harry's been teaching him spellcasting, like we do, and he's been getting pretty good. And of course Bel's supposed to learn more at Oxford—"

"It's not Hogwarts, you know." Because they spoke of Bel's time away like it would send him back a completely different person.

"Well, it is the way Bel's doing it. So anyway, I asked Harry, and Harry and the others agreed. When we do the spell—the one that breaks you completely free—we'll all pour some of our power into you. Enough to lengthen your lifespan, you understand? We haven't asked Emma and Leonard—they've given plenty. But Suriel, Beltane, me, Francis, Harry—that should be enough."

Mullins blinked, discomfited by such practical discussion of power, as though it were food or water or electricity or something else mundane and replenishable.

"So you'll be bringing me to your world as your lover—"

"For as long as we both shall live." Edward's smile suddenly reminded Mullins that he *wasn't* young. That his optimism was hard won and defended by the formidable strength in his heart. "I wasn't kidding about not being able to lose another lover, Mullins." He held up his hand, and Mullins answered him, lacing their fingers together. "You and I are going to be bound for many, many years. Are you ready for that?"

Mullins had to laugh. "I assure you, Edward, if I didn't love you enough for that to sound like a perfectly wonderful arrangement, I would have told you." His laughter faded. "I would have told you from the very beginning not to try for me. Watching you and your brothers labor, watching you working with all your heart to bring me back to your side—only a truly evil person would have let you do all of that with no intention of loving you for eternity."

With his other hand, Edward traced Mullins's lower lip with his thumb.

"Not evil, beloved. Desperate. Tired and sick and terrified of hell. You've proved to us again and again that you are more than just a task. I have faith. Are you ready to walk by my side forever?"

"It's the hope that fed me," Mullins confessed brokenly. "For the past hundred and forty years, it's the hope that kept me sane."

Edward smiled slightly and pulled Mullins in for a long, heated kiss of avowal. The kiss was about to become so much more when Edward yanked back sharply. "Bacon," he said, pulling away and running to the stove. "Almost overdone."

Mullins laughed softly, somehow feeling lighter now that they'd had that conversation. As he sat down at the table—already set with flowers and place mats in an absolutely charming fashion—he had a thought.

"Will I be a cat too?" he asked. "A familiar bound to you as you were to Emma?"

Edward grinned at him over his shoulder. "Do you want to be a cat?"

Mullins scratched his nose. "I'm rather fond of Beltane's dog," he confessed shyly. "I… I mean, I don't have to have a shape, it's just, you know, watching you all fall asleep in the minivan over these weeks… a dog or a cat would be—"

"Convenient," Edward told him archly. He sobered. "And damned helpful if we're to resume the family business."

Mullins felt something more than hope bubbling up in his chest. He felt purpose. "Freeing the enslaved?" Oh yes. "Yes, Edward—this is a thing I would love to assist with."

Edward smiled reassuringly. "Then we shall come up with a way. I'll tell Harry after breakfast." He finished plating up their food and served Mullins with a flourish. "Here. Breakfast. Most important meal of the day."

Bacon, scrambled eggs with cheese, toast, and fruit. Simple and perfect.

Mullins paused in front of it, inhaling.

"What?" Edward asked anxiously.

"Food. I… I'm hungry. I haven't eaten in 450 years."

Edward grinned again. "Suriel hadn't eaten *ever*. I swear, Harry learned the boomerang just so he could go to the market and get him fresh whatever, because he lights up like a little kid."

Mullins took a bite of the bacon and closed his eyes, shuddering. "Oh… poor Suriel," he mumbled through a mouthful of bacon. "Never? Because I remember this. Warm bread—" He took a bite of that and chewed blissfully. "Emma made this?" He'd seen modern breads. Most of them weren't really… substantial. This was homemade, simple, wheat flour, water, yeast.

"I made it," Edward told him, a delighted smile on his face. "Because I am Emma's son."

"You're wonderful at it," Mullins told him. "In my day, the baker could bake and the townspeople bought from him. Very few people had an oven that could make all of this."

"Where are you from, originally?" Edward asked, frowning. "You have an accent, but…."

"So do you." Mullins arched an eyebrow. "Actually, you six, talking mostly to yourselves for so much of your lives—it's taken you all an appallingly long time to *not* sound like British immigrants from 1860. Even Bel."

Edward's cheeks pinkened, and he took a bite of his own bacon. "Well, that's humbling, but you dodged the question."

Mullins chewed thoughtfully. "Somewhere in England?" he hazarded. "When you're a peasant in a small village, you don't really get schooled in where you are. You just sort of live your life, you know?"

"Could you read and write?" Edward asked, all curiosity.

"No," Mullins said promptly. "Not beyond my name. But Leonard saw my… my induction, as it were. He was… I think I shocked him out of his spiral. He grabbed me the moment I entered hell and put me to work as a scribe. He had to teach me then, how to read and write, how to reason. Having a friend there, having someone to give me purpose… that's why I never really lost my soul." He paused, his food suddenly less appetizing. "I hope. It's not like we have it in a jar or anything to check to make sure it still lives."

Edward's look was all compassion. "It's there," he said kindly. "Your soul. You're our friend, Mullins. You're my lover. Nobody who touched me like you touched me last night can be soulless."

Mullins nodded, still worried, but Edward cleared his throat.

"Eat," he commanded. "After breakfast, I need to review our spell and look over some maps. As soon as Harry's back online, we'll need to be ready."

Mullins gnawed on his bottom lip. "It's odd, isn't it?" he asked, before taking an ordered bite of eggs. "That Leonard noticed me—he said himself that he was a heartbeat away from giving up. That mentoring me, keeping me out of trouble, it's what gave him back his heart."

Edward twisted his mouth. "Honestly, it's no more odd than three boys being in the underbrush when Emma needed three familiars to survive. It's one of those random twists of fate—"

"That almost feel destined." Mullins could feel what he was hinting at, but he couldn't bring himself to say it. There seemed to be a blank place in his mind whenever he thought about it. He shook his head. The breakfast was lovely, and Edward was so full of plans. He'd been a young man before he went to hell, and he was feeling young again.

But Edward surprised him—as he often did. "If there was another hand—a kinder hand—in the things that happened to us, I certainly wouldn't turn down any help now," he said graciously. "Whoever tampered with the spell to get you here gave us last night. They gave us this breakfast and the things I plan to do to you afterward. They gave us many years of a friendship that sustained us. Perhaps not angelic—Suriel's people don't feel especially warm to me, although Suriel is a charming exception—but… but something important. I'm going to count my blessings and be grateful."

Mullins smiled shyly at him. "You have plans for me afterward?" he asked, taking a bite of perfectly crispy bacon.

Edward nodded and took his own bite. "I do indeed."

Oh. Mullins's brain—always the part he'd relied on to keep him safe in hell—took a long deep breath and kicked back to enjoy the show.

He was warm and comfortable, clean and fed, and his skin still tingled from lovemaking of the kind he had never thought to have again.

And Edward—his boy—the boy he'd guarded and avenged, the boy he'd taught and loved—was there, across from him, a wicked gleam in his bright green eyes.

"I'll enjoy that," Mullins said simply. He took his cue from Edward and shook some sriracha sauce on his eggs. A little spicy, but some milk to wash it down? Perfect.

"Good."

Mullins had seen many moods on Edward's face over the years, but this one, this playful smugness? He shivered deliciously. This could be his favorite.

Never Enough Touch

MULLINS OFFERED to clean up while Edward looked at maps to try to find the possible whereabouts of a fairy hill in the middle of the Sierra Nevadas. It wasn't going well. After the tenth try, Edward looked up from scrying over the most recent map he could find, to see a stunningly handsome young man washing dishes in the cabin kitchen, and had a heart-thumping moment of disconnect.

This is Mullins. I've loved him forever. He's mine.

Mullins bit his lip in thought, and Edward felt another terrible pressure on his chest.

He can't go back. He never should have been there in the first place.

Everything Edward had learned thus far, both of heaven and of hell, told him that a person's self-perception, their empathy, their forgiveness, all had a hand in determining where they should end up. Nothing about Mullins's story the night before told Edward he should have been in hell.

Mullins was right—something about his fall, his stay, his association with Leonard felt both random and destined. Right down to Mullins's rather crafty and dogged determination to not do anything he couldn't forgive himself for.

Nobody with that sort of integrity deserved to be in hell. Even the hell of his own making should have been forgiven and absolved when time and experience and maturity had shown him that what seemed to be an unforgivable sin had been a painful lesson, exacerbated to insanity by mob rule.

It all seemed so odd, and Edward's mind wandered to and glanced away from the most random part of the story.

He gritted his teeth and focused on that thought. Dammit, he was too old a wizard to allow his attention be… what? Deflected? Abruptly the thought came into focus.

"Mullins?" he asked, feeling out of sorts. "Did you ever figure out who the red man *was*?"

"He was blue at the end," Mullins said. "Wait… no… sunset orange."

Edward heard it then.

There was a blankness to Mullins's voice. A magic-induced blankness.

"That's not an answer, love," Edward said, keeping his voice gentle and firm. He needed Mullins to see it.

"He came to my sister's window," Mullins said.

"You told me that. Why?"

The blankness eased. "She was so sweet." There was a smile in his voice. "Everybody loved Ruthie." And now, sudden animation. "I wonder… we'll have to see what happened to her. I mean… I know it was the last thing on the list, but… but we'll get to find out what happened to her!" He turned toward Edward then, all thought of the red man or the blue man gone. "Do you think—when Harry's better, I mean—we can scry for my descendants? I mean… I had other sisters but…." His face fell. "For some reason, I just keep thinking…. Ruthie was supposed to survive. She was supposed to grow old and have children, and they were to have children, on down the generations. Four hundred years in hell—I have to think he kept his word and let Ruthie survive. Surely she must have lived, loved, had children. I would love to see my Ruthie's children." He turned his face away. "Sorry—you've all been so focused. It's not fair of me to—"

"I think we have to," Edward said, to make him smile. "It's part of the spell."

Mullins brightened. "Oh, it is! Good."

Edward stood and moved toward him, dismayed when Mullins turned his shoulders, warning him way. "But it's okay if you want it just for yourself."

"Only if it's necessary," Mullins said, still looking away.

A century and a half of falling in love and a month of playing boomerang around the planet, and Edward was going to let him get away with that?

Edward moved behind him, invading his space, wrapping his arms around Mullins's waist and digging his chin into his shoulder. He felt a restless twitching against his leg, and while part of him thought, "Aha, *there's* his tail," most of him was focused on the feeling of Mullins in his arms and the necessity of having him open up.

"There's no sin in the question," he murmured against Mullins's ear. "Harry looked up his sisters about seventy years after we came to live with Leonard and Emma." His voice dropped. "They both died in their twenties.

No children. He… he was hurt. I understand—the hope and the fear. But I think… I think that the interference in our hunt was sort of a good sign. So was your story. Your midnight lover promised your sister would be safe. He might even have come to save you from that demon."

"In which case I'm the dumbest fucking—"

"Shut up," Edward said gently. "You wouldn't let us destroy ourselves over our mistakes—you don't get that option either. You were young and scared and hurt—and in over your head, I might add. If a blue man appeared next to my window when I worked at the Golden Child and said, 'Hey, let me make this not suck for you,' I would have been all over that shit like a clean diaper. Don't be angry at yourself for wanting to enjoy something new and exciting. Fidelity is a luxury of maturity, experience, and self-knowledge, none of which you had a zillion years ago."

Mullins half glared at him. "You're so damned reasonable! You make it sound like it's all so normal."

Edward felt the flush of embarrassment wash over his cheeks. "I… I was not reasonable as we were searching," he admitted. "I… I drove Harry. I didn't say anything and he'll never blame me for it, but I… I worried about you, beloved. I was so afraid to hope for so long, and then… I was impatient, love. It's why I'm not champing at the bit now."

Mullins's mouth twisted wryly. "Is it the only reason?"

Edward kissed him, savoring his taste all over again, and then pulled back. "Finish the dishes," he said a little breathlessly. "I need to write something down—carve it into the table if I have to. Then…." He raised his eyebrows suggestively.

"Plans?" Mullins asked, a flush washing his pale cheekbones.

"I *will* see that tail," Edward vowed. "I have to. I'm walking funny after last night, and it's your turn."

Mullins turned away, completely mortified, so he could upend the washtub and clean out the sink.

And Edward went back to the table and wrote carefully on his legal tablet at the same time he wrote on the tablet in his mind:

Who is the red man and why is he trying to help us?

Mullins wiped down the counters and Edward went back to the map, scrying with a clear mind. In a few moments, a wash of triumph heated his skin, and Mullins's arms around his neck felt so much a part of that, he didn't even startle.

"You see that?" he asked, excited.

"I see I'm being extremely forward here," Mullins pouted, and Edward grinned and turned his head for a brief, hard kiss.

He pulled away and rubbed his lips against the back of Mullins's hand before pointing to the map.

"You see that?" he asked. "That spot right there?"

"Yes—you haven't marked it once."

Edward laughed, almost manically. "Nope. I've marked to the north, the south, the east, the west. Twelve times I cast a scrying spell, and twelve times the charm landed decisively—*decisively* I tell you—everywhere but this quarter-sized spot *right here*."

Edward glared at it, because ha! He had it now, dammit!

"It's...." Mullins moved a hand so he could trace the spot with a finger. "It's oddly blank, isn't it? This is a fairly detailed map, and something this size should show changes, a mountain, a gulley, a road, a driveway—something. But no—just the same graded green."

Edward snorted grimly. "I would imagine if I looked this up on the computer, I'd find the satellite just handily doesn't intersect any bit of this. Nothing to see here, folks—trees and brush right off the road, driving by a full-blown fairy hill with nothing to show for it."

Mullins leaned further, his chest heating Edward's back, his cheek rubbing against Edward's ear. "That is some serious power," he said in awe. "For one thing, that's nearly twenty thousand acres, if the proportions are right. For another, that's not just us. That's...."

"Everybody," Edward breathed, nodding. "That power keeps everybody out."

They were quiet for a moment.

"Your mother trusted him," Mullins said, as though he was trying to keep his fears at bay.

"Of course." Edward rubbed his cheek against Mullins's barely stubbled jaw. Shaving. He would have to learn. "I'm not thinking that this is a fearsome thing. I'm wondering what our thirty or so acres here in Mendocino would look like if someone were trying to scry for *us*."

Mullins let out a little chuff of air into his ear, and all Edward's skin began to tingle.

"You're thinking it's protection."

"Absolutely. Think about it, Mullins—an elven king, and more than that. Vampires? Werewolves? Brownies? In 1850 he was willing to go to town and risk exposure to try to keep his land and people safe. If he's gotten more powerful—and more people—what do you think he'll try to do now?"

"Mm...." Mullins let out a strained chuckle, and his hands moved to Edward's chest, where he started kneading. Edward's brain—so clearly focused until now—became a pleasant blank. "I'll be honest, beloved. I want to puzzle this out like you do, but at the moment, I've developed more pressing concerns."

Edward stood and stepped around the chair, then caught Mullins's chin between his fingers. "Seems we have the same interests," he murmured, a sweet shiver coursing down his spine. Mullins closed his eyes and raised his face for the kiss, impressing Edward with that implicit trust he'd shown all along.

Edward and his brothers *would* finish what they'd started. They *would* break off all ties to hell, leaving Mullins free and clear and safe in the Youngblood family circle.

But now, this moment right here, was not the moment for great quests.

It was the time to take his lover to their bed and make him truly, irrevocably Edward's.

Edward kept kissing, backing Mullins up to the bed, still rumpled from the night before. He grabbed the hem of Mullins's shirts, dragging them up over his head and steadying him as he went over backward before yanking at his own sweatshirt, his jeans, his boxers, letting them puddle on the floor in his urgency.

His fingers trembled as he fumbled with the faded pair of Francis's jeans Mullins had put on when he dressed. "These look very good on you," he said, finally freeing the button-fly. "You look better with them off." With a yank he added the jeans to the puddle on the floor and stretched out, pressing his lips to Mullins's soft, bare neck.

Mullins shuddered in the open air, pulling Edward closer to him, like Edward would cover his nakedness. "We just did this," he murmured, tilting his head back, giving Edward access.

"Not enough." Edward took a pink nipple into his mouth and sucked hard, waiting for Mullins to writhe and moan.

He was not disappointed.

Mullins's body had learned from their adventures the night before. He moved a little slower now, like he had just enough space between thought and sensation to fit some self-control.

Good.

Because Edward wanted to take his time.

He took Mullins's cock into his mouth—but he didn't suck hard, didn't squeeze. Just laved, putting enough pressure to keep things interesting, but not enough to amp up the excitement, to raise the stakes.

He tortured.

Mullins's quivering body started to jerk—his arm, his hand, his foot—as he pressed against the bed, trying not to take over.

"You want something?" Edward taunted, his own erection pushing against the bed. "Anything in particular?"

Mullins gasped, inarticulate, and Edward kept laving. He dribbled enough spit between Mullins's thighs to run his fingers through it.

Very carefully, he traced a path between Mullins's cheeks.

"Edward!" Mullins protested, just as Edward breached him. "Ah! Oh sweet hells!"

He bucked up, then down, the momentum of his hips driving Edward's finger in farther.

Edward lifted his head and wiggled his finger. "Now, Mullins," he panted, trying to keep his voice even, "you need to be clear. Was that 'Sweet hells, yes!' or 'Sweet hells, no!'"

He pushed in a little more. "*Yes!*" Mullins cried, and Edward rewarded him with another finger.

He could feel Mullins's tail thrashing under his knuckles, but he ignored it.

What was important was that Mullins let Edward love every bit of him—the flaws, the moments of weakness, the tail, and all.

Mullins moaned, and Edward licked his cockhead with lazy intent.

"Was there something you wanted?" he asked. Two fingers, moving back and forth. But not stretching. Not really fucking. Just… tormenting.

"Augh! Edward! Please!"

Edward pulled back—but kept his fingers where they were. Mullins was naked, thighs spread in the pale daylight of the room. One wicked hand had moved to his pink nipple, where he plucked and pinched while Edward ministered to him with clever fingers and willing mouth.

The other hand was knotted in the sheets, pulling rhythmically as Edward moved inside him.

"Please what?" he taunted.

Mullins opened blue eyes and snapped hotly, "Fuck me, Edward. God, I need!"

Edward grinned with satisfaction and squeezed Mullins's cock slowly, base to tip, while Mullins thrashed below him.

"Edward!" he wailed.

"Of course, beloved," Edward said mildly. He let go of Mullins's erection, reached for the slick on the dresser, and prepared himself cursorily.

Then, with a little more care, he drizzled some on his fingers and penetrated Mullins again, stretching with purpose.

"Nnn…." Mullins went absolutely still. "I'm going to come," he panted.

"Not. Yet."

Edward pulled his fingers and moved into position between Mullins's spread thighs. "Look at me, beloved," he rasped.

Mullins's eyes flew open again, and Edward pushed against his entrance. "Edward?" Uncertain and aroused, he tugged at Edward's heart.

"I'm here," Edward said gently. "I see you. I see all of you." His pale skin was blotched with arousal, and he needed activity and food to shore up his muscles, give his wiry, muscled body substance and weight.

But he was beautiful, wanton, generous in bed, and Edward loved him, tail and all.

Mullins nodded, eyes fluttering shut. "Please," he whispered, and Edward pushed gently in.

Ah! Hot! The furnace of his body almost undid him. But Mullins pulled on his thighs and let out a terrible, wonderful keening sound, a begging sound, the kind of inarticulation that begged for more.

"Good?" Edward asked.

"Harder," Mullins begged.

"Yes!"

Like a horse let loose on the track, Edward plunged forward, harder, faster, thrusting in to the hilt. Mullins cried out deliciously, needing every inch, every thrust, clenching and rippling around Edward's hard flesh.

"Ahh! Please! Everything!"

Edward couldn't have held back if he'd wanted to. Again and again, his movements became frenzied, almost violent as Mullins bucked beneath him begging for more.

Edward slammed forward, stopping deeply embedded in Mullins's body, and took the hand knotted in the bedding very carefully. "Stroke yourself, beloved," he urged. "Don't hold on to the bed or you'll never fly."

Another one of those glorious sounds and Edward watched as Mullins stroked his own cock hard and slow.

Edward pulled back, back, back… then slammed forward hard, and Mullins broke loose, his hand a blur, spend spurting from his tip.

"Now!" Mullins begged, and Edward lost himself in the frenzy of the fuck, back and forth, sweat running into his eyes as he performed the sweetest labor of all.

Mullins's cry of completion was nearly a scream, and his clench and ripple around Edward's cock aroused Edward to the point of pain.

Edward cried out, orgasm blinding him, all sense leaving his limbs. He poured come into Mullins's spasming heat, rewarded by the hot jet of semen that coated both their chests.

Edward fell forward, burying his face in Mullins's neck and letting out a happy, laughing moan.

"Gah! Beloved! That was glorious. It almost killed me, but it was glorious."

Mullins half laughed into his ear. "We're both dead," he panted. "Dear hell, that was intense." Their breathing grew calmer, and Mullins nuzzled his ear. "You didn't see the tail," he murmured.

"Feeling it was the point," Edward told him, pulling out and rolling to the side. "I know it's there, Mullins. I'm not frightened yet."

Mullins's eyebrows attempted to knit themselves, reminding Edward of when they'd twitched as a beast's. Edward laughed and smoothed them back, blushing with the intensity of Mullins's blue eyes.

"I've killed for you, you know," Mullins said baldly, as though trying to gauge a reaction.

"You're expecting me to be surprised?" Edward had looked up the massacre at the Golden Child after Mullins had let slip that everyone involved was dead. Blamed on a madman with a fistful of knives, the carnage had been horrific.

But not a working girl had been touched.

Other crimes, other deaths—traffickers who had gotten away from the Youngbloods and had simply disappeared. Once they had busted a ring belonging to a fairly large crime family in Kansas City. The girls had been freed, and Harry, Francis, and Edward had been in hiding while Edward and Harry tried to hack into the ringleader's computers and find some way to bring the whole lot of them up on charges.

An unknown enemy had burst into the boss's favorite restaurant and taken out every made man, St. Valentine's Day style.

Not an innocent person was touched.

Harry had read the reports and arched eyebrows at Edward, who had shrugged. "He doesn't like it when we're threatened," he said in explanation.

"Given the lack of collateral damage, we'll call it good," Harry replied, and they'd gone back home.

Now, Edward looked into Mullins's wide eyes and tried to reconcile that knowledge with what he saw within.

"You were protecting us," he said softly, and Mullins bit his lower lip and looked away.

"My boys," he said after a moment. Then he smiled slightly, meeting Edward's eyes again. "My *boy*. If I'd interceded for good, I would have been taken from you. But vengeance—vengeance is a top-tier sin. Nobody minded if I went in and protected you under the guise of vengeance."

Edward felt a wicked smile coming on. "That's very devious, Mullins."

Mullins's answering smile was freer, bolder—and just as wicked as Edward's. "Well, I *am* a demon, you know…."

Edward leaned over and took his mouth—wide and smiling and unpinched by the worry that seemed to so consume Mullins as a beast. "I never would have known," he said softly, and then the kiss deepened.

And they made love again.

This time Edward got to stroke his tail.

THE NEXT morning, Leonard showed up at their door in the ancient pickup truck that he kept running with a combination of mechanics, science, and magic.

Not even Leonard could say how much of which.

Edward had packed a couple of changes of clothes for them both, and Leonard told them cheerfully that his brothers were packing another new minivan with Edward's beloved case and plenty of snacks.

"Beltane went out this morning and came back with several boxes of doughnuts. You should probably eat one just so he can pretend they aren't all for him."

Edward squeezed his eyes shut and shook his head. "The amount of sugar that boy can put away boggles the mind!"

"Sugar? I swear, thirty-six ounces of meat last night. Emma said she felt like she'd broiled an entire cow."

Mullins chuckled, as he was meant to. "Francis doesn't eat like that?" he asked curiously.

"No," Edward replied in disgust. "Francis only eats fish. From the very beginning—even when we were in the Golden Child. Fish and vegetables. And eggs and milk, but mostly fish. It's like he really is a cat."

Leonard and Mullins made twin grunts of a noncommittal nature, and Edward cocked his head. "That was… disturbing," he said in revelation. "You both make the same sounds when you're avoiding talking about something. Did you get that from hell?"

"Revealing too much about your emotions isn't prudent in hell," Leonard said mildly. Then he took a fortifying breath. "You just made another piece of Francis fall into place. Elves are mostly vegetarians, you know."

Edward's eyebrows went up, and he felt a moment of sadness for his littler brother.

Leonard patted his arm in sympathy. "No worries. I suspect your meeting with the elves might be very productive in more than one way." Leonard paused in the act of swinging into the pickup truck. "You *do* know where to find the elves, don't you?"

Edward nodded smugly. "Damned straight I do."

He and Mullins piled in, Mullins on the outside, head practically hanging out the window.

"I really do need to see about how to let him shapeshift into a dog," Edward said, realizing he hadn't even looked up how that would be done.

Leonard cocked his head. "It's not a conscious thing," he said surprisingly. "I think it's… compensation. The Goddess's get can be bitten. With witches and wizards, I think it's more of a… a predilection, if you will."

"Good," Edward said, liking the idea. "We already have four cats. Two dogs will make us much better balanced."

Leonard let out a chuckle, but it sounded strained.

"What?" Edward demanded.

"You and Beltane should drive there," Leonard told him. "Harry needs to sleep."

"Is there something wrong?"

Leonard shook his head but then sighed, indicating the "no" was a lie. "We *think* it's just fatigue and healing. He was shot and then dragged through several dimensions. And while Suriel healed him—"

"Francis healed him," Edward said, remembering that had been yet another surprise.

Leonard grunted. "Of course. Of course, that explains it. Francis doesn't know what in the hell he's doing. He's never even had a cold."

"Harry and I have had plenty," Edward grunted resentfully.

"Yes, I know. Very human. Being familiars didn't spare you both until your human immune systems built up, just like Emma's. But Francis never suffered what you did—"

"But he did get sick!" Edward remembered. "Remember—right when we were expanding the house! For about a year he was thin and pale and constantly threatening to puke. You and Emma were at your wit's end."

"I remember," Leonard said softly. "He got better right after we wallpapered your room. Emma was so excited—she liked the colors and, oh my God!" He shook his head. "Edward, you don't use guns."

"I know," Edward said, as though speaking to a child. "We have magic."

"I mean Francis has never held a gun. Did he touch the bullet in Harry's shoulder?"

"No," Mullins said, like he knew where this was going. "He just pushed it out with his healing."

"Elves don't do lead," Leonard said simply. "They don't do guns. It makes them sick. He's not all elvish—he's at least half human. It's probably the only reason he can get in a car. But we painted the house—back then, paint had a considerable bit of lead in it. So he doesn't understand immune systems. When we heal you boys from bullets, and Suriel as well, I'm sure, we take into account the possibility of infection. Harry's shoulder was healed of trauma, but his immune system wasn't." Leonard shook his head. "Hold on while I talk to your mother."

Leonard's attention turned inward, and Edward and Mullins exchanged glances.

"Harry *is* coming with us, right?" Edward said worriedly, after Leonard's eyes focused on the dirt road again.

"He was coming anyway," Leonard replied. "But this way, Emma knows what to send with him so he doesn't overdo it."

"He'll be all right," Mullins said softly, and Edward turned to smile at him. It was such a kind thing to say.

"I'm pretty sure your soul is fine," he replied, hiding his own worry. Dammit, Harry!

HARRY WAS getting last-minute instructions from Emma as they drove up to park next to a gleaming white Toyota Sienna. Edward made an unhappy sound.

"White? Really? It's so boring. Remember when cars came in colors?"

Leonard rolled his eyes. "Remember when cars were pulled by horses and this trip would take you boys three weeks instead of two days? Because I do. How do you like our new minivan, son?"

"It's glorious, Dad," Edward said dryly. Mullins smirked as he got out of the car, and both of them walked to where Suriel stood, looking anxious.

"Every four hours," Emma warned, waving a small thermos. "Every. Four. Hours. Do not skip. Do not tell Suriel it tastes bad. If you're feeling queasy, tell Edward to pull over. If you start feeling feverish, Suriel—"

"I have it right here." Suriel held up a bag with home-made tablets that Edward remembered from childhood. He also held up a bottle of over the counter ibuprofen, because sometimes science could be fun!

"Good. Now this trip should only take eight hours. That's one dose in three hours, one dose an hour before you get there, one dose three hours after you arrive—"

"I can tell time, Emma—"

"Shut up, Harry. I don't care if you're all in the middle of an elvish orgy, what are you going to do when the alarm on your phone goes off?"

Edward saw Harry's body jerk as the obvious adolescent answer almost popped out of his mouth. He took a deep breath, though, and was respectful to his mother. "I shall get up, buck naked, go to the car, and get my medicine," he responded dutifully.

Emma shook her head in irritation. "I. Am. Not. Shitting. Around. You were some place the earth was blue and the sky was red—"

"And the air smelled like barbecue chips and lilies," Edward supplied.

Emma grimaced. "See? And you all get here, and nobody bothers to even tell me you were shot and then dragged to an alternate dimension. Just, 'Oh, Harry's tired from spellcasting and blood loss,' and no shit Harry's tired from spellcasting, that boomerang is not an easy thing, and you were *sick*, and you'd lost blood, and I'm so angry at you for getting in that car right now I can't even speak!"

"As if," Leonard muttered under his breath, but Harry was up to defending himself too.

"Elves, Emma," he said wistfully. "You may be over them, but we're not. Please?"

"Fine," she muttered, kissing him fiercely on the brow. She pulled away and looked at Suriel. "Go get water and give him the febrifuge and ibuprofen now. He'll sleep the whole way there."

Suriel nodded unhappily. "Harry—"

"Elves," Harry repeated stubbornly. "Also"—and he looked almost melancholy—"I really would like to know how the brownies are doing. I mean, we're only guessing they ended up at Green's."

Edward watched as both Suriel and Emma slumped forward in the classic posture of defeat. "Aw, Harry," Emma said softly, kissing him again, but this time with tenderness. "Take the medicine, get some sleep. You'll see elves when they get there, I promise."

Suriel loaded Harry into the back of the minivan and came out to load backpacks and suitcases—and Emma's small cooler of food and whatever was in the bottle that she'd insisted he drink.

"You boys are going to find a place to stay, right?" she nagged, and Edward nodded once, because Harry was out of commission and it was his job now.

"Yes. Don't worry."

"Oh! Wait!" Emma reached into her pocket and pulled out an envelope that she handed to Edward. "It's a letter, and three strands of my own hair in trade—"

"Mine or Mullins's would probably be more appropriate," Edward said, "but I'll tell him." He kissed Emma on the cheek. "We'll take good care of Harry—"

"And Francis and Beltane," she said, looking worried.

Edward shook his head. "Emma, we've done far more dangerous things than—"

Emma shook her head. "No. You don't understand. Elves are perilous, Edward. Elves are always perilous. And this is no ordinary elven king. This is Green—a hundred and seventy years ago, he had thirty people to protect. I made some enquiries last night—remember that bloodbath in Redding two years ago?"

Edward nodded. He'd mentioned it to Mullins.

"That was Green's people—and they weren't killing for sport. They were hunting a rogue vampire—one who turned children."

They all shuddered as the implications hit them.

Emma nodded. "See? Apparently Green turned his best fighters loose on the little vampire kiss in Redding, and only the pure of heart walked away. This is serious. Take this seriously. This isn't a poor drunken fraternity of brownies in your room. These are elves, and vampires, and for all I know every shapeshifter under the sun, and they work on different rules than we do, and I don't know how to prepare you."

Edward nodded soberly and then grinned. "But then, we're witch's familiars. We might be new to them too. And an angel. And a demon. It will be a triumph in interspecies communication."

Emma cocked her head and widened her eyes. "So reasonable," she muttered. "And so deluded. I love you, Edward. Take care of your brothers. And for fuck's sake, drive safely—if we wreck this one I'm going to have to assume another alias to buy another car." She looked up suddenly. "Beltane, Francis, come here and hug me. My God, you boys, have you forgotten everything?"

"Sorry, Mum," Bel said, lifting his mother up in a rib-cracking hug. Francis waited until he was done, pretending it didn't matter, but when Emma turned toward him, he launched into her arms, rubbed his cheek against hers, and bussed her on the forehead.

"Yes, Francis, I still love you," she said softly. "Keep your brothers safe. And Beltane too."

Francis twitched a little when she said it, but neither he nor Beltane responded. Emma rolled her eyes—and then hugged him even tighter. "Love you," she said resignedly, and he smiled as she let him go.

And finally they were loaded into the minivan, Edward at the wheel. As he pulled onto the road and onto Hwy 1 he felt the tingle of the wards on his parents' property and then a sudden oppression, hitting his chest hard enough to stop his breath. In the air around the minivan, spots danced, thin places in the membrane between the hell dimension and the earth dimension, showing only the shadow of the grotesque denizens searching the air frantically for them.

"Wards, everybody!" Harry shouted hoarsely. "Protective magic up! Jesus, can you feel that?"

Everybody's personal wards against demons went up so fast the minivan probably glowed from outside.

Edward kept the van going and felt their shields for gaps because the demonic presence pounded at him, searching, searching, searching for their missing number.

"Mullins, Harry—pull out."

Harry smirked from the back, and Edward felt a flare of anger. "We are *not* twelve. You are weak, and not only will the shield drain you, they can feel your weakness, so just drop out of the spell. Mullins, if they think it's you, we're toast."

Their power wavered and then stabilized, and probably thanks to both the van's movement and the strength of the four people pouring power into the wards, the air around them brightened, became strong again as the dimensional wall was shored up.

Next to him, Mullins let out a strained breath. "That was bad," he rasped. "So bad. Do they know where we are?"

"Nope," Edward said with grim satisfaction. "They know where we *were*. And they probably knew that anyway. They couldn't penetrate the wards of our property, so they were lying in wait."

Beltane's booming laugh was a comfort. "Well they weren't ready for our shit, that's for certain. Damn, that was a strong shield. You know, when my class in Oxford tries to do a co-op like that, we usually can't keep a puddle at bay—that was really amazing."

"Good," Francis said shortly. "Maybe Emma will stop trying to send you away."

Bel's laugh went evil. "So, can we have this discussion now? You can't keep up the force field and go cat on us, and you can't block my voice like you can my telepathy. I'm going to repeat this: I don't want to go.

Maybe if we act grown-up and talk to my parents about why we don't want me to leave, they won't keep putting their foot down."

Francis let out a yowl of exasperation—but he stayed human, which was great, because Edward could feel the force field around them, and while it was strong—damned near impenetrable—now, he wasn't sure what losing one more person would do for it.

"Bel!" Francis hissed. "We don't want to talk about this now—"

"Oh yes I by God do," Beltane said grimly, and Edward had a chance to reevaluate all those moments of thinking about him as his little brother. He was an adult now, of what? Twenty-two winters? He would live immortally, as Emma would have if she hadn't given her power up—first for Leonard and her three familiars, and then in order to live as a mortal to have Bel—but that didn't make him any less able to know his own mind now. "Is there anyone in this car who does *not* know that Francis and I are lovers?"

"No," Harry responded behind them. "And there's nobody back home who doesn't know either."

Francis's mewl of unhappiness was very catlike—but his control over his human form and the shield that kept them safe never wavered. "That's not fair!" he wailed. "You're not supposed to—"

"What?" Edward demanded. "Know? Because you both made it damned hard to miss. Say anything? Well, we haven't, but apparently living in the shadows isn't good enough for Beltane, and it shouldn't be good enough for you."

"Jesus, Francis," Harry said, his voice rasping as he coughed. "The whole family celebrated Suriel's return. We're welcoming Mullins with open arms. Don't you think we'd want to celebrate you two as well?"

"But I like home," Francis said softly, and Edward's chest ached.

"So do I," Bel told him, voice assuming a patience Edward was damned proud of. "I wouldn't make you leave. There's enough room in the house for us as brothers if we can't be lovers. Don't you have some faith in me?"

"You're not the one who can't be human," Francis said shortly. "And I'm done. I can't. I can't have this conversation anymore."

Bel let out a sigh of frustration, and then, to the car in general, said, "If you're not human, then human isn't what I want. I've met other warlocks, Francis. I've met other witches too, for that matter—that's why Mum wanted to send me to Oxford. But I haven't met another Francis. I haven't

163

met anyone who does the things to my heart that you do. Don't tell me that's a bad thing because I won't believe it."

The silence in the car was electric.

Finally Francis let out a breath. "Fine. Whatever. They know anyway."

Edward could practically feel everybody's patient eye roll, but it was Mullins who spoke up.

"Francis, you may not be Bel's brother anymore, but you are definitely Emma and Leonard's son. Remember, nobody in this car is strictly human. That doesn't seem to be a sticking point with them."

"That's kind, Mullins," Francis said, and even Edward could hear his voice soften. But when he spoke next, he was obviously done for the moment. "This is a thing in my heart. There are many things there—it's a confusing place. Someday, maybe I'll tell you all of them. But for right now, I just... just want Bel. He's my one clear thing. Can I have Bel and not talk for now?" He sounded near tears. "Harry's sick. I got used to him not being close to death. And there's bad things after Mullins. And he's not a beast anymore. I liked the beast, Mullins. He comforted me. The world is changing; can I not keep my one clear thing?"

Bel's sigh filled the car. "Okay, beloved," he said gently. In the back there was shifting, and when Edward checked the rearview, he saw Bel and Francis in their customary pose—Beltane with Francis in his arms, drawn back against his broad chest. "But please sort out your words in the next ten to fifteen years. Forever is a very long time in this family, and I'd rather spend it happy than waiting."

So grown up. In his head he felt the gentle mental nudge of Mullins, who had spoken to him like this sometimes as a demon, but never as a man.

What are you thinking?

Beltane is an adult. We watched him be born—Harry, Leonard, and I acting as midwives. We watched him take his first steps. These last months, we've been thinking, 'What will we do about Beltane and Francis,' but the fact is, they're grown. Thinking about Francis as the one to protect is many long years of habit—but his heart has obviously been protecting itself just as long. I'm thinking their road together is probably more fraught and more difficult than we ever imagined, but that it is—of all of us—most singularly their road. I needed help to claim my beloved, and my brothers all jumped in a minivan and chased me around the world. But Francis needs help claiming his beloved, and first he must claim himself, and there's nothing any of us can do about that.

Mullins's very warm hand on his knee surprised him, and he had to remember to keep his eyes on the road.

But that didn't stop him from taking one hand off the wheel for a moment so he could briefly lace fingers with Mullins, who apparently had known all of that in Edward's mind, but had wanted to hear him say it anyway.

California's topography changed drastically between Mendocino and Foresthill. From rich green forests with giant redwoods to sparse hills filled with oak and scrub. From the oak and scrub to the flat farmlands, and from the farmlands to the Sacramento valley—more farmland, but with the delta and the river to give some hope and some greenery to the scene. And then up again, to the foothills of the Sierra Nevadas, to red dirt and pine, dusty in the summer, and now, in the spring, rich and ripe and cool with promise. There were lakes here, and the memory of snow.

Mullins looked about eagerly, remarking upon each change, upon the temperature outside when they stopped for gas or to use the bathroom. He would remember places—Sacramento in the 1800s, for example—but he'd been released from hell spottily, and his journeys had always been missions.

Watching him enjoy himself, take time to see where he was and how it connected to where he had been, marked quite a change from the young man who hadn't even known where he'd lived during his earlier mortal life.

Edward's heart filled with quiet delight each time he remarked on the changes of the age, the people, the landscape.

And it filled with purpose every time he felt a charge against the shields that kept them all safe, as long as they stayed close together when they were stopped.

Harry slept for much of the journey, but when Suriel woke him for medicine, Edward noted that he gave the febrifuges again too.

At their second stop—this one for food too, since Bel and Francis were both starving—Edward helped Suriel out of the back since his long legs were cramping, and looked in on his brother, still asleep.

"How's he do—"

"Worse," Suriel said shortly. "He's responding to the medicines but…." Suriel shook his head. "Like Leonard said—infection. This one seems particularly stubborn—and I think he's right about it being supernaturally driven too. You boys have successfully warded off a variety of diseases—starting with the ones I healed you of the night Emma found you. Every little cold you got, every sniffle, was driven away by the magic in your bodies giving your immune system a tremendous boost. This isn't earthbound, and it's not like the other viruses that have evolved, and your systems along with it. I'm pouring what I can into him but…." He bit his lip, uncharacteristically uncertain.

"You're helping to shore up the wards in the car," Edward realized. "Well, maybe we can have Mullins do that so you can heal Harry—"

But Suriel was shaking his head. "No. Because if we sustain an attack right now, he'll be helpless."

Edward swallowed. "Dammit. He had to see the elves—"

"He had to be here for you." Suriel's usually serene face sharpened. "Please tell me you understand that, Edward."

Edward swallowed, remembering that meeting in the Market, when he both cursed his brothers for interfering and blessed them, because damn if he didn't love them.

"I do," he said softly. "Let's get to Foresthill and see if maybe Green can help. Emma seemed to place a lot of faith in him."

Suriel nodded. "He's strong, your brother. We can hope."

Of course Suriel had always been made of hope, but Edward and Harry, they'd needed help.

After they'd gotten gas—and sandwiches, of course, for Beltane and Francis—and they were on the road again, Mullins turned down the roar of 90s grunge rock—Harry's favorite musical time period to date—and asked him softly, "How's he doing?"

"Not well," Edward told him, gnawing on his lip. He didn't want to tell Mullins about the hope that Emma's Elven King could heal him. They were going to ask him for three hairs—it seemed invasive enough without adding, "Oh yes, and help our brother out too because getting this far was rough going."

"You know this isn't our last stop, don't you?" Mullins asked him anxiously. "Maybe we should have Emma pull Harry back and we can go looking for my sister's descendants instead."

Edward shook his head. "Have a scrying spell all ready," he said. "I put it together before we even started the quest. We need to talk to Green and get Harry better, and then we'll be good to go."

"Edward," Mullins said, his voice sharp and sober. "Look—if it's a choice between Harry's health and me spending more time in hell—"

"Who makes that choice!" Edward muttered, stomach sinking. "Why would you even say that?"

"Because the world's an unfair place, and when you dabble with angels and demons that kind of thing shows up," Mullins retorted. "And look, I have hope now. I can go through another four centuries if I know I have you at the end. Don't sacrifice your brother because you think this is your only chance. *That's* all I wanted to say."

Edward shook his head. "I refuse to believe we have to do this again," he growled. "I *would*. I'd do it a thousand times over. I just…." Even over the music, even over the engine noise, he heard the tenor of his brother's breathing change, grow a little bit worse. "I'd just rather not visit corn chip and lily land again," he muttered. "I just…." His heart constricted. "I love you more now than ever, Mullins. How am I going to say goodbye one more time?"

The heat of Mullins's hand on his knee shored him up. "By knowing it's not the last time. Knowing it never will be. I will always come when summoned, Edward. Always."

Edward remembered that discussion—how summoning a demon when he was being detained in the depths of hell could be the cruelest torment of them all.

"I don't want to hurt—"

Mullins shook his head, his voice trembling. "Remember how well that worked for Suriel and Harry?"

Because it hadn't. Harry had refused to call Suriel, knowing what it cost him—and Suriel had fallen in love anyway.

Edward swallowed, his throat tight. An hour—they had an hour up Highway 80 and then half an hour on Foresthill Road. Surely God, the fates, Goddess, or even the mysterious other could not gang up on them for an hour and a half, right?

He felt a hit to the wards outside the minivan and fought it off, then faced what Mullins had just said.

"We will never give up," he said, meaning it. "Even if we're sent reeling all the way back, at least we know the way."

"Exactly," Mullins said, sounding strong. "They can keep my body in hell as long as they need to. We both know my heart is free and sound in your hands, Edward. That alone will sustain us."

Edward nodded and laced his fingers briefly with Mullins's.

Then he put both hands on the wheel and stepped on the gas. They were so damned close to help.

ONCE THEY took the turn into Highway 49 and drove over the double bridge spanning the canyon, the entire minivan took a breath.

"Oh my God," Beltane said on an exhale of relief. "Can you feel that?"

"It's like… not wards, exactly," Suriel said in wonder. "But like the wards we're near are so damned strong they sort of scrubbed anything in the area."

"I can feel them," Francis said dreamily. "Can you all see it? That mountain over there—it's glowing."

Edward kept his eyes on the road—but he eyeballed the mountain Francis was talking about. "I see a faint shimmer," he admitted. "But not a glow—"

"It's practically blinding!" Francis objected, then let out a breath. "But at least you can see it," he said, almost disconsolately.

Beltane shifted his knees into Edward's seat for the umpteenth time, which probably meant he was pulling Francis closer. "I love that you see things differently," he murmured. "It gives us all better vision."

Oh, bless the boy for being Emma and Leonard's son. Until the two of them had their confrontation that morning, Edward had no idea that part of the peril of elves would come from within.

A FEW miles past the bridge, before the start of the town proper, Edward saw a small service road winding between two hills and turned left onto it. The road was graveled but not paved, and as Edward drove, he had to fight an almost uncontrollable urge to turn around.

"No!" he said after a moment. "I'm not turning around because you are as plain as day, and dammit, we can see you! Please! We don't mean any harm, we're just asking a favor!"

As if in answer, a large wooden gate appeared, as though a veil had been torn off of it, and Edward had to screech to a halt, leaving just enough space for it to swing open.

The gate had a spring latch and looked as though it swung both in and out, and Edward looked at Mullins—and then at Francis through the rearview.

"Francis? Given that you're seeing a glow when we're seeing heat distortion, maybe it's less dangerous for you to get out, you think?"

Francis pulled out of Bel's embrace, almost eager. "So, like I can help?" he asked, excited.

"You're always a help," Harry wheezed from the back. "This time, you have very special qualifications." He hauled in a deep breath then and coughed, and Francis turned toward the back seat.

"You sound like Suriel," he said almost gently. "We need to fix you so you sound more like Harry."

And with that he opened the door and trotted to the gate, swung it toward Edward, and then ran to secure it and gesture them in.

"I'll close it behind you," he called as Edward rolled down the window. "Don't worry—I'll come find you after you park."

A balm rolled in through the window—that's the only way Edward could describe it. Soothing, fresh—a spring smell. Sun on rocks, cinnamon and roses, mustard flowers, pine trees and solid red earth. All of it combined headily, and Mullins and Beltane struggled to roll down their windows to flood the car with the freshness of hope.

From the back, Harry took one of his first decent breaths for the last hour.

"Oh wow," he mumbled. "That's amazing."

The driveway was lined for the first quarter of a mile—a sort of ground cover, rich and pale green with pink or yellow flowers, seemed to spring up between pine trees on one side and oak on the other.

"That is so wrong," Beltane said flatly.

"What? I think it's pretty!" Suriel responded.

"Yes, but it's not natural!" Mullins shook his head. "I scribed a lot of botany over the years—that is Scotch Heather, and it usually grows in the sandy soil of the coast, where it's temperate. It gets mighty hot here—"

"But it's not," Edward pondered. "It was getting to be around eighty degrees after we cleared Redding. It's much cooler here."

Bel let out a low whistle. "Temperature control—I like it! That's nth level shit right there." He looked behind them. "Francis has turned. Can I go out and run with him?" He let out a wistful sigh. "Please, Edward? It's been hard on us both. We don't talk well with words."

Edward slowed enough for Beltane to get out, and in his rearview mirror he watched the big blond dog run to touch noses with the small Siamese cat.

"They're going to need to find words eventually," he muttered, but they all knew he was as helpless as the rest of them.

Instead, they looked forward, to the end of the path, and Edward missed Bel's low whistle.

"Look at that," he said softly, and behind him, Harry struggled to sit up.

"That house is built into the top of the hill," Harry said in wonder. It appeared as though a window wrapped around half the mountain—probably the main living level—and most of the rest of the hill sloped up to a smooth dome.

"Those trees up there are… unusual," Mullins said. And then, "But damn. Look at the gardens."

As the minivan rounded the last bend, they saw the driveway passed directly in front of the house to a garage that seemed to be the ground floor of the house—completely under the hill. A smaller house sat across the driveway—fairly large, in fact, a red-painted farmhouse complete with white trim—but dwarfed in comparison to the greatness of the house inside the hill. Beyond the driveway sat what should have been the front yard, if a front yard was bigger than a football field and boasted its own pond, complete with a small orchard and a great stretch of grass surrounded by patches of flowers planted in orderly chaos around the lawn.

"That's stunning," Suriel said in awe. "Just… oh my word. Harry. That's beautiful. I have no words."

"Look," Harry murmured, weak but happy. "Elves."

Elves having a picnic, from the looks of it.

Under the shade of several of the trees in the orchard, by the pond, someone had laid a large quilt for people to sit on. As Edward parked the car near the entrance to the underground garage he counted three men, two gigantic wolfish dogs, two young women, and two children.

Infants, actually, complete with car carriers set beside the blanket.

One of the young women was nursing, talking to her companions freely, and as Mullins and his brothers disembarked and waited for Bel and Francis, Edward frowned.

"Does that look… doesn't that look…." The people were arranged in a loose circle, and the young mother was the focus.

The much taller men on either side of her were part of it, but *she* was the one the others were deferring to.

Even the big wolflike dogs.

"She's their queen," Mullins said with no hesitation whatsoever. "And the men on either side of her—"

"Are elves," Harry said happily. "Look, Suriel. We're going to meet elves."

One of them had butter-yellow hair, so long even the braid pooled next to his thigh as he sat. The other had dark hair just long enough for the sides to be pulled up into a partial queue. The dark-haired one was holding the other infant, smiling at it with complete attention, and Edward had another moment of trying to make sense of the scene.

The woman nursing the infant looked up at them then, and from this distance it was hard to gauge her expression, but after a few words to the man with the butter-colored hair, he turned and beckoned them all to the intimate little picnic.

They completely disembarked—Suriel carrying Harry more than supporting him—and Beltane and Francis trotted at their heels as they approached.

When they drew near, Edward saw that the woman nursing the infant was not small just because she was sitting—she was small period. And she wasn't just sitting on a pillow—she was sitting on a clever cushion, meant to shore up her back and give her arms support as she nursed. She smiled up at their group as they approached and then frowned as one of the dogs leaped up and trotted over to rub noses with Bel.

And turned abruptly into a naked, glowering human with dark-blond hair, green eyes, a tattoo on his wrist, and various scars on his bantam-weight body.

"What are you?" he asked Beltane, in a tone that brooked no nonsense. "You don't smell wolf or shapechanger that I know, and you are not human."

"I am too!" Beltane snapped, abruptly six feet three inches of angry blond human. "And at least I wear clothes!"

The werewolf met Bel's eyes with a no-bullshit glare, and to Edward's surprise, Bel's head drooped in submission.

"My apologies," he murmured, and Edward half expected him to turn into a dog and roll over to his back. "You were rather abrupt."

"You are on our turf," the werewolf said. "And we don't know you. How did that happen? How did you even see the entrance to this place?"

Behind him, the blond elf stood up gracefully, and the dark-haired one gave the infant he'd been cooing at to a young man with rust-colored hair and did the same. Together, blond one slightly in front, they approached Edward's party, and Edward leaned his head back and tried not to swear.

And they thought Beltane was tall.

"And they're still walking toward us," Harry muttered. "Jesus."

"You can stop there," the woman called behind them, and Edward was relieved to see the men smirk a little. They were being intimidating on purpose—that was actually good to know. "We don't want to scare them off."

The two men were stunningly beautiful.

The one with blond hair—it had to be Emma's Green—had grave emerald-colored eyes, and the elvish features Emma had described: pointed chin, pointed ears, wide-set, over-large eyes. His skin had the faint greenish cast of peaches in the shade. The elf next to him had the same features—but his pale skin had a hint of tan, and his eyes were the colors of a pond in the shadows.

Suddenly the blond one frowned. "There is... dammit." His eyes unfocused, and Edward knew that look. Behind the Youngbloods, a set of stairs came down from the level with the wraparound porch, formed a landing, and then made their way to the ground. Another man—elf—trotted down the stairs and screeched to a halt next to the blond elf.

"Who in the fuck are they?" he asked, and thank God he wasn't as tall as the other two, but his eyes swirled with turquoise and copper, the same disconcerting sparkles that Green's emanated.

"That, Arturo, remains to be seen," Green said quietly. "But this one is very, very ill, and we need to care for him first." He approached Harry gravely and then looked at Suriel, his eyes widening. "May I?" he asked, and it was unclear which one he was talking to, but Suriel nodded unhappily.

"Please. He was exposed to… to unknown bacteria. We… we should have left him at home but—"

"I wanted to see elves," Harry said wistfully. "They're beautiful, aren't they, Suriel? How are the brownies? We missed them."

Arturo and the elf next to him burst out laughing. "That was you?" the shadow-eyed one asked. "Oh, they were so sad for a while. They adored your household."

"Our fault," Harry said, smiling faintly. His cheeks were alarmingly pale. "We wanted to reward them with pie. But they got drunk, and we could see them, and it just didn't seem right anymore."

"Well that's one mystery solved," Green said, laying his hand on Harry's brow. Harry shivered, and Green nodded at the other two. "He needs me," he said softly. "Arturo, Bracken, could you stay out here and entertain our guests? Suriel, was it?"

"Yes, sir—I'll come with—"

"Please do," Green said. With a simple movement, he scooped Harry into his arms like a child. "And after he's asleep, some of your brethren up in the Goddess Grove would love to visit with you."

"Oh!" Bracken said, palm to forehead. "Of course! That's what's missing. They practically leave a void in the sky! Oh, my brother—what happened to your wings?"

"He gave them up," Harry said, unhappy. "He gave them up for me."

"Mm." Green nodded to Suriel. "Come with me, my children. When we're done with you, we can attend to everybody else. That includes you, little brother," Green said grimly, not even looking behind him. "We need you to be yourself for this meeting, no matter how uncomfortable you are."

"The hell!" Francis suddenly stood, indignant, on the edge of the quilt, where he'd been batting at one of the baby's hands with a sheathed paw.

"The *fuck*!" said the young woman on the cushion, and then, as Edward turned to exert some control, he watched as the other young woman on the quilt turned into a cat.

Not a small housecat like the Youngblood brothers did.

A giant housecat, like no housecat Edward had ever seen in the world.

Her sundress puddled around her back end, and she began to methodically clean her paw, gazing at Francis with smug eyes.

Harry let out a weak chuckle, and Green kissed his brow. "So hot," he murmured. "And brave too. Teague, you and this one will be fast friends, I think." Abruptly the naked man who had greeted them was a wolf again. He let out a woof and placed himself at Green's heels. "The rest of you, have fun. Learn about each other. Arturo, Bracken, make sure to keep the defense system strong—there is something out there beating at our periphery, and I'm not in the mood to fuck around."

"I am," said the young woman with the infant at her breast. "Can I kick some ass, Green? Just a little? It's been over a year."

"Not without company, beloved," Green called, and even as he turned back to the house, Edward saw the small, grim smile. Apparently he knew about warriors who ran headfirst into situations without backup.

Not fun for anybody involved.

Edward smiled hesitantly and extended his hand to Arturo. "Hello. I'm, uh, Edward Youngblood. That's my brother Francis over on the quilt, my brother Harry who just got carted into the house, and our brother Beltane behind me. And this is Mullins, my…." He bit his lip and caught Mullins's eyes. "My beloved," he said. "We're… well, we have a boon, of sorts?" The antique word embarrassed him. "We have a huge favor to ask the guy who's about to do us a huge favor and hopefully save Harry's life."

Arturo broke the awkward silence after the speech with a rich laugh. "That's amazing. I can't wait to hear this story—you bring an angel and a shapeshifting half-elf to our place—"

"Don't forget whatever is beating at our shields," Bracken said, frowning.

"Yes, Goddess forbid whatever the hell is beating at our shields. And you just drive up our driveway like it's no big deal? This is going to be the most entertainment we've had in a year."

"Entertainment is good," Bel said, nodding.

Arturo glared at him. "The last entertainment we had was not good. People died. Many. Many. People. And the entertainment after that was when the twins were born, and that was not good either."

"Many people died?" Bel asked with a wince.

"Only one," said the girl on the cushion. "But he was trying to be my obstetrician, so that was fun. Come over here, you guys. Are you hungry—"

"Starving!" Beltane said eagerly. "Do you have food? We like food!"

"A big yellow dog?" she said, tilting her head. "Why of course you were a big yellow dog. I don't see why you wouldn't have been a big yellow dog. It all makes sense now." She turned to the other werewolf next to her. "Jack, honey, could you go ask Katy if she can throw together a big plate of food for everybody? She can have the sprites or brownies send it down. I know she's busy."

Jack woofed and nodded, then looked around, grimacing.

"You don't have to change until you get to the house," the woman said, but the wolf shook his head in resignation.

He changed form. Not nearly as smoothly as the giant cat—who remained a giant cat—or as fast as the other werewolf. It was a slower process, not a magical instantaneous shift. Edward realized that, in this matter, it was the difference in the magic.

In the wolf's place, a tall young man stood, with dark hair framing blue eyes from a part in the middle. "Nice to meet you," Jack said with an awkward little bow. "You've met Arturo and Bracken. This here is the Lady Cory, her uh, consort, Nicky"—the young man with rust-tipped black hair and freckles who was now holding the other infant nodded—"and her lady's maid, Renny." The giant cat turned her paw over and spread her claws. "I'm Jack. I'm naked, and I've learned not to care anymore. This is what I get when I go on a run with my husband and we decide to come see what's doing on the big quilt, and I swear to Goddess, next time we'll just be rude and run back to the house and put on clothes."

Cory and Nicky burst into laughter and leaned against each other, chortling. "Oh my God!" Nicky burbled. "Jack! That was amazing! We're gonna make you open the fucking door like Lurch the butler from now on!"

"Fuck off," Jack said resignedly, starting for the stairs. "I give up. There is literally not a soul in this place who hasn't seen my balls."

Cory and Nicky continued to chuckle as he started up the stairs, and Bracken grunted and came to sit next to Cory again.

"Come on," he muttered. "Sit." He glared at Francis, who was looking around wildly, as though trying for an escape. "You too, little brother. If he took away your cat, he took away your cat, and you're going to have to be human for a while. We'd really like to talk about that as well."

"How'd he do that?" Francis asked almost desperately, and Beltane threw his arms around Francis's shoulders and held on tight until they both sank down on the edge of the quilt.

"How'd you become a shapeshifter without going totally batshit insane?" Cory asked, no longer the little earth mother. "Because we're really curious about that."

"That's a problem?" Beltane asked, frightened.

"Has been with us. How long's he been like that?"

"A hundred and forty years," Edward said levelly, and to his relief Bracken and Cory both laughed.

"You're probably safe, then," Cory said, looking soothed as well. "So you can settle down, little brother."

"Why do you keep calling me that?" Francis snarled.

"Because you're half-fey. You didn't know that?" Bracken arched dark eyebrows, looking skeptical.

"We only just now began to suspect." Edward swallowed, feeling the onus of being the leader with Harry out of commission. "It's been a lot of years since we all became familiars—we figured he would be okay."

Cory tilted her head, suddenly compassionate. "He's not okay," she said softly. "But it's not because of you. Family isn't defined by blood—believe me, this hill knows that lesson very well. But there are things about elves that it helps to understand. Between physiology and software, life can be very difficult in the human world."

"We're not precisely human," Edward reiterated.

"Neither am I," she said amicably. "Come. Green's going to be a while—your brother's going to need some healing there. And I'd really like to know what keeps beating at our shields."

Mullins made an unhappy sound. "Would you believe the forces of hell?"

"No!" Cory clapped the hand *not* holding the infant to her mouth. "Fucking seriously? You hauled the forces of hell to our doorstep so your brother can see elves? Oh my God. You guys have *got* to tell us this story!"

"And quickly," Bracken muttered. "Aren't we going to have company soon?"

Cory opened her mouth to answer, and then looked down at her breast in surprise. "You little shit," she murmured happily to her baby. "You just popped off there and fell asleep, didn't you, little lady?"

Deftly she tucked herself back into her bra and her T-shirt one handedly, and held the baby up to her shoulder.

"Barf rag," Bracken muttered, grabbing a square of flannel from the car seat next to him and repositioning the baby on it. "You know she's gonna need it."

Cory nodded and spoke to the Youngbloods. "Almost a year old, and her stomach's too delicate for anything not me. C'mon, Silver, let's have that burp so you can go sleep under the trees." She smiled happily at them as she patted the baby's back, and Edward got a chance to see her up close.

By conventional beauty standards, she was really very plain—freckles across a broad peasant face, that tumble of blonde/brown/red hair pinned over her crown, and a wide, generous mouth—but her smile as she talked about her daughter was... lovely.

"How's Drian?" she asked Nicky.

"Asleep, thank Goddess." Nicky leaned forward and placed the child he was holding into the car seat. As he did so Edward realized the baby seemed much longer than Beltane had at ten months, although his face seemed just as mature—and that he had pointed ears and the triangular features of the elves but, oddly enough, freckles across his delicate little nose.

He looked up at Cory, who was still patting her daughter on the back, and realized that Bracken was sitting intimately close to her, and so was Nicky.

Green had called her beloved.

Green, Bracken, Nicky, Cory—these children were theirs.

He blinked hard and had a thought to his brother in Green's care.

"What healing methods does Green use?" he asked, and Cory tilted her head back and laughed softly. The laugh did more to transform her from simply lovely to stunningly beautiful, and Edward swallowed.

This was a woman like Emma—a woman to be reckoned with.

"None that those being healed would object to," she said cryptically. "Don't worry, Edward. We have few laws here, but sensual and consensual is one of them." Her mouth twisted. "Now about those demons from hell—we've got a guest coming. Is he going to have trouble getting here?"

"Oh shit," Bracken muttered. "I completely forgot about Sam." He banged his forehead gently on her shoulder while Nicky groaned.

"Because the son of chaos and man is going to do *so* much to help this situation," he said. "The other. Fuck a bird, people—we were just having a goddamned picnic."

"The other better not be fucking you," Bracken snapped back. "You're taken."

Nicky grinned. "Yes, husband, yes I am."

Cory rolled her eyes. "You two flirt all the damned time, but do I have twenty-four seven live porn in my room? I don't think so."

Edward felt heat wash his face, and he couldn't even look at Mullins. Next to him he knew Beltane's eyes had grown really large, and Francis was practically catching flies.

Across from them, the cat who used to be a girl let out a feline snicker.

Cory put her hand over her mouth. "Oh dear. I'm sorry. You guys, I think we've sort of… I don't know. Short circuited their brains. Edward, are you okay?"

Edward swallowed hard, not sure how to tell her that in *his* day, orgies were private affairs. "We're… we're sort of a monogamous bunch, my lady," he said after a moment. "Sorry—"

"No, I'm sorry," she murmured graciously. "Most people who can see this place, enter this place, they're not put off by sex in any of its forms. We were being rude." She let out a sigh. "And off topic. We really *do* have the son of chaos and man on his way, and we've got about four or five hours before he gets here because that little shit learned how to drive, and I'm betting he's going to make San Diego to Foresthill in record time—"

"We could tell him not to come," Nicky said reluctantly, and Cory shook her head with some violence.

"Are you shitting me? He woke up this morning and said, 'Oh, hey, I have to be at Green's Hill *right the fuck now*,' called us, and stole his mother's car. When that kid's got a pull under his breastbone you don't fuck around. Does everybody remember Redding?"

Even the cat groaned.

"Fucking Redding," Bracken said with feeling.

"So I'm thinking it's time for us to stop blowing the guest's fucking minds and start listening to how we have the forces of hell pounding at our shields." She shuddered for a moment—a full-body, visceral shudder—and Bracken and Nicky responded immediately by putting a hand each on her arm. Bracken leaned forward and kissed the back of her neck, and Edward saw the subtle glow of power around her and made a connection.

She was holding the shields together. They were feeding her power.

No wonder she swore like a sailor. If Edward wielded that much power while parenting two infants, he'd have a one-word vocabulary.

"I think," Edward said carefully, "that we have to start at the beginning."

"It's a good story," Beltane said, arms tight around Francis. "The first time I heard it I cried."

Suddenly the cat across from them was a girl again, not even bothering to pull her sundress modestly against her barely-there breasts. "*You* are someone's precious little summer child and honey baby sweetie face, aren't you?"

Beltane nodded at her, smiling. "Yes—my parents and brothers adore me. How did you know?"

The girl shook her head and turned back into a cat, the better to look superior while she washed her hind leg.

Edward realized what that position would look like if she stayed a girl and blushed.

Cory let out a sigh. "I'm sorry, Edward. If you wanted to continue?"

Edward opened his mouth, and Mullins put a hand on his, lacing fingers, making him pause.

"My beginning," he said softly. "Then yours."

Oh. Edward brought his knuckles to his lips and kissed. "Of course, beloved. Bel and Francis haven't heard this. It is time."

He yearned for Harry next to him, being caustic and steady, but looking at the Lady Cory and her men, he thought maybe they would help fill the void while Harry was being healed.

Mullins squeezed his hand again and began.

When he got to the part about the red man—or the blue man, as it were—making love to him in a field of night-blooming flowers, and then confessing to his lover the next day, Cory sighed.

"That sucks," she said softly. "I'm sorry. I mean, no, it wasn't okay to go kiting off with the next supernatural being at your window, but seriously. Supernatural. I mean, I bet he fucked like a god."

Suddenly she stopped and looked at Bracken, who widened his eyes.

"Yes," Bracken said, so shocked his voice came out stiff, like wood. "Your lover fucked like a god. Of course he did. No reason he wouldn't have. Fucking Christ."

They stared at each other for a fraught moment, speaking bibles full of truth without a single word, and then turned their attention back to Mullins.

"Go on, sweetheart," Cory said with renewed purpose. "Besides company, the kids are really only asleep for another forty-five minutes or so. Burning daylight."

Mullins continued, and Edward felt his hand grow damp when he spoke of selling himself into servitude.

Cory nodded. "Okay," she said softly. "So, you were a demon. That's the shit right there. I'm impressed. Tell me about hell. Was there a grand pooh-bah there, or was it mostly run by demons?"

"Run by demons," Mullins said promptly. "That's one of the first things you figure out. There is no grand pooh-bah. You end up in service of whoever recruited you. There's no compulsion to do evil. There's punishment if you disobey, but you're immortal. You'll survive. Escape is possible—Edward's father and I worked as scribes, and we wrote the spell down, verbatim, to file away. It was trivia, given to us to annoy us into screaming boredom, but what we scribed was real."

Cory's mouth pulled up. "Oh, I don't doubt that for a moment," she said grimly. "So, tell me about Edward's father."

Mullins talked then about how he and Leonard covered for each other, and how Mullins had gathered Leonard up and taken him to the clearing that fateful night, because he was afraid Leonard might be too weak to answer the summons, and he didn't want to see the hordes of hell loosed on Emma.

"So, once Leonard was human, completely, that was it? No hordes of hell?" she asked, meeting eyes with Bracken again.

"No. I fled into the forest, to lead them away while Suriel and Emma finished—"

"So, Emma knew Suriel too?" Nicky asked, looking at them like they were reading his favorite romance book aloud.

"Yes," Edward said, picking up the thread. "She and Suriel had helped Mullins and Leonard gather the ingredients to put in the hex bags—"

"How come you don't use hex bags?" Nicky asked Cory.

"Because Goddess is kind, and I'm just a sexually powered nuclear fusion generator," she retorted pertly. "Seriously. Can you see me organizing a fucking hex bag? Following a list? She knows what sort of weak clay she has to work with and doesn't give me any goddamned more to worry about than I've already got."

Nicky held up his free hand in self-defense. "Okay, you're right. If that's the difference between God's magic and Goddess's, I'd have to admit, it was apportioned appropriately all around. They seem better suited for all that spellcasting stuff, and you're pretty damned good as a power generator. I can deal."

"I'm so relieved," Cory responded dryly. "Now go on—how did you boys end up being there? I mean, you're telling the story—I assume you were there."

"All except Beltane," Edward said, and Bel smirked at him and piped up.

"I'm Emma and Leonard's actual flesh and blood son. I'm the only one here who's as young as I look."

Nicky snorted. "Twenty-two?"

"Yes—"

"I'm twenty-four. *Cory's* twenty-two—"

"Three?" she said. "Please—I have to be twenty-three already."

"Fine," Nicky sighed, rolling his eyes. "Twenty-three. Grandma."

"Fuck off. Edward, go on."

Edward raised his eyebrows, and he and Mullins exchanged self-deprecating glances. Okay. Emma squared. She was Emma on speed. She was literally a small goddess, sitting in the garden nursing her children.

Humbling was not even the word for it.

"We had just escaped a brothel," he said, biting his lip.

The people on the blanket sobered immediately. "How old were you?"

"Well, Harry and I were around fourteen, and Francis was a few years younger. We... we were trying to get Francis away before he had to work for his living too."

The concern on Cory's face sharpened, and she and Bracken had another one of those eyeball-to-eyeball conversations. She turned to Francis, a study in gentleness.

"Were they in time, little brother?" she asked softly.

Francis looked away.

"That's… that's a terrible thing for one of the Goddess's children." She grimaced. "It's a terrible thing for *any* child, *any* person. But elves are… are wired very sensitively. You've survived, sane. Well done, little brother."

Francis seemed to melt into Beltane's arms at the praise, and Edward's heart ached a little. Maybe he needed more of that and less of their actively voiced worry.

"So, about the cats," Cory said, pulling them from their lapse into quiet. "Was that part of the spell to bring Leonard back?"

"It demanded a great deal of power," Edward said. "And she was the only one there. She knew that it would strip her completely if she didn't store the bulk of it somewhere. We were hiding in the bushes, and she stored it in us, making us her familiars. Then she offered us sanctuary, if we would only stay with them long enough to teach us what to do with our new power." Edward looked at Francis. "Leonard only just told me that they did that more for us than for Emma."

Francis rolled his crossed blue eyes. "Even I knew that," he said, as though bored.

"For you?" Cory asked, smiling.

"They… they made us into a family," Edward said after a moment. "And later, when she and Leonard wanted to have Beltane, they knew they'd have to give some of their immortality into making him. We all… shared, I guess. So they didn't become old overnight. And we learned—it's more an art, really. But the thing is, I think with all of us here—my brothers and Suriel—we can bring Mullins over and… you know. Redistribute. It wouldn't be too big a sacrifice for any one of us. I think it's a ratio of—"

Cory held up her hand and smirked. "Oh please. No math. Believe me, Edward, you don't have to break down power distribution and collective sharing. I know you have no idea who we are, but if you believe nothing else, believe me when I tell you we know. So, why did you all come here anyway? You could have done this from home!"

This sounded so trivial in the face of Lady Cory's competence. "We need three hairs from an elven king," Edward said grimly. "That's all. But as soon as we left home, we felt the forces of hell slam into us. We hadn't been planning to bring them here but—"

Bracken rolled his eyes. "They would have shown up here sooner or later," he grunted. "And your sick brother?"

"We didn't think he'd be quite so ill," Edward said with a sigh. "At first we thought it was because he'd exhausted himself. He was teleporting us all over the world to get the damned ingredients, and then he got shot by poachers and—"

"He sent us somewhere so he could rest, and it was sort of an alien dimension," Beltane said. "It smelled totally disgusting, and we think he picked up bacteria there that he can't kick."

Nicky shook his head, enchanted. "It's like every time one of them opens his mouth, a better story kicks in. How do they do that?"

Cory eyed him grimly. "Nicky thinks they're entertaining, Arturo. Do *you* think they're entertaining?"

The powerfully built elf with the copper-lightning eyes gave her a measuring look. "Remember when you set those infected werewolves on fire and catapulted them into the lake?"

"Yeah," Cory said, a beatific smile on her plain face. "That was fun."

"That was mildly entertaining. I have the feeling that was like watching a video on television compared to what's about to happen."

"Which will be?" Cory cocked an eyebrow at him, and Edward got the feeling of two seasoned generals, sizing up a battle.

"It's going to be a grand stage spectacle," Arturo said grimly. "Like Cirque du Soleil without the hot women."

Cory's eyes grew wide. "Awesome." She turned back to Edward. "So, are we your last stop? Because I've got to tell you, I don't see you leaving this place until we've changed this one fully human and gotten rid of the motherfuckers pounding at our shields right now."

"No," Mullins said, looking at Edward unhappily. "We need... well, a descendant, or a descendent of one of my family members—"

"Don't worry," Cory said. "We've got it handled."

Bracken smirked. "I was wondering about that—the resemblance is uncanny."

"Right?" Nicky nodded animatedly. "She said his name, and I was like, 'Holy shit!' It's like... well, fuck."

"Fate," Cory said grimly.

"Or the *other* hand of fate," Bracken retorted, and she rewarded him with a grin.

"Wait!" Edward held up a hand. "Please—what are you talking about?"

"Oh." Cory rolled her eyes. "Mullins—his descendent is currently speeding toward the hill in a stolen car. The resemblance is fucking freaky. Don't worry. Sam—he's the son of a human and the other. He's a pain in the ass, but you'll love him. Sweet kid. Has your eyes." And then, before they could collect themselves, she turned to Edward. "I have one question."

"Fine." Well, not fine. Mullins's descendent was on his way? What in the hell?

"Okay, I've got several questions. I'll try to go slow. Number one—I'm going to assume that you're using... well, God's magic, which doesn't sound right because I went to church, but it is basic spellcasting that's based on a patriarchal world view. So that's what you're using to shapeshift, right?"

"Right," Edward said, wondering where this was going, even as Cory breathed a sigh of relief.

"It's not blood-based," she said to Bracken. "Little brother's change. All of our problems have been with blood-based changes."

"Oh thank Goddess," the girl on the blanket said, suddenly a girl again. "Because seriously, I was waiting for him to wig out on me."

"If you don't let him turn into a cat soon, he might," Edward said frankly, but Cory shook her head and turned to Francis.

"Little brother? You may wander the grounds. You may walk up the hill and get an education. You may even swim in the pond, although there is something in there that might eat you. You can go in the house—stay away from the darkling. But you need to stay human until Green says otherwise. Don't worry—the cat isn't his to control, but this is his home, and he will have his say. I know this is hard—very hard." Her firmness softened. "Even Renny there knows how hard it is because Green's done it to her. But there are things in your heart that Green needs to address, and he can't do that if you're not yourself, understand?"

Francis nodded unhappily, his eyes tearing up. Beltane wrapped his arms around Francis's shoulders, and it was a testament to how rattled Francis was that he simply rested his head on Beltane's chest and patted it disconsolately.

Cory met Edward's eyes with grim compassion. "How long has he been allowed to do that? Retreat into the cat when things got uncomfortable?"

Edward shrugged. "A hundred and forty... one. One hundred and forty-one years."

Her eyebrows went up. "It's good, living forever."

Wait. "You *don't* have an extended lifespan?"

And she tried to make her own shrug insouciant—but failed. "My only regret is that I'll be dragging Bracken into mortality with me. Nicky will live as long as Green does, so they won't be alone. We take what we can get. I'm only saying that your brother is wet-wired to respond to a king—and a king's job would be to make him face himself. I know...." She grimaced. "Mothers like to think that they're all their children need. But Francis needs Green in his life—at least for a little while—or he'll never be able to fulfill the promise of him and Beltane. Your family needs to think about that and decide how you want to proceed. Green will be available whenever he's ready."

Edward swallowed, heart aching in spite of the other things going on in his life. "Beltane has three more years being educated at Oxford—there's a coven there related to Emma, and he's promised he'll stay out his training. Francis... we can come with him, here, while Bel's away."

She leaned forward and patted his cheek. "So good. You all are so good. You all work that out how you need to. This isn't a prison sentence. Think of it as a stay with relatives if you want. But you do need to think of it."

"What's your other question?" His heart hurt too much as it was.

"It can wait until after lunch," she said, scrambling to her feet and moving the cushion to make room. Out of nowhere, several platters of food arrived—crusty home-baked bread, cheese, thick cuts of meat—even a trencher of sausage patties that Bracken eyed with distaste but everyone else looked excited about. "I'm starving—but when we're done, you need to explain how you make hex bags. Because the minute Sam gets here with his big blue eyes, we're gonna scalp Green and it'll be game on."

The food was delicious. Edward and Mullins sat shoulder to shoulder, making quiet conversation about everything, from the seasoning in the sausage to the softness of the bread. Even Francis came out of his funk a little to lean forward and eat the cheese sandwich Beltane made for him.

Bel, of course, would have eaten the entire repast—but Bracken and Nicky kept snagging food and slipping it onto Cory's plate. It almost seemed to be a game with them, except sometimes Cory would catch them and scowl. As lunch was wrapping up, Cory held her hand out, and Edward watched in fascination as a tiny being, surrounded by sparkly silver light, landed on her palm.

"Hello there," she said softly. "I wanted to thank you for all your hard work today. Can you thank your brothers and sisters for me?"

The little creature nodded excitedly, and Cory smiled. "Would you kindly ask Katy and Jack to come out, then? I was going to spend the day out with the children, but I think I'm going to need some help today."

More excited bouncing, and this time Cory grimaced. "No, my love. I think we're going to need to work in the new vampire room for the time being. The children hate that room, and I don't blame them. If you could have some science tables and a cauldron and maybe some Bunsen burners moved in there—remember not to touch the iron or steel, my darlings. Ask Teague to organize the werecreatures for you, okay?"

More happy nodding, and little sparkles seemed to fly from the tiny winged person. "Also, if nobody's done so yet, tell the angels in the grove that there is another angel here on the hill. His beloved needs healing, but they may want to say hello before all this is over."

This time the thing in her palm drooped and made a sad little buzz.

"You've seen him, then? Yes, his wings are missing. But that is his story to tell. We have enough new stories to work with—you should ask him yourself. But wait for his beloved to feel better. Nobody's happy when their lover is ill."

The creature's nodding turned more subdued, and Cory made an air kiss at it.

"You're perfection. Can you remember all that I told you? Good. Thank you again for all you've done, yes?"

And the thing flew off, leaving loopty-loop trails of sparkle glitter in its wake.

"Do you think he… she—" Edward floundered.

"She," Cory said. "She will remember everything I just told her, and will even remember what I let Nicky and Bracken sneak me for seconds and what I did not. She will also remember to bring me root beer on ice, which makes me sound like the queen of everyfuckin'thing, but I asked for it once after lunch and they haven't forgotten it in the two years since." She nodded. "The sprites are lovely people, but I live in fear of ever offending one. Their memories are longer than Bracken's johnson."

"That's saying something," Nicky told him sincerely. "How do you know we're going to need all that science stuff, by the way?"

Edward had been wondering the same thing.

"Look at him," she said, nodding at Edward. "He's practically got a frock coat and those little steampunk extend-glasses. You *do* need a science station, right, Edward?"

Edward felt his face wash hot. "I understand some witches just sort of throw things in the pot—"

"But you are much too sensible for that," Cory said with a regal tip to her head. "We all understand."

"It's a good thing you don't have to do any of that," Nicky muttered in disgust. "You'd probably blow us all up."

Cory let out a snort. "Like I need a spell book and a cauldron to do that." She grew serious and turned to Bracken. "Nicky and I can help the boys cook up the hex bags—I want the elves to stay clear."

Bracken shrugged. "I'll sit in the outer room."

"Bracken—"

"You're keeping our shields running too," he said implacably. "I will be nearby."

She let out a frustrated sigh. "Arturo—?"

"I'll be listening for Sam," he said, nodding. "I'm not sure what's going to happen when that boy gets here, but I'm pretty sure it will make 'very interesting' look like an afternoon sorting your socks."

"She doesn't wear socks," Nicky said blankly. "She makes them for all of us but doesn't wear them herself."

"That, birdman, is the point."

"You're all hilarious," Cory muttered, then scrambled to her feet to give Nicky and Bracken a hand up. Renny—the girl who preferred to be a cat—had slid her sundress back on, and she stood too, checking to make sure her hair was in a ponytail. Once they were all standing together, Edward got another shock.

Nicky was a smaller than average man—maybe Edward and Harry's size. Bracken was well over six feet tall.

Cory and Renny were tiny women, standing five foot one or two at the most. Cory had wide hips—hell, she'd borne twins—and a smallish bosom, and was, in general, a lot smaller than her sizable personality.

"What?" Cory asked, wiping at her mouth self-consciously. "Did I spill food down my shirt?" She checked that too.

Edward did it unconsciously—he came from an age where men bowed to women. Mullins followed suit, and so did Beltane and even Francis.

"Thank you, my lady," Edward said when he'd straightened. "We came asking for a favor, and you've given us everything. You're our salvation. We… we're in your service."

Cory nodded in return. "Do you boys have any idea that there is a ring of vigilantes rescuing victims of human trafficking? The victims have turned up, safe and sound, counseled and placed with foster families—but the men can never be found. Sometimes, the smallest of children talks up a storm about a fluffy white cat." She stuck out a gentle finger and booped Francis on the nose. Francis turned his head and blushed. "You've saved a few half-elves who have found their way to us," she told them. "Good guys have to stick together."

With a sigh she walked to where Nicky had placed the car seats in the shade and crouched to kiss her children on the cheek as they slept.

Edward got a good look at the little girl this time, and realized that she looked… well, almost completely elfin. There were no freckles, no broad cheekbones. When her eyes had been open, they'd been brilliantly blue.

Two people approached from the steps as Cory straightened—Jack the irritated werewolf and another tiny woman, this one Latina with a soft, heart-shaped face and enormous sloe eyes.

"No playing in the garden today?" the woman asked sadly.

Cory shrugged. "Not today. Thank you for lunch, Katy—I was sort of hoping you and Jack would join us."

Katy shook her head. "No—I like this new kitchen job. Sometimes, it's just nice to sit *in* the kitchen and eat with your husbands, you know?"

"It's a perk," Cory said, and then her mouth quirked. "It's a perk for shy people who don't like to meet strangers."

Katy gave a lethal grin, and Edward's heart stuttered a little. She was stunning. "You know Teague, my lady."

Cory met Jack's eyes over Katy's shoulders. "Yeah. Teague."

Jack shrugged. "Do you want us to keep them outside?"

Cory let out a sigh and fidgeted. "I…. It's a lovely day," she said plaintively. "Or rather, a lovely late afternoon, almost evening."

Edward looked around and realized she was right. Lunch had stretched on—stories had made it longer. Evening was perhaps an hour away on this early spring day.

"They're just going to want to play outside for a bit before it gets dark," Cory said. "I… the shields are being poked at constantly, though. I don't want some sadistic pus-pile jumping out and grabbing one of them instead of Mullins." She looked over her shoulder. "No offense, Mullins."

"None taken, my lady. If I may—they can't actually touch children. They can lure them, they can tempt them, but they can't touch them. They can't cross thresholds, so the house is safe.

But even in the gardens, I'll be honest—I didn't even know elves existed until recently. I don't think they'd go after an elfin child even if one was given to them in a box."

Cory gave a sigh of relief before speaking to Katy. "Excellent. Just don't wrap them in any boxes and they'll be fine."

"Not a problem, my lady. And you know me and Jacky—we stay close."

"You're the best," Cory said with a hug. "Thanks, you guys. I think Teague and Arturo are going to be checking the borders, so make sure you keep in touch with them. At the first sign of wonkiness—"

"We take them inside and watch a movie. We're good at the nanny thing, Cory. You know us."

"And I'm a micromanaging hosebeast." Cory shrugged and then turned to the group. "Okay, folks—we're going in through the garage. You can get the full Green's Hill tour later—you'll love the place, I'm sure, but right now, let's make some fuckin' magic."

WHAT MIGHT HAVE BEEN

MULLINS LOOKED around the "new vampire room" in surprise.

It was, essentially, a stainless steel vault, with scouring marks on every surface. They'd passed through the garage, much bigger than he'd expected, to a landing. A set of stairs led up from the landing, but they'd taken the set that led down, into the roots of the hill.

And yet not cavernous.

Even while underground, the feeling of this place—from the grounds to the garage—was that of complete freedom.

They'd leveled out to what appeared to be a giant sitting room, complete with couches in black and oxblood leather, big fur rugs, and a giant wide-screen television in the center.

And two on the sides.

"Pardon the decorating," Cory said as they passed through. "For some reason—"

Bracken cleared his throat.

"For reasons of controversial conclusions based on human behavior," Cory corrected, "most of our vampires are male. About seventy-five percent. I can't even… well, I could probably explain it, but then people would argue and other people would discuss, but we'd be here all day. Anyway. Lotsa guys. So their sitting room looks like a man cave. I've commissioned a sitting room designed by the female vampires, but you know. Busy. They're getting to it. But that's why that room is so frickin'…."

"You're their queen, Cory," Nicky said delicately behind her.

"Male," she finished flatly.

"You're queen of the vampires?" Beltane said avidly. "Awesome! How'd that happen?"

Cory gave them all a look so filled with pain, Mullins felt his breath stop. "Terrible, terrible loss," she said quietly. "And more time than we have to tell."

He remembered then, Emma's story that Green's lover, Adrian, had been a vampire. Perhaps their story was like his—filled with tangles of lovers, filled with regret.

He was glad that they'd seemed to find some peace, though. This place—this lovely, chaotic, peaceful fairy hill—was such a balm to his soul.

He wasn't sure what had been racing through Edward's mind since they arrived—there'd been no time to exchange their thoughts in private.

But Mullins knew that for his own peace of mind, seeing the people here—bawdy, gentle, kind, stern, sometimes all in the same breath—had opened his eyes somewhat.

Cory had given him a gentle absolution for his sins.

Yes, Edward had forgiven him, had put his wrong in the context of being young and stupid and filled with remorse. But Cory had told him that it wasn't just a lover's kindness. She'd told him that the world was large enough for a man to be both evil and repentant. That Mullins's transgression was minor. That his soul, his feelings, were important, not invalidated because he'd screwed up.

He wanted to cry. He wanted to exult. He wanted to celebrate that his humanity had never really been gone—that he'd been a victim of his own guilt.

But mostly what he wanted to do was grab Edward's hand and thank him for his faith, for the implicit faith that had never once wavered, that Mullins was a man worth loving.

Unfortunately, first, they had things to do.

"So, here we go," Cory said with a shiver. "Gotta tell you, guys, we really hate this room. Elves can't come in here because of the metal, but the werefolk can, so I'm going to have Teague and Renny and a couple of other weres in the corners. Don't mind them—they'll read a book or something. I just need my people in here while we work."

"But they can ride in cars?" Edward asked, and Mullins was both proud of his practical brain and eager to get started. Of course, though. He was worried about his brother.

"Half-elves usually can," Cory said frankly. "They're not great with long trips. Green needs a special herbal infusion in all his clothes to fly, and all the cars are washed with it."

"So when we painted our house with lead paint about sixty years ago—"

Cory looked at Francis with sympathy. "Oh, you poor baby. Yes—that would have made him sick eventually, just like human children if they ate it. For right now, there will be a few elves outside and one in the panic room—"

"You have a panic room for a…." Beltane looked around. "Panic room?"

Cory shook her head. "You guys, just… just, you do not want to know. Anyway. There will be someone monitoring us from outside in case something tries to get in. Are we good now?"

Everybody nodded.

"Now, is there anything you need?" she asked.

"My case from the back of the minivan," Edward said. "You can't miss it—it's nylon over a wooden base that has a core of plastic cubicles, each one is marked—"

"It's out here!" Bracken called from the open door. "The brownies also brought some sort of staff that is totally disgusting and feels like a live snake."

"Yeah!" Edward called, trotting out of the room to retrieve the items. "You might not want to touch that."

Mullins snickered, and Cory caught his eyes and winked. "Everybody's got their stories, right?"

"Well, this is the one that almost got Harry killed," Mullins told her. And then, as Edward brought the case in and organized, asking the air occasionally for an item they'd forgotten, such as linen squares and ribbon, he *told* her, relating the boys' adventures as he'd seen them through the small bit of glass that had tethered him to Edward's reality.

"Ohh…," she breathed happily, Nicky nodding by her side, "I really want to meet Harry when he's feeling better. Me, him, Teague—we could do some serious damage."

Nicky grew sober. "No, please, beloved," he said softly. "I thought we were beyond—"

She shook her head. "Never beyond that," she told him. "What kind of mother would I be if I killed the part of myself that made them?"

"Lady Cory!" Edward called, interrupting. "My lady, may I ask you something?"

"Of course," she said, stepping forward and away from the uncomfortable thing Mullins hadn't meant to bring up. "What do you need?"

"It's not necessary," Edward said humbly. "The thing is, Emma had only Suriel and us to bring Leonard fully into the human world. This time it was going to be myself and my brothers, and we were going to spread our power around, grant him the same long life we have."

"But Harry is out of commission," she said gently.

"I could call Suriel—"

Cory looked over his shoulder for a moment, her eyes unfocused. "It's done," she said. "He'll be down in about an hour."

Edward nodded, unfazed. Of course he was—he and his brothers had learned telepathy as their first spell.

"Anything else?" she asked kindly.

"Help," Edward said, and Mullins could tell the admission cost him. "I… I think I could protect you all from getting power-stripped, but God, if we could just have some more power feeding us… I…." He gave Mullins an unhappy look. "You don't understand. We *watched* Emma and Suriel do this, and it was… huge. There was so much power involved. I'm… I just can't let him down, is all."

Cory nodded gravely, then stepped forward and took his hand. "Look—we'll put an elf on every corner, if you want. You make as many hex bags as you think necessary, and someone will be there to anchor them. We'll make the first Goddess get/wizard combined ex-demonizing task force—I'm there. It'll be a hoot. But I think you're forgetting the main ingredient that saved your father, and it's the thing Mullins is going to need the most from you now."

"What's—"

Cory held up a finger. "'Scuse me, my pocket's buzzing."

Edward jumped. "So is mine," he muttered. He pulled out his phone and looked at Mullins. "It's Emma," he said softly. "I'll have to tell her about Harry."

"She's going to want to be here."

Edward shrugged. "I should probably ask the Lady, or Green, if they can come."

Mullins nodded, gesturing to him to proceed, and went to work on the hex bags himself. The ingredients were divided into five categories—one for each point of the pentacle. Earth, wind, fire, water, and spirit—of course.

Edward's cunning little box—Francis's creation—had put the items into separate sections for each category, because Edward was exceedingly clever that way, and Mullins was about to reach into the box when Edward held out his hand. "No touching!" he snapped. "Mullins, this spell is *for you*. You could completely contaminate it!"

Mullins yanked his hand back and blew out a breath. Edward had put everybody to work on some part of the spell—Nicky was firing up the distillery, Cory had started warming up the cauldron. Even Renny was busy wiring together a tiny strainer so they could use some of the items to infuse the potion like tea.

He was completely superfluous, and with a sigh he wandered past Cory, who was talking excitedly to someone named Max. "Look, asshole, I don't care how fast he was going. We've got fucking *demons* banging at our shields! Yes, they're real. What, you think you're a shapeshifter and you know everything? No, it surprised me too. But the point is they're not going away until that little car thief gets his ass on the hill and donates blood or spit or hair or something so we can complete this spell. I don't know why a spell. It's just how the God people roll, man, I don't know what to tell you."

She paused and took a deep breath. "Is it worth your job?" she asked, and like everything Mullins and Edward had said, she seemed to take it seriously. "I'd rather you keep your job. You're handy where you are. But if it's a choice between losing your job and detaining that kid for another hour, I'm going to have to say retire, sweetie. I'm sorry. Max, this shit is getting fairly out of hand. Do you need an elf there to do a mind-wipe?" She paused. "Seriously? It's that late? Fuck! Where in the fuck did my day go! Yeah, sure—baffle your guys with bullshit for ten minutes and I'll send Marcus and Phillip to do a brain wipe when they wake up. Jesus fucking Christ—I could swear we just sat down in the fucking garden to eat."

She hung up and looked around. "Edward, do you have a time frame, here? Any specific pull of the moon that's gonna make this shit go easier?"

"Midnight's always a kick in the ass," Edward said, "but anytime we're ready to roll is good."

Mullins covered his mouth, because even Edward was affected by the Little Goddess.

"Excellent. It's seven o'clock now, apparently—the vampires are almost up. If we can get this show on the road by ten o'clock I will be *really* fucking excited." She went back on the phone, and Mullins wandered out the door.

Bracken was sprawled on one of the ugly couches in the common room, reading something on his phone. He looked up as Mullins wandered in and gestured with his chin to the nearby chair. "Too much going on?" he asked perceptively.

"I'm not allowed to touch anything," Mullins said, tail twitching as he sat. "And yes." He shrugged. "I… I'm used to hiding away from chaos, you know?"

A slight smile flickered over Bracken's beautiful features. "She tries to do that. Doesn't always work."

Mullins nodded. "I can see that. What's that room for, anyway? I know she said it was the new vampire room but—"

Bracken shook his head. "Oh, little demon. So young. So naïve. So totally not prepared for what a new vampire is like. Especially when the whole damned kiss is about to wake up and get up in our business."

Mullins let out a little moan. "I miss Edward's house," he said softly. "The family was big enough. This… this is exhausting. It's intimidating. It's… confusing. All of the brothers are in disarray. Edward's trying to convince his mother not to come. Bringing Leonard back took three people— and Leonard."

"And three boys hiding in the bushes," Bracken reminded him. "Families grow. Friends too. Be glad she took your side, because—" His jaw firmed up, and he braced himself like someone taking a hit in the stomach. His entire long, muscular frame shuddered, and he took a deep breath and met Mullins's eyes. "Do they really not like to lose people that much?"

Mullins shrugged. "Pisses them off. Makes them question their world. It's not an easy thing, you know?"

Bracken nodded, and they continued to speak. Surprisingly enough, the big elf was decent company. He didn't talk a lot—and often in grunts— but what he had to say was relevant and often funny. About twenty minutes had passed when suddenly… just like that, the room was full of people. Mullins shrank back on the couch, prepared for an onslaught of questions, but Bracken shook his head no at two men who stood side by side and appeared to be the leaders of the group. One stood shorter than the other, with curly brown hair and a sweet Italian face, while the other was a cool six feet plus, with long legs and a Dracula widow's peak. Almost in sync, they nodded at Bracken and moved into the new vampire room to talk to Cory, and Mullins breathed a sigh of relief.

He caught Bracken's raised eyebrow and said, "I'm sure they're very nice."

Bracken smirked. "They're total assholes, and their romance almost tore apart the hill—but they're totally devoted to Cory." His smirk faded. "And they survived something really painful, so I should probably not be a dick. Anyway, don't worry. There's a lot of us. You are not required to meet nor get along with everybody, particularly not in the same night. Particularly not *this* night—"

As he was speaking, they all felt it.

Everybody in the room jerked, like they'd passed through a force field, and from the new vampire room came shouts of, "Oh hey!" "The *hell?*" and—from Cory—"Holy fucknuggets in a shitbasket!"

Mullins stood and looked at Bracken in alarm—and was surprised to see a familiar face standing between him and the couch.

"Who in the holy fu—" Bracken's full-throttle attack was warded off with a flick of the wrist. Bracken went flying backward to hit the wall, and struggled grimly to his feet.

"Sorry to do that," the red man said, smiling slightly—no longer red but lavender. Mullins knew him, though. Knew his smile, knew his skin, knew how his flesh felt moving inside of him. "You're really very strong, you know." He threw an ingratiating smile over his shoulder to Bracken and then turned to Mullins conspiratorially. "They're *all* amazingly strong. It's why I had to wait for my son to cross the shields so I could get in to speak to you."

Mullins stared at him in panic. "Edward!" Oh God. He was *here*. The man who had made love to him so sweetly and then thrown him to the wolves. "Edward! He's—"

"Hush." The red man held his fingers next to Mullins's lips, and Mullins suddenly couldn't open his mouth to even breathe. "You and I need some quiet time to talk."

And with that, he put his hand on Mullins's shoulder, and the chaos and kindness of Green's Hill disappeared.

Quicker than a heartbeat, quicker than an eye blink, they were back, snug and cold and alone, in Mullins's cell in the twelfth sphincter of hell.

Magic, Faith, and Blood

"Edward!"

At Mullins's shout, Edward dropped the test tube he was holding, vaulting toward the door to the common room before it even shattered on the floor.

He got there just in time to see Mullins, back to him, standing in front of the most beautiful man Edward had ever seen.

His skin color was pale lavender, and his face—square-jawed, strong-chinned, with delicate cheekbones and a decisive nose—was beautifully proportioned, absolutely symmetrical.

His almond-shaped eyes were brilliant turquoise. He caught Edward's eyes over Mullins's shoulder, then reached out and touched him.

And they disappeared.

"The… oh my God. *Mullins!*" All thoughts of the spell, thoughts of rescue, flew out of his head. All he could remember was the bleakness and the sorrow in Mullins's eyes every time he'd been banished back to that cold, blood-dripping little cell, to the beatings, to the screams that he never mentioned but Edward knew made up the soul-shredding reality of every moment.

Unless he was with Edward.

"*Mullins!*"

"Stop it!" A woman—*Lady Cory*—was shaking him by the arm, yelling at him. "Goddammit, Edward, fucking stop!"

The profanity, of all things, penetrated his haze.

"You swear a lot," he said, his throat hoarse with screaming.

"You fucking think? Look—he's okay. For right now, he's okay!"

"How do you know?" Edward all but sobbed. "He's back in hell—"

"Well if he is, it's not because a demon got him." She closed her eyes and shuddered. "Although, goddammit, it would have given me room to think. Bracken, you feeling this?"

"No, Cory, I'm just along for the fucking ride. Of course I feel it. You're right—it wasn't a demon. We know who it was."

Edward stared at them blankly. "It was the red man," he said, feeling out of his league. "Or, you know. Purple now. It was the demon who got him in trouble—"

"Oh, honey," Cory said, patting his face. "Sweet baby. That wasn't a demon. The demons are still clamoring to get in. To get in and out of our shields like that? That was something much older and much more powerful than those fucking asswipes clawing at the hill right now."

"What—I don't understand."

"It was a god," Harry muttered, coming slowly down the stairs.

"You look like hell," Edward said, his throat thick. His brother was still pale, and he looked as though he hadn't eaten in a month. "What are you doing out of bed?"

Harry was wearing a pair of sleep pants and nothing else—it was clear he'd been resting. But his face wasn't flushed, and he wasn't sweating with fever. While pale, he wasn't waxy with sepsis. Edward could almost forgive him for being sick.

"The whole hill heard you scream," Harry muttered. "Did you tell him yet, my lady?"

"You stole my line," Cory said, taking Edward by the arm and setting him down in the corner of one of the butt-ugly couches. "Suriel, sweetie, do you have him?"

Suriel grunted, scooping Harry up into his arms and cradling his head against his shoulder.

"Idiot," he muttered.

"Did she tell me what?" Edward asked, feeling lost. "What do you mean, god?"

"Edward," Harry said with exasperation, "who do you think sent us on a special extra side mission to make a penis staff out of a snake?"

Edward gaped, all of his attempts to remember suddenly paying off. He'd tried—he'd worked so hard, but finally the addition to the spell list and the big gaps in his memory were making an awful sort of sense.

"Did I miss him?" The voice snapped Edward out of his shock and he looked toward the stairs again, this time seeing a young man—seventeen at the most—taking the steps at a sprint. He was followed by a man in a law enforcement uniform, a little older than Cory and Nicky.

"Miss your father?" Cory said with a grimace. "Yes, Sam, I'm sorry. He used your blood-link to get past our shields, grabbed Edward's boy here, and took off."

Sam grunted in disappointment, and Edward got a good look at the kid who'd apparently stolen his mother's car to get here.

"Oh dear God," he muttered.

"Yup," Cory said, moving around the couches to give Sam a hug. "It's freaky as a fuck in a fishbucket, ain't it."

Edward stared at the young man as the others in the hill—including Bracken, Teague, and Nicky—stepped forward to embrace the young man.

Who was a dead ringer for Mullins.

"Please," he said loudly, voice breaking. "Please—somebody explain this to me."

Cory put her hand on his shoulder. "Me and Suriel are going to go make sure your hex bags are good to go—we need to get him back ASAP, and you've had a shock. Sam, you come talk to Edward here and explain shit, 'kay?"

"Any time, my lady," he said with a head bob. His hair was dark and curly, which was already familiar, but his eyes—Mullins's shape, Mullins's color—rested on Edward's face with a wealth of compassion. He stepped out of the embrace of half a dozen people to come crouch in front of Edward's seat, while Suriel set Harry down on the couch Bracken had occupied.

"You'll be okay?" Suriel asked anxiously, and Harry looked up at him and smiled tiredly, squeezing his hand.

"Go help," he ordered. "I've been enough of a hindrance—"

"Sh." Suriel kissed his temple, his red-gold hair streaming down over his shoulder like a curtain. "I'll be back when we're done."

He left, and Harry and Edward were there with Bracken and a young man who looked enough like Mullins to make Edward doubt his sanity.

"You saw him?" Sam said, before they could say anything. "You saw the other?"

"Wait," Edward said, feeling dense. "That's... the red man or purple man or whatever—"

"The other," Sam said matter-of-factly. His eyes—so much like Mullins's—were older than their years. "You saw him."

"I don't understand," Edward said faintly, and Bracken laughed.

"I'll help. Mullins's little sister—you needed something from an ancestor, right? Well, Sam looks just like him—cheekbones, chin—there's even a little mole by his ear. It's frightening. So for the sake of coincidence, we're going to say Sam is a long-ago descendent—"

"But the odds of that would be—"

"Astronomical," Sam said promptly. "A terrifying coincidence. So improbable that I would be coming here the exact day you arrived that it should be impossible."

"Yes," Edward said, shaking out of his funk. "Exactly. How is it possible at all?"

"Well, that's my other bloodline," Sam told him, his mouth going flat and grim. "That red or purple or blue jerkoff who took off with your boyfriend is also my father. You got yer God, you got yer Goddess, you got yer other. That's Pop. He's the god of random fucking chaos. My guess is, he gave me the call to come here because you needed my blood for your spell. You do, right?"

"Yes," Edward said again, the hair on the back of his neck lifting up. "We do."

"So I wake up this morning with a pull in my stomach to cut school and drive seven hours to say hi to Lady Cory. I peed in a bottle, the urge to get here was so strong. Seriously. The garage fey are going to love me."

"Possibly more than you ever dreamed," Bracken said dryly. "They're weird that way."

"Squick. Ee." Sam rolled his eyes. "Anyway—so Dad knows I'm coming, he knows the shields are going to be up, and he just bides his time. The minute my car hit the shields, he slides in. We're related by blood, right? The shields are friendly to Sam, so they're friendly to Sam's dear old fucking dad. So he sneaks in here, grabs your guy, and goes." Sam met Bracken's eyes. "How'm I doing?"

"Spot on," Bracken said dryly. "Sorry you missed him."

Sam blew out a breath. "Well, it would have been nice to meet him, period. But I take it I need to go bleed in a jar?"

Edward smiled a little. "Hair, fingernail clippings, spit—"

"Semen," Sam supplied, because he was a teenager, and he apparently had the same filter Cory did.

"Keep your love life to yourself," Bracken told him, and then snickered. Apparently it wasn't just teenagers.

Sam grinned, showing a mouthful of unnaturally straight and even teeth. "You stay you," he said, and Bracken nodded before the kid turned on his heel and went to spit in a jar.

Edward sagged against the couch.

"He just disappeared," he whispered.

Harry leaned forward and patted Edward's knee awkwardly. "I remember the feeling," he said. "But you know what to do now, right?"

Edward tried to smile. "Jump naked into a shootout with coke-addled human traffickers armed with semiautomatic weapons?"

"Mm… good times," Harry said, nodding, and Edward had to laugh. It was exactly what Harry had done.

But he'd also confronted the scariest moment of their past.

"Confront your inner demons?" Edward guessed then, not sure why this hadn't occurred to him.

"What are yours?" Harry asked, voice so low only Edward could hear him.

Edward swallowed hard against the lump in his throat, and two lifetimes of love and loss opened up to devour his heart whole.

"Remember?" he asked, voice hoarse. "Remember what I was like after Dorothy?"

"Yes, my brother. I remember."

Edward looked into his eyes for judgment—and found only understanding.

"If I lose Mullins… it will take decades to fish me out of that well," he said, knowing this fear so intimately, it was like it wore his skin.

"Centuries," Harry supplied cheerfully. "One at the least. I'll look forward to hauling you out."

Edward half laughed. "I'll be in the depths of depravity," he told Harry—but he couldn't stay earnest in the face of Harry's steadfastness.

"And Francis and Beltane and Suriel and I will be there," Harry said, suddenly sober. "But we would miss Mullins too. Let's see what we can do to get him back first."

Edward's eyes burned, and he wiped them on his palm. "I'll do my best," he whispered.

"Think of the things you'll say to him." Harry's shrug told of his pain when Suriel had gone missing. "Think of all the actual words you want him to have etched in his heart."

Edward startled. "Oh my God." He remembered Leonard's last advice about the spell Edward would have to cast—and he remembered his own thoughts about how to get Mullins back if he was ever snatched back to hell.

"You just figured out what to do?" Harry asked.

"Yes!" But oh hell. Oh no. "How do you feel?" Oh God. His brother was so pale.

"Top of the world." Harry's smile was just a tinge crazy. As it always would be.

"Can you boomerang me to Mullins using Sam's blood?"

Harry cocked his head. "Challenge accepted. You realize you could end up spattered among every descendent of Mullins's little sister on the four corners of the earth, right?"

Edward grimaced. "Maybe you should write that spell down on paper first."

"Right," Harry conceded. He put his arm underneath him as though he were about to get up, and then fell back against the couch. "Hells."

"Stay there," Edward told him, standing. "I'll go get you pen and paper—"

And like that, pen and paper materialized on Harry's lap.

"Thank you," they both said in unison, and then met eyes and laughed a little.

"I should really ask Green if we can send some brownies back for Emma's kitchen," Harry said fondly. "It might make up for the worry of the last month."

Edward nodded again, the thought of home soothing him.

"I'll come up with the spell," Harry added. "And the spell to get you back, since it's on the tip of your tongue."

"I've got an idea," Edward told him firmly. "To get back, I mean. But will you be strong enough to get me there? That's all I'll need." He wouldn't sacrifice Harry for Mullins. He couldn't.

He'd never be able to look his lover in the eyes afterward.

"I'd better," Harry laughed. "Emma would never forgive me if we had to go collecting your DNA from the four corners of the earth in another treasure hunt."

"It's your DNA I'm worried about!" Edward wanted to smack him. "Harry, you almost died." It was the truth, and no amount of his brother's posturing could hide it.

"Greatly exaggerated," Harry lied. He waved Edward away. "Go on. I'm trying to be heroic."

Edward watched from the corner of his eye as Bracken wobbled slightly, as though he'd taken a heavy blow to the knees.

"We have no time," he said, angry. "Dammit, Harry, you'd better be fine." And with that he stood up to go help with the spell.

LATER, FRANCIS and Beltane told him he was amazing. Crisp, logical, reasonable. He gave clear instructions and had an easy-to-follow plan—the people of Green's Hill were eating out of his hand.

Green apparently handed over his three strands of hair—over five feet long and smooth as spun gold—with a faint smile. "Ah, Emma. Lovely woman. I'm sure she's an amazing mother." And Edward added it to the hex bags—under spirit.

Sam had extended his wrist, and Bracken had drawn a gentle finger across it, painlessly freeing just enough of what apparently was very potent blood.

But Edward didn't remember any of that. One part of his brain was engaged with what he had to do, what was *necessary* to do to get Mullins back. The other part was screaming, and no amount of common sense could silence that part of his brain.

And Edward worked, going up to the now darkened orchard and laying out three five-pointed stars, one within the other, with unerring precision.

Cory and her people came out and assumed a place, one at each point of the pentagram circle that was now nearly twenty feet in diameter. Suriel and his brothers took their places at four corners, making sure they were aligned with spirit as well, and Harry watched unhappily, sitting in Cory's nursing cushion and propped up against a tree.

"Blood yet?" Beltane asked, pulling out a small scalpel that they had for just that purpose. Edward saw Green's people pulling out blades of their own—steel for the werefolk, silver for the elves, vampire fangs for anybody who wished them.

Cory was holding her wrist in front of Bracken, waiting for him to cut her flesh with his touch alone.

And suddenly Edward was right there in the moment.

"Not you, my lady," he said softly. And then, with the eyes of a crowd of people—some of them strangers—looking at him for leadership, he felt—truly felt—what it was to be a leader.

"No, my lady," he said, his voice stronger than he could ever remember it being. He had to make sure these people knew what he was and what he wasn't—and what they were offering with their blood on the hex bags.

"I'm sorry?" Cory asked, affronted.

"This ritual—it took years from our mother's life. And yes, she was an immortal, and the years were hers to give, but I'm sorry. Your people need all the years you have."

Cory's twisted smile of acquiescence hurt—but she backed out of the circle, and a dreamy-eyed elf with hair that seemed to shift color with every breeze stepped in after her.

"You should all know that," he said, his voice carrying across the suddenly quiet yard. There were vampires surrounding them, he realized, hands joined. He wondered if they were there for protection—he'd noticed Cory's eyes unfocused a lot, as she ordered people around. Perhaps they were hers. "This spell was done once with two people—but one of them was an angel in active service. The other was my mother, and she sacrificed years of her life. I realize you all have extended lifespans, but so do I." He shrugged. "Every moment is precious. I have the feeling you all know this, probably more than most mortals. So right now, decide if that's a sacrifice you're willing to make for a complete stranger. My brothers and I were prepared to make it alone—we could do that again."

Not a soul moved, and Edward bent his head humbly.

"I have no words," he said. "My family is indebted to you for your kindness."

"The brownies miss you," Green told him from behind the vampires, arm wrapped firmly around Cory's and Bracken's shoulders. Nicky was in the circle—because he was as immortal as Green. "If we could send some of them to your home, they will be happier, and you'll have discharged your debt."

"But that doesn't make sense!" Beltane muttered loudly. He was glared into silence by Francis, who, for once, seemed to understand.

Edward pulled his heart from his throat. "So Harry's going to send me to where Mullins is, and then…." Edward thumped the snake-and-rhinoceros-horn staff in his hand next to the mirror at his feet. "Then, when you see this coming through the mirror, please pull us out."

There was general laughter.

"And when Mullins is situated in the middle, I'll start the spell. Are we clear?"

General assent then, and Edward took a deep breath. "Harry, you ready?"

Harry pushed himself standing. "You'd better not get lost, you prick!"

"You'd better not send me to the place with the big blue corn, idiot!" Edward snapped back. He saw Harry's lips curve wickedly and knew that they'd both said "I love you, brother," in front of an entire crowd of people.

And then everything—elves, werecreatures, vampires, brothers—all of it disappeared.

CLYDE

"HELLO, CLYDE," said the… well, now the purple man. "I hope you don't mind a little bit of privacy."

"I hate this place," Mullins said flatly. He'd been Clyde for twenty years and Mullins for nearly four hundred. Whoever Clyde had been, Mullins wasn't like that anymore.

The purple man looked around sadly, taking in the jagged edges of stone dripping thickly with blood and the tiny, safe bed in the middle of the cell, pristine. "I can see why. Why would you choose to stay here?"

Mullins gaped at him. "Because I was in *hell*. Remember? I was making a deal to save my little sister!"

The purple man nodded. "But I was coming to save you both!"

"But I didn't know that!" Mullins pulled away from him, feeling a reluctant burst of attraction coursing through his blood. He was still perfectly made—wide shoulders, lean hips, muscular arms and legs.

No clothes and a prodigious manhood.

"Well, true." To his horror the purple man wrapped strong arms around Mullins's shoulders and nuzzled his ear. "I mean, I *did* save your sister. That's her offspring who just hit that infernal fairy hill. Proof, right, Clyde?"

Mullins's senses—newly awakened in Edward's arms—kicked up about a thousand notches. In the back of his mind he heard, *This is a god. Who refuses a god?*

But his heart constricted.

Edward. He remembered the loneliness he'd felt, realizing he couldn't even help with his own redemption spell. All he'd wanted was Edward's touch on his hand, his bright eyes smiling back.

One hundred and forty years as Edward's friend, mentor, avenger had not been enough. Two nights, one glorious day in Edward's arms had not been enough. All it had done was tell Mullins an eternity would never be enough.

Mullins twisted his body and broke away from the embrace. "I'm not Clyde anymore," he said, feeling a sense of relief. He'd been so young! So easily enchanted. He'd seen wonders since—an exploding bathtub, an angel delivered from torment, the desert at night.

Four young men he'd come to love, embarking on a tremendously difficult adventure—for him.

One of them growing, falling in love, being hurt, falling again.

Falling for him.

Mullins.

Not Clyde—not the shallow boy who didn't know any better, but Mullins. The demon who'd learned to lie, to cheat, to kill—and who still doggedly hung on to his own soul.

Oh, Edward. I've seen so many marvels and so many abominations. But the most marvelous thing I've seen in four hundred years is your love, and my only abomination would be to betray that love, even for a god.

"Thank you," Mullins said stiffly. "For saving my sister." He relaxed a tad. "That was well done. She didn't deserve any of what happened."

"And you did?" the other asked silkily.

Mullins felt his lips contort and knew this was nothing like the smile he'd become more and more used to in the past few days. "I did not," he said simply. "But I set those events in motion, and they could not be unset. Ruthie lived a long life?"

The other took a step back and eyed him warily. "She did. Over eighty winters, lively and blithe. She married a good man—three of them, actually—and outlived all three."

Mullins nodded. "As long as she loved." His Ruthie, young and sweet and kind. Not knowing of the perfidy of adults, of the hatred of... the other.

"She did," the other told him quietly. "And your heart—still just as pure as I sensed when I showed up at your window, offering you sweets."

It had not been this man's fault that their evening together had erupted into chaos. His penchant, perhaps—even his curse—but the chaos, the danger, his parents' house, all of that had been the gullible, panicky humans who would rather destroy what they didn't understand than have a little faith.

"The sweets were... costly," Mullins said, and he realized that all those years spent minding his tongue, minding his expression, waiting to see which way the whip would fall, all of that experience was paying off here.

He wanted to fall to his knees and scream Edward's name.

What he was doing instead was discovering what this man would do to harm them.

Or help them.

"Well, yes." The other nodded. "I hadn't meant for you to become a demon." He grimaced. "I really don't...." He waved his hand around the cell, indicating the dank stone, the bloodstains, the vast vaulty echo of a mostly deserted hell. "I don't really mingle with the folk down here. They seem to have their own agenda."

Mullins let out a short bark of laughter. "Yes. People really do make their own hell and their worst selves possible, don't they?" He'd learned that too. "But that doesn't mean a signature into servitude isn't binding."

The other shrugged. "But hey—I gave you the means to unbind it, and here you are." He smiled winningly. "And there are *so* many promising things we could do with your tail."

Mullins felt anger congeal in his stomach. "Nobody touches my tail but Edward," he snapped, and the other backed up, hands held out in mock surrender.

"Okay, okay! He can play too!"

"No," Mullins told him. "No. It's not playing. Not now. It never should have been playing in the first place. I hurt somebody. Somebody dear to me. He was kind and good—and maybe I've seen marvels and maybe I'm not the ignorant peasant boy I was all those years ago. But it came at the expense of breaking a friend's heart, and that was not my price to pay. Maybe someone else could have many lovers with no hard feelings—Cory, Green, Bracken, Nicky—they seem to have found a way to love each other and to not let their love crumble from the weight of the four of them. But I'm not that strong. I love Edward—and I won't hurt him, not for the world."

"What about for your freedom," the other asked harshly. "Because I'll be honest—as much fun as those people in that fairy hill seemed to be having, you know they were just screwing around. There's no way they can save you from here. The demons were going to get in sooner or later, and then where would you be? Hundreds of years of torment and no what's his name—"

"Edward," Mullins insisted. He hadn't even mentioned Jonathan's name before. Edward would be a real person between them. Edward would be a force for the other to fear.

"I mean, you disappeared," the other reasoned. "He's going to think you're gone. And I can take you away from here as my consort. We play around a few years, you have the rest of a mortal lifetime to explore the world as it is. How bad can that be?"

Mullins closed his eyes and heard Edward promising to try again. And again. And again. If he had to start over again for his entire longer-than-mortal lifetime, he wouldn't give up on Mullins.

Mullins believed that. Believed that help was coming with all his heart. It may not be this night. It may not be this decade.

But Edward would come.

"No thank you," he said softly, closing his eyes against the awfulness of hell. Inside his heart, he saw the mirror of hope Edward had given him.

He still had it in his pocket.

His eyes flew open as he realized it was warm.

Edward.

"But Clyde—"

"Mullins. Clyde died in that stream, signing his name in blood, believing the lies of a soul as small and petty as Menoch. Mullins was reborn. He's seen and done terrible things—but he's still a good man."

The other rolled his eyes. "Well, *Mullins,* you can come with me and be my love, or you can rot in hell and await your precious wizard kid. Just remember—I gave you the staff. I gave you the bloodline to finish off the spell. I saved your little sister and her descendants for you—this is a really shitty way to say thanks—"

"Thank you," Mullins said again. "Thank you for saving my sister like I begged you to do, despairing with my last breath. Thank you for teaching me the difference between love and lust in a field of flowers, no two the same. And thank you for reminding me now that I'm not a fool. Not anymore. I refuse to pay anybody else's broken heart for my sins, and I will *never* betray Edward."

The other gazed at him, turquoise eyes alight with an unholy glow. "Done," he said softly, as though this speech was the thing he'd waited 400 years to hear.

And then he disappeared, blinking out of existence in the space of a heartbeat.

Mullins covered his face with his hands and sank to his knees on the stone floor.

"Edward," he whispered, and then, as the full extent of his loss hammered at him, as he realized how long he'd have to wait for another touch from his beloved's hand, he screamed it.

"*Edward!*"

He managed to crawl onto his bed, alone, all alone in the twelfth sphincter of hell, yearning for one more breath, one more touch, one more moment of peace from the heart of his beloved.

AN HOUR passed.

Maybe two.

Mullins crouched on his bed and tried to reason.

Where *was* everybody?

From what he could hear, none of the demons were actually *in hell*. Maybe, off in the distance, in the first through tenth sphincters, he could hear the screams and wails of hell's usual doings, but not here with the scribes, and not next door with the beast-makers. But these two units—these were deserted, and Mullins was alone.

Which meant they must be still breaking down the magic and psychic barriers that guarded the fairy hill.

Why would they do that? Unless… unless they didn't know he was here.

But Edward would know, certainly, wouldn't he? But wait. Would Edward *have* to know? Edward had his blood—or Sam's blood—and Harry could….

At the thought of Harry Mullins's heart sank. Harry was weak. Edward wouldn't ask his brother to help them at the expense of Harry's life, would he?

The thought tormented him, around and around, as he listened to the far-off tortures in places he'd done his best for 400 years not to explore.

He might be here for 400 years more.

"Edward…," he moaned, covering his face with his hands.

"Mullins!" Edward cried, and Mullins gasped.

His boy, orange hair mussed, green eyes shadowed, gave a whoop and embraced Mullins with all his formidable strength, falling to his knees across from him, both of them clinging together in the twelfth sphincter of hell.

Edward smiled at him, eyes red-rimmed, as he smoothed Mullins's hair back from his face.

"I told you I'd come for you."

Mullins nodded and tried not to sob. "Oh, you did. You did indeed."

"I'm sorry I'm late—you knew I was coming, right?"

Mullins broke, laying his head on Edward's shoulder and holding him so tight he gasped for air. "Oh, I did," he hiccupped. "I did. With all my heart, I took you at your word."

REDEMPTION DAY

EDWARD PICKED the staff up from where he dropped it and pulled Mullins close one more time.

"You ready?" he asked. His heart still thundered in relief from seeing Mullins alive and unharmed.

Mullins looked unhappily at the staff. "We're using that? You know it was a gift from… from…."

"Your ex-boyfriend? Yeah. We figured. Congratulations, Mullins, your lover was a god."

Mullins's laugh sounded a little unhinged. "But other than that, he wasn't a bad man."

Edward paused. "What happened?" he asked softly. "What did he want?"

Mullins gnawed on that lush lower lip, thinking carefully. "He wanted to… tempt me," he answered at last. "He wanted to offer me an easy way out of hell."

The smell of blood, of entrails, of despair washed over Edward then, suddenly strong.

"And you didn't take it? Oh, Mullins—you're a stronger man than I am!"

Mullins seized his hand and gazed intently into his eyes. "Don't you believe it, Edward Youngblood. You gave me the strength to say no."

Edward had to turn away, humbled. "That's an amazing thing to say," he mumbled, charmed even more by his Mullins's kiss on his cheek.

"It's true," Mullins whispered, before pulling back. "But we should leave soon before everybody comes back."

Edward shook his head. "They're still waiting for you on the hill. I don't think they'll go until you are well and truly transformed. Do you have your mirror?"

Mullins nodded. "It was the oddest thing that I grabbed it this morning. I… it was on the floor of Leonard and Emma's after I came through. I couldn't imagine leaving it there."

"I didn't even remember holding on to mine," Edward said. "But it was in my pocket this morning when we dressed." He grimaced. "I spelled another one to both of ours and left it on top of the hill. We need to use them because…." His brother's pale, strained face as Harry had stood to cast that spell was terrifying.

"Harry?" Mullins said unhappily. "Well, then. Let's go."

Edward kissed him. Hard. "I'll do it all again if I have to," he swore. Then he grinned. "Let's hope we don't have to."

And with that he set the mirror on the ground and thrust the staff through it, clinging to the staff with one hand and Mullins with the other.

With a terrible heave, he and Mullins were dragged through.

He almost dislocated his shoulder with the pressure of hanging on to Mullins, and Mullins clung to him so tightly they'd later realize he'd cracked Edward's ribs.

There was a terrible friction this time, a physical reluctance to the relocation, and it wasn't until Edward found himself hauled to his knees in the center of the multiple pentagrams on Green's Hill that he saw what the problem was.

"Mullins?" he cried, touching his beloved's face.

Or the beast that had taken over as his face again.

"Oh no." Mullins lay on his back, where apparently rescuers had placed him after prying his arms from around Edward's waist. His eyes were closed, and he lay flat on his back, legs like a goat's, hands like a pig's, a face like a horse. Still. Abominably, deathly still. "He's not breathing!"

"Edward!" Suriel was there, hauling him to his feet. "We have no time. We have to perform the spell now. Edward, after you disappeared, the shields slipped a little more. The demons are making it through!"

Edward looked around the garden wildly, appalled. The ring of spellcasters remained, but they were all facing outward. The fey were glowing, their bodies impossibly tall, giants crouched and ready to fight. Around them was a mosh pit of demons and werecreatures—wolves, giant dogs, jaguars, mountain cats, giant housecats, and giant birds fought with snarling, howling intensity. As Edward watched, the werewolf he'd known as Teague and a giant housecat with crossed blue eyes like Francis's took one end each of a creature with a fly's bloated white body and ripped it in two.

"Oh, heavens! Suriel! What have we done?"

"Nothing intentional," Suriel said sternly. "And it's time to make it right. Now Cory's got a plan to leave you unmolested, but she says it can only buy you a few moments. We're all in position. Can you use that time?"

Edward nodded and bent for a moment, touching Mullins's still cheek. "Hold on, beloved. Trust me."

"Are you ready?" Suriel asked. "Because on your count, we'll blood the hex bags, and after that, Cory's going to work her magic. Give us the signal, Edward—we need this done now!"

Edward didn't ask about Harry—he could only hope.

"Ready, my lady?" he called to the darkness, standing as strongly as he could.

"Ready, Edward!"

He looked up, mouth open. She was... flying. Directly overhead, Bracken and Arturo at her side. The wind whipped through their hair, and she held her hands out toward the circle of vampires hovering in the air outside the circle of people on the ground. Edward gasped and tried to pull his attention to his job instead of the spectacle above.

"As soon as the hex bags are blooded—you'll see the glow. That's when we need you."

"You hear that, guys?" she called, and the vampires all called back various versions of "Got it!"

"All right! Everyone in the circle turn around and face me, then blood your hex bags. Go!"

He felt it.

He'd laid the chalk for these three pentagrams, and he felt the power—the combined power—of everybody giving their life force to Mullins's transformation. It flooded him, overwhelming, like a spotlight through a bedroom window or an ocean through a spigot.

Their circle became a glowing orb, half of it buried below his feet in the earth of this holy place and the other half arching overhead in a golden bowl of light, and Edward remembered the words of the spell and opened his mouth to chant.

As he spoke, he looked above and then shut his eyes so he could think.

The Lady Cory was pouring power into the vampires above, and they in turn were glowing blue, their very light destroying every demon who came through the air around the hill. In that moment that he looked, he could see the flicker of lights and the carnage of the demon dead, a chaos of battle and the hellish joy of the vampires as they threw cold fire from their hands and killed and killed again.

The chant ended, but the spell was not yet closed, and Edward knew the thing he had to do next.

Of this, and this alone, he was not afraid.

Mullins, there are people fighting all around us and demons destroying themselves to do us harm. And I regret their pain, and I regret this chaos, but my beloved, nothing in this world or beyond this world can make me regret loving you. You were the dry, funny voice in my head as I truly grew and came of age. You were the avenging angel when my blood or that of my brothers was spilled. And in the past years, you have become my true companion, the other beat of my heart, the better part of my judgment, the sureness of my convictions. I would start this quest again and again and again for just one more day at your side. If the most we can manage is one night every hundred years, then I will be there, ready to love you, my love as fresh as summer rain to wash away our sins and our fears and make us clean for one more touch.

Come back to me. Be my beloved. I give you a legion of brothers and friends, new family of the heart for our betrothal, if only you'll be mine.

Several things happened at once.

The spell closed, that tremendous power shutting off, leaving Edward staggering from the effort of channeling it into Mullins.

The people in the circle all gave a little gasp, as though they'd been pricked by a needle, and several of them stumbled to their knees. The werecreatures all became abruptly human, shivering and pissed off and naked.

The demons in the ring of battle simply disappeared, the destroyed bodies fizzling into the air in a noxious vapor.

Cory cut off her flow of power abruptly, and her vampires fell randomly out of the sky, many of them laughing drunkenly as they landed, lying on their backs and belching softly as Cory, Bracken, and Arturo descended slowly, landing very carefully *not* on any fizzling demon corpses.

Francis, Beltane, and Suriel stepped into the circle, looking at Edward hopefully as Edward turned and found Mullins on the green. He crouched, heedless of the pain in his ribs, to see Mullins open his eyes.

"Beloved?" he asked, because it was, once again, the Mullins he'd made love to, the beautiful man with the lake blue eyes who loved him back. He was sitting up groggily, looking surprised.

"We got out of hell, then?" he asked, and Edward fell to his knees and laughed a little.

"We did indeed," he said, touching Mullins's face. "Did we manage to lose your tail this time?"

Mullins thought carefully—

And turned into a small gray housecat.

And then turned back, looking surprised.

Edward kissed him on his befuddled nose and then took his mouth, shoulders shaking with suppressed tears.

Mullins pulled back and whispered, "That was marvelous. I'll have to do it again sometime on purpose."

Edward nodded and looked up at the circle of brothers around them. "Did you see that?" he asked. "Sorry, Beltane. We were hoping for a dog."

"No worries," Bel said happily, offering them a both hand up. "I'm just happy for a brother."

And then they were surrounded, their brothers embracing them soundly, laughing with joy.

Except for one.

Edward pulled away from the rejoicing, worried beyond belief. "Harry?" he asked anxiously, only a little relieved when Green left the shadows of the nearest tree to come toward them, Harry in his arms.

"Exhausted," Green said tenderly, kissing a sleeping Harry on the forehead. "I'm afraid I was much out of the battle this time, so I could feed him strength. But he'll make it." He grimaced. "But I think it's best if you boys honeymoon here, just to give him time to recover. Do you mind?"

Edward shook his head, eyes burning, and pulled Mullins into his arms before grimacing. He took a deep breath and stopped, coughing. "Dammit," he muttered. "Mullins, I think you cracked my ribs."

"Doing what?" Mullins asked, still out of it, and Edward would have laughed, but his ribs hurt too much to breathe.

"Oh, dear boy!" Green cried, concerned. "Suriel, my lad, come here and take your lover. I think Edward needs a little help!"

Green helped him sink to the ground, laying hands on his ribs while the rest of Green's people… cleaned up.

Legions of tiny fey came out with equally tiny buckets of water which they poured over the remains of the demons, rinsing those areas clean.

The elves tended to the shapeshifters, healing them of their hurts in small multihued explosions of light, and when that was over, the shapeshifters wandered to the lawn and started to drag the vampires back inside.

"I don't wanna go," belched a tall one with a black widow's peak who looked astoundingly like Dracula, while draped half over a short, bandy-legged werewolf's shoulders.

"That's cute. I'll throw your boyfriend in with you, will that make it easier?" Teague—the werewolf—asked, naked and bleeding, while an elf tried to grab his arm. "Lambent, the bloody hell!"

"You're bleeding, wolfman. Yes, I know, you're fucking badass and all that shite, but for sweet fuck's sake can't I just close this fucking wound before you drag that idiot inside?"

"Yeah. Fine. Whatever."

"Your graciousness overwhelms me. Now stop moving."

At that point Green put his hands on Edward's shoulders, and a soothing, peaceful surcease of pain practically melted him into the ground, made even better by Mullins sitting, warm and real, at his side.

At that moment, Lady Cory's voice penetrated his haze. "Are you shitting me?" she asked, and the man Edward had last seen in a police uniform nodded earnestly. He was naked now, which made Edward wonder which shapeshifter he'd been.

"Serious," he said. "I swear to Goddess, Cory. We're all fine."

Cory closed her eyes and bounced on her toes. "Did you hear that?" she shouted to the world in general. "People, that's zero casualties! *Zero fucking casualties!* And I just might get inside in time to kiss my children before they sleep!"

The whoop that went up from the people on the hill was deafening, and Edward found his eyes closing, even as he sat on the lawn.

"You remember, Francis?" he asked, hoping his brother was right there. "After Leonard was turned. Emma and Leonard walked back to town with us in their arms and found us a place to sleep and some mice to eat."

"Harry found the mice," Francis said, yawning and collapsing abruptly by Edward's feet.

"Yeah, but they did all that, and I'm so tired I can hardly move."

"*That's* because I'm spelling you all to sleep," Green said with a weary laugh. "I don't trust the lot of you not to start another war if you don't get a nap in first."

"Mullins?" Edward mumbled, slumping to the ground.

"Right here," Mullins mumbled back. "Never leaving you. Never."

"Never's not good enough," Edward whispered, but then he fell asleep, so it would have to do.

After the Hard Rain

EDWARD AWOKE in a room full of sunshine, Mullins asleep next to him, curled on his side, facing away.

Edward reached out an arm and pulled him closer, full length of naked man flush backward against Edward's front.

A quiet chuckle rumbled in his chest.

"What?" Mullins asked hazily.

"No tail." Just a bare and slightly furry backside. Edward could rub it all day.

But as Mullins moaned deliciously and thrust against Edward's hand, he thought maybe he had better things to do than rub his lover's bottom.

He kissed the back of Mullins's neck, scraping lightly with his teeth, and Mullins breathed out sharply through his nose.

"Have I ever told you how much I like that?" he asked.

Edward leaned over and nuzzled his ear. "How about that?"

"Mm… that too."

Edward reached around and brushed a tan nipple with his thumb. "That too?"

"Mmm… yes…."

"This could be my favorite game ever," Edward whispered, rolling his hips so Mullins could feel his erection pushing thickly against his backside.

"Can we play the short version this time?" Mullins asked breathily. "Suddenly I need you very much."

Edward moved his reaching hand down Mullins's stomach, not surprised in the least to find his cock hard and thick in his palm.

He squeezed and stroked, liking the way Mullins arched his hips very much.

"You need me?" he whispered.

"Inside me," Mullins begged. He reached across the bed for a tiny plastic bottle sitting on the end table in plain sight. As he handed it off to Edward, Edward couldn't help but ask.

"That was just *there*?"

"There were two cups of water too," Mullins moaned. "I drank one in the middle of the night."

Edward remembered that too. Simple human things, both of them drinking water, getting up to pee, stumbling in the dark.

Coming back to bed and cuddling together and falling asleep.

"Yes, but…." Edward couldn't finish the thought as he slicked up his own cock and then probed between Mullins's cleft.

"Ahh…." Mullins thrust back against his fingers, and Edward shuddered. So perfect, so easy. Life wouldn't always give them each other, perfect and easy. This moment was something they'd worked for, had earned.

It was so much sweeter for all of that.

They could savor this moment and remember to always come back to it.

Mullins shifted his hips and pulled his knee up to his chest, giving Edward access, and there, ah! So tight. So warm. The haven his body had always needed.

Edward pushed inside him slowly, letting Mullins's noises be his guide.

His head popped through, leaving Mullins to clamp down on his shaft as Edward slid all the way in with a delirious "*Yesss!*"

Oh yes.

He fucked.

Such an animal thing—hips forward, hips backward, cock forward, cock backward—skin and nerves and electrical stimuli….

And trust.

And joy.

And physical exultation.

And love.

Oh, so very much love.

Forward and backward, he built momentum, their bodies pulsing in waves of pleasure, high pitches of sensation.

Mullins groaned, hand moving to his own cock, and then, the best thing of all, he begged some more. "Faster, Edward. Harder. All. I need it all."

With a growl Edward shoved against his shoulder blade, pushing him flat and facedown against the bed while he fucked him furiously, the pressure of pleasure building up in his loins until he was desperate for release.

"Augh!" he cried out. "No! Too soon—"

"*Now!*" Mullins demanded. "Now! I need... oh yes! Oh God yes! Please!"

Edward could deny him nothing. He howled, his arms shaking as his climax rocked him, shattered him, and he poured himself into his lover's body, sweating and panting and joyous.

Mullins convulsed around him, milking him flaccid, pulling his seed inside, keeping all of him safe.

Edward collapsed on top of him, facedown on the bed, and licked the back of his neck.

"Didn't we just do this?" Mullins mumbled.

"But it ended up so well the first time," Edward said, and they were still connected when Mullins laughed, so it reverberated through his entire body.

The feeling was delicious.

"I'd like to kiss you now," Mullins told him, and Edward lowered his face to where Mullins had turned his head.

"I'd like to kiss you forever," he whispered.

"That too."

But they started with now.

Eventually they made it out of bed in what appeared to be a suite. The floor and walls were paneled in glowing golden oak, and the coverlet—a detailed quilt, they realized as they looked at it—was all lake blue. They had a window that looked out over the hill and across the highway, to the canyon beyond.

Their windows were opened, and forest green curtains billowed into their room in the early morning breeze.

"It should be colder," Mullins said as they made their way out of a deliciously prolonged shower. He was bare, with a towel wrapped around his waist as he hunted for sweats in a set of drawers that looked hand-carved to match the bedframe.

"I think Green controls the temperature," Edward told him, biting his lip. He could go again. He could. They'd had sex waking up and sex in the shower, and he could have gone one more time if Mullins hadn't begged for food to sustain him.

Half laughing, yes, but also serious.

Edward knew it was the first of many meals to come.

"He can *do* that?" Mullins pulled out what looked to be a clean pair of comfortably worn sweats and a long-sleeved T-shirt in a man's medium. He threw them at Edward—with boxer shorts to match—and grabbed a set for himself.

"He apparently shopped for us," Edward said dryly, sliding the clothes on.

"These could fit half the men here," Mullins told him. "It's like we got the shared laundry pile Emma used to use for you three."

Edward grinned and bounced his bottom on the bed. "Now us six," he said, overwhelmed with the joy of having them all—brothers and lover and parents—all in one heart.

"Four," Mullins corrected, pulling on his bottoms. "Suriel and Beltane need totally different sizes."

Edward laughed. "So you, my demon lover, are really the most average man of us all!"

Mullins finished dressing and walked into the vee of Edward's legs. "Not too average, I hope," he said softly, closing his eyes and lowering his mouth for a kiss.

"Perfect," Edward said against his lips. "Absolutely perfect."

Mullins sank into the kiss, and Edward was about to let his good intentions about finding breakfast fly out the window when there was a knock on the door.

"Guys? You got breakfast arriving." At Cory's words, a tray of everything—toast, fruit, eggs, sausage, everything—appeared on the dresser they'd just used, and Mullins moaned in gratitude as he moved toward the food. "And I hope you're decent because I've got to come in."

"All dressed, Lady," Edward said. He couldn't begrudge their hostess a damned thing—not after everything her people had done for them.

"Excellent." Cory came through the door dressed… well, much the way Mullins and Edward were. The men's sweats were snug across her hips, and the enormous white T-shirt—likely one of Bracken's or Green's—hung down to her knees. Her hair was pulled up in a practical ponytail behind her head, and she carried the little girl—white-blonde of hair and silver-blue of eye—on her hip. "Can you say hello, Silver?"

The child hid her face against Cory's neck, and she kissed the top of a perfectly braided blond coif.

Apparently the sprites did more than just cook.

"Too shy," Cory apologized, smiling. "So, guys—come out when you're ready. They'll drop food in on you and clean up if you don't, and get mad at me if you don't eat, so definitely eat. We have snacks out in the kitchen if you get hungry between times—make yourself at home. Green wants to meet with you this evening, and we're going to have a celebratory feast tomorrow. You may want to invite your mother, Edward, because that's the other thing." A buzzing filled the room, and Cory grimaced, pulling Edward's phone out of the pocket of her sweats. "Your mother's been calling. She wants an update. She seems to think we've cooked you and served you up as scraps. Francis and Beltane don't count—and Suriel got us about an hour's reprieve. She needs to talk to you."

Edward frowned. "What about Harry?"

Cory sobered. "Still sleeping. He'll be okay, but Suriel and Green both thought they should let him stay that way. So there you go. You have a banquet in your honor tomorrow, and your only chore today is to call your mother. You're welcome."

Edward shook his head and accepted the phone. "My lady—I have a debt I can never repay—"

"Ha!" she laughed, and Silver repeated the sound. "Ha! Ha! Ha!"

"Yeah, they'd better laugh," Cory burbled. "Oh, honey, don't you worry. I'm not sure how or when or where, but we will come knocking on your door someday—or even on your phone—and say, 'Oh, guys! We've got a thing only you can do!'"

"And I'll say 'We'll do it.' In a heartbeat. Without question," Edward said, bowing, Mullins at his side.

Cory grinned. "Excellent. We'll try not to bring the forces of hell down on your heads when we do that—because yeah, it was novel, but it was a little too damned interesting for a picnic in the garden, you think, Silver?"

"Dammit!" Silver said proudly, and Cory grinned at her.

"Anything else you want to say, little lady?"

"Dammit! Dammit!"

"Awesome! Let's go see Nicky and we can blame this on him!"

"Dammit!"

"That's right—once more with feeling!"

Mullins and Edward both laughed, and Cory turned around and left the room.

"So," Mullins said, going back to the food and starting to dish up their plates. "Food first or conversation with Emma first?"

Edward looked at the phone.

Fifteen messages, forty phone calls.

"Could you make me a plate?" he hedged. "I think I'll do both."

The room had two stuffed chairs near the window, facing a small television, and Edward sank into one of them and hit Emma's number.

Time to face the music.

"Are you dead?" she asked before the phone had even finished ringing.

"I'm pretty sure Francis and Bel told you I'm not!"

"But they must have been mistaken," she responded sweetly, "because here you are, not dead, and yet I haven't spoken to you by phone or brainwave in almost twenty hours. There's a block around the hill, you know. Harry was sick—I get that—which means you're the one I trusted to tell me you all *aren't dead*."

For a moment Edward thought of brushing it off, Harry style, and saying, "Not even a bruise. Maybe a little one," but he couldn't.

"Harry got really sick," he told her honestly. "Emma—I think he almost died. And… and he could barely stand, and he did anyway, and sent me to hell to bring Mullins back. And we got back and there was"—he had to use the word—"fucking chaos, and battle, and Mullins wasn't breathing and… and I did it. Mom, I did it, but I don't know how…."

His voice broke, and Mullins's hands on his shoulders grounded him as Emma soothed.

"Now see?" she said when both of them had calmed down. Her voice sounded shaky and broken. "This is why I talk to *you*, Edward. You're the one who tells me the truth. Now what's your plan from here?"

Edward took a deep breath.

And a bite of toast.

And remembered his belief in truth and his belief in reason.

And remembered who had taught him these things.

"I think Francis is going to need to stay—"

"No," she interrupted. "Bel will come back with you all, and Francis should come with him. He needs to be with Bel until Bel returns to England. When Bel goes back, he can return to Green's."

Emma knew best. Oh God, she really did.

"And Harry needs to sleep here for a week," Edward told her, his voice wobbling.

"Ask him when he's ready to return," she said softly. "Green's consort—"

"The Lady Cory?"

"No, I got an impertinent young man named Nicky. Does he have more than one?"

"Yeah...."

The conversation continued as Edward told his mother about the hill and she told him about how to make sure his brothers were as whole as possible.

When he finally hung up, his plate was clean and Mullins had placed it on the dresser with the tray. Mullins had flung himself across the bed and was facing him, eyes half-closed. He heard Edward sign off and opened them.

"So?" he asked softly, swinging his legs over the edge of the bed and sitting to face Edward.

"We stay here until Harry's ready to travel. We rest. We make love. We enjoy our break." He grimaced. "Bel and Francis are going to... to need to figure things out on their own. Francis will probably come back here after Beltane leaves again."

"Until he's ready," Mullins said softly.

Edward swallowed and looked away.

"You'll miss them."

Oh, he felt so foolish. "I... I had this vision. The six of us, the family business—"

Mullins's laugh was so gentle, Edward almost missed the tone of an older lover. "My darling," he said. "We have so much time for that to be our reality." He smiled, and it was blinding. "Your brothers will always be your brothers. I think if yesterday showed anything, it was that you will always be inseparable."

In his head Edward could hear Harry calling him a "worrier princess," and he took a deep breath. "Harry's going to be okay," he said, remembering Green's kiss on his brother's brow.

"He will." Mullins stood and moved to between his knees again, then took his hands.

"And Francis and Bel will find their way," he realized.

Mullins smiled and nodded, kissing the backs of his knuckles.

"And you and I will be together until death do us part," Edward said, the revelation seeping into his bones.

"I wouldn't have left hell if it wasn't to be by your side," Mullins told him reverently.

Edward's eyes burned. "I'm so very glad you did," he rasped, and Mullins bent to take his mouth.

The kiss wasn't passionate—although there would be plenty more of that. It was a blessing, a promise, and a prayer.

It was their future as two, their more-than-mortal lifespans made beautiful, sustained in their hearts, by being lovers side by side.

They would be two, and their family would follow, and there was happiness—such happiness—to hold gently in the palms of their hands.

AMY LANE lives in a crumbling crapmansion with a couple of growing children, a passel of furbabies, and a bemused spouse. She's been nominated for a RITA, has won honorable mention for an Indiefab, and has a couple of Rainbow Awards to her name. She also has too damned much yarn, a penchant for action-adventure movies, and a need to know that somewhere in all the pain is a story of Wuv, Twu Wuv, which she continues to believe in to this day! She writes fantasy, urban fantasy, and gay romance—and if you accidentally make eye contact, she'll bore you to tears with why those three genres go together. She'll also tell you that sacrifices, large and small, are worth the urge to write.

Website: www.greenshill.com
Blog: www.writerslane.blogspot.com
Email: amylane@greenshill.com
Facebook: www.facebook.com/amy.lane.167
Twitter: @amymaclane

Choose your Lane to love!

Purple

Amy's Alternative Universe

Some lovers are as familiar as the family pet.

FAMILIAR ANGEL

Amy Lane

"Fantastic...a transcendent
love story that will sweep you
off your feet."
CINDY DEES,
NYT and *USA Today*
Bestselling Author

Familiar Love: Book One

One hundred and forty years ago, Harry, Edward, and Francis met an angel, a demon, and a sorceress while escaping imprisonment and worse! They emerged with a new family—and shapeshifting powers beyond their wildest dreams.

Now Harry and his brothers use their sorcery to rescue those enslaved in human trafficking—but Harry's not doing so well. Pining for Suriel the angel has driven him to take more and more risks until his family desperately asks Suriel for an intervention.

In order for Suriel to escape the bindings of heaven, he needs to be sure enough of his love to fight to be with Harry. Back when they first met, Harry was feral and angry, and he didn't know enough about love for Suriel to justify that risk. Can Suriel trust in Harry enough now to break his bonds of service for the boy who has loved his Familiar Angel for nearly a century and a half?

www.dreamspinnerpress.com

IMMORTAL

AMY LANE

www.dreamspinnerpress.com

When Teyth was but a child, a cruel prince took over his village, building a great granite tower to rule over the folk. Greedy and capricious, the man will be the bane of Teyth's existence as an adult, but as a boy, Teyth is too busy escaping his stepfather to worry about his ruler.

Sold into apprenticeship to the local blacksmith, Teyth finds that what was meant as a punishment is actually his salvation. Cairsten, the smith, and Diarmuid, his adopted son, are kind, and the smithy is the prosperous heart of a thriving village. As Teyth grows in the craft of metalwork, he also grows in love for Diarmuid, the gentle, clever young man who introduces him to smithing.

Their prince wants Diarmuid too. As the tyrant inflicts loss upon loss on Teyth and Diarmuid, Teyth's passion for his craft twists into obsession. By the time Teyth resurfaces from his quest to create immortality, he's nearly lost the love that makes being human worth the pain. Teyth was born to sculpt his emotion into metal, and Diarmuid was born to lead. Together, can they keep their village safe and sustain the love that will make them immortal?

www.dreamspinnerpress.com

AMY LANE

A SOLID CORE
OF ALPHA

In an act of heroism and self-sacrifice, Anderson Rawn's sister saved him from the destruction of their tiny mining colony, but her actions condemned the thirteen-year-old to ten years of crushing loneliness on the hyperspace journey to a new home. Using electronics and desperation, Anderson creates a family to keep him company, but family isn't always a blessing.

When Anderson finally arrives, C.J. Poulson greets him with curiosity and awe, because anyone who can survive a holocaust and reinvent holo-science is going to be a legend and right up C.J.'s alley. But the more C.J. investigates how Anderson endured the last ten years, the deeper he is drawn into a truly dangerous fantasy, one that offers the key to Anderson's salvation—and his destruction.

In spite of his best intentions, C.J. can't resist the terribly seductive Anderson. Their attraction threatens to destroy them, because the heart of a man who can survive the destruction of his people and retain his sense of self holds a solid core of alpha male that will not be denied.

www.dreamspinnerpress.com